The Brookes Babes

Thomas Brant

ISBN 978-10683106-6-9

CHAPTER 1 – Queueing Like Madmen

Saturday 20th September 2003

Everyone at Brookes Vibes knew that Adam Banks, the promotions coordinator, was a sex addict, and that his advertisement for the Brookes Babes, a new street team which was meant to drum up attention for the station, was less about marketing and more about his ego. It was a poorly-kept secret that Adam enjoyed being surrounded by young women, under the guise of "team leadership," while the rest of the office rolled their eyes and carried on with their day. But when the applications for the Brookes Babes came flooding in, even the most sceptical staff had to admit that Adam's hare-brained scheme had caught the attention of the student population.

Brookes Vibes, after all, was a competitor to Fox FM, which was owned by Capital Radio, a giant in commercial radio, and Fusion 107.9, which was owned by Fusion Radio Holdings, a smaller but fiercely competitive independent network. Brookes Vibes, by contrast, was owned by the Home Counties Radio Group, a group of stations across Buckinghamshire, Berkshire, Oxfordshire, and Surrey, known for its modest budget and reliance on creative, grassroots strategies to stay relevant. While Fox FM and Fusion 107.9 boasted slick branding and high-profile presenters, Brookes Vibes leaned heavily on its connection to Oxford Brookes Univeristy and the student population, trying to carve out a niche in the crowded radio market.

The idea of the Brookes Babes had divided the office from the moment Adam pitched it at the weekly programming meeting. Sarah Linton, the station manager, had grimaced but ultimately signed off on the campaign, muttering something about "desperation breeding innovation." She had hoped the stunt would generate some buzz without crossing too many lines, though she had little faith in Adam's ability to keep things professional.

Standing outside the studio building in the Summertown area of Oxford, Kevin Lenkhirst, one of the senior presenters who was responsible for the Saturday Soundcheck, a pre-drinks show which was intended for students at both Brookes and Oxford University, smoked a cigarette and watched as Adam strutted across the car park with a stack of application forms. Kevin shook his head. "This is going to end in tears," he muttered to himself, taking a long drag and blowing the smoke into the crisp September air.

The fact that there was a queue a mile long of hopeful students outside the building spoke volumes about the allure of Adam's so-called marketing brainchild. The line stretched from the station's modest entrance all the way down the road towards a nearby kebab van that was doing brisk business. Most of the applicants were young women in their late teens or early twenties, dressed in outfits ranging from casual to club-ready, each carrying the hope of making it onto the team that Adam had promised would be "the face of Brookes Vibes."

"He'll hire that one, and that one, and that one," Mark Harrison, a 19 year old who was one of the electricians in the station's engineering team, said with a smirk as he leaned against the doorframe, pointing discreetly at the more glamorously dressed applicants. Most of the female applicants were the ideal women for Adam's mind, having worked at Trent FM as a Promotions Assistant with their Black Thunders, Mercia FM as a runner, and Kix 96 as a tea boy. The fact that the station management was formerly of GWR Group, and so acted like a fleet of Churchill dogs, nodding whenever Adam pitched an idea, only made the situation more predictable. Brookes Vibes was a place where ambition and cynicism collided daily, and everyone knew that Adam was a product of his environment as much as his own inflated ego.

"Fiver says he hires the blonde with the bikini top and ultra short skirt next to the kebab van," Kevin said with a wry grin, flicking his cigarette butt into the ashtray nailed to the wall. "Tenner says he makes her lead Babe."

Mark chuckled as he observed the woman in question, an obvious jailbait candidate who looked in her early teens and not a day over sixteen, despite the minimum age requirement being eighteen. "You're on," Mark said, shaking Kevin's hand with exaggerated solemnity. The mood was light-hearted on the surface, but beneath it was an undercurrent of unease. The Brookes Babes campaign wasn't just another cringe-worthy promotion; it was a litmus test for how far the station would go to remain relevant in a cutthroat market.

A man in a suit and tie walked in, and Mark recognised him as Antony Peckham, one of the senior management team, a former GWR Bristol station manager who was now the Group Director for Promotions. Antony, Mark knew, was GWR through and through, which meant that

Adam would get away with murder, the old boys club of radio ensuring that his questionable antics were swept under the rug as long as the ratings didn't suffer. Antony surveyed the queue with a tight-lipped smile, nodding approvingly at the sight of the eager applicants. "Ah, Mr Harrison, enjoying your fag break?"

"Just wrapping it up, Mr Peckham," Mark replied with a quick nod, stubbing out the cigarette and stepping away from the doorframe. His tone was polite, but there was a faint edge to it, the unspoken understanding that Antony Peckham's presence usually meant trouble—or at the very least, an impending lecture on "innovative thinking" that most of the staff had learned to ignore.

Antony adjusted his tie and turned to Kevin, who was still lingering with his arms folded. "Lenkhirst, isn't it? Saturday Soundcheck?"

"That's me," Kevin replied, his voice nonchalant but firm.

"Good, good," Antony said, his eyes scanning the queue again. "Quite the turnout, isn't it? Proof that we're onto something with this campaign. Mr Harrison, I want you to be on the panel. You're 19, right?"

Mark raised an eyebrow, unsure if he'd misheard. "Me? On the panel? I'm just an electrician, sir."

Antony dismissed his modesty with a wave of his hand. "Exactly why we need you. Young, reads lads mags, no doubt has a Jordan poster on his bedroom wall and shags half his way through the Brookes campus. We need a student's perspective on what will appeal to the demographic. You're a perfect fit for the panel, Harrison."

Mark felt his stomach drop. This wasn't exactly the career progression he'd imagined when he took the job at Brookes Vibes. "Uh, sure. If you think I'm the right man for the job, sir," he replied, forcing a tight-lipped smile.

Antony clapped him on the shoulder. "That's the spirit! Meet us in the conference room in thirty. And bring your sharp eye."

As Antony disappeared into the building, Kevin gave Mark a look of mock sympathy. "Congratulations, mate. You've officially been roped into the circus. You know the gaffer was at GWR when the Black Thunders started, and unofficially defined the look of the female promotions team? I'd bet good money he's expecting this to be just as 'memorable.'" Kevin's air quotes around "memorable" dripped with sarcasm.

Suddenly Adam rushed out, dressed as if he were Pete Waterman on a budget: an oversized leather jacket, sunglasses perched atop his gelled hair, and keys to the newly liveried Babemobile – a bright yellow van plastered with the Brookes Vibes logo and a cartoon of a radio microphone surrounded by sparkles. He looked like he was about to introduce a boy band on Top of the Pops circa 1997.

"Mark, Kevin, I need a hand getting the uniforms out of the van."

Kevin raised an eyebrow. "Uniforms? For the Babes? Dare I ask?"

Adam grinned, his teeth gleaming with an enthusiasm that bordered on manic. "Oh, you'll love them. Branded crop tops, miniskirts, and knee-high socks. Very on-trend, very now. This is gonna make us the talk of Oxford!"

Mark exchanged a glance with Kevin, whose expression hovered somewhere between bemusement and exasperation. "Yeah, 'talk of Oxford' is one way to put it," Kevin muttered under his breath as he followed Adam to the van.

The so-called "Babemobile" was parked haphazardly across two spaces, its garish paint job practically glowing under the early autumn sun. Adam unlocked the back doors with a flourish, revealing boxes stacked high and marked with "Brookes Babes Uniforms" in thick black marker. Next to them was a few boxes marked "Vibes Condoms", all resting on what looked like a mattress.

Mark raised an eyebrow at the sight of the mattress, which looked brand new as it was still in the plastic wrapping. He gestured towards it with a half-hearted chuckle. "What's that for, Adam? The Babemobile's boudoir?"

"Yup. Back in my Trent days, the Thunders would often nip out of the TSA to hook up with other GWR stations," Adam said, as if it were the most natural thing in the world. "Bit of networking, you know? Well, when we're taking the Babes out on the road, you never know where the night will end. Best to be prepared."

Kevin let out a low whistle. "Class act, mate. Truly the pinnacle of professional radio marketing."

Adam either missed the sarcasm or chose to ignore it, hoisting one of the uniform boxes out of the van with a grunt. "We're not here to play it safe, boys. We're here to make waves. We're here to disrupt."

Mark muttered to Kevin as he grabbed another box, "Disrupt? He's gonna end up disrupting Radio Authority when someone complains about this madness."

"You know, I saw a second Babemobile parked at the back car park when I pulled in," Kevin continued, grinning slyly. "Reckon you've got one for emergencies, or just a backup in case this whole thing goes up in flames?"

Adam smirked. "That's so we can run two events, one at say Whitney and one at Banbury. Double the exposure, double the impact," he said, puffing his chest out like a general unveiling a war strategy. "That's got the promo kits in, the free pens, notebooks, carrier bags, all the usual stuff. Just need to empty some into the other Babemobile and grab the speakers and banners, Bob's your uncle, Fanny's your aunt, and we're getting pussy tonight!"

Mark shook his head, suppressing a groan. "You're something else, Adam. You know that?"

Adam winked, clearly mistaking Mark's exasperation for admiration. "Stick with me, Harrison. You'll learn a thing or two about how this industry really works."

Kevin, still holding a uniform box, leaned in close to Mark as Adam turned back to fiddle with the van's sound system. "Learn a thing or two? More like get yourself blacklisted from every respectable station in the country. Honestly, mate, this whole operation has 'HR disaster' written all over it."

"Trust me mate, we're tame compared to the old mob within GWR. Last year when I was there, sex in the studio was the norm, not the exception," Adam said with a grin that Mark knew was meant to be mischievous but came off as deeply unsettling. "That's why I love this business. It's wild, it's unpredictable, it's…" He gestured grandly at the queue of hopefuls outside, "…this."

Kevin rolled his eyes and whispered to Mark, "I give it a week before this turns into a full-blown scandal. You watch—some fresh-faced student's going to call their mum crying, and that'll be it for the Babes."

"Or Radio Authority's hotline will be lighting up like a Christmas tree," Mark replied under his breath, smirking despite the unease gnawing at his gut.

The trio lugged the boxes into the building, navigating the cramped corridors of the station, which was abuzz with activity. Presenters were rehearsing links, producers were shouting over each other about scheduling conflicts, and interns scurried about with armfuls of CDs and promotional flyers. It was the usual controlled chaos, but the energy felt heightened today, charged with a mix of anticipation and trepidation.

"Right!" Adam said, clapping his hands together as they reached the conference room. "Let's get these uniforms unpacked and ready for the panel. The first round of interviews starts in two minutes, and we need to look sharp."

Two minutes?! Mark knew that he was totally unprepared, his clothes obvious to anyone he was an electrician and not a fashionable student. But before he could voice his concerns, Adam was already tearing open one of the boxes, revealing a pile of branded crop tops, dolphin shorts and skirts, and Mark assumed that the two different choices were so the upcoming applicants could "mix and match." The clothes were emblazoned with the Brookes Vibes logo in glittery lettering. Mark winced, imagining the complaints that would roll in if anyone saw these as anything less than 'empowering.'

Kevin let out a low whistle. "If I were any less charitable, I'd say those outfits belong in a nightclub, not a promotional campaign."

"Fashion is subjective, mate," Adam shot back, holding up a crop top against himself and striking a ridiculous pose. "This is the future of radio branding."

"The future of a tribunal, more like," Kevin muttered, earning a stifled laugh from Mark.

Before the uniforms could be laid out, the door burst open, and Sarah Linton stormed in. The station manager's face was a picture of barely controlled fury, her usually tidy bob slightly frazzled. "Adam," she snapped, her tone low but dangerous. "What are those?"

"Uniforms," Adam replied, unfazed. "For the Babes. We discussed this at the meeting."

"We discussed branded clothing, not… whatever this is," Sarah said, gesturing to the skimpy outfits. "I've just had a call from Antony Peckham. He wants to make sure this campaign is 'memorable.' But if this is your idea of memorable, Adam, you'll be lucky if you're not remembered in court."

Adam laughed nervously, clearly trying to gauge whether she was serious. "Oh, come on, Sarah. It's just a bit of fun. The students will love it. Anyway, the big boss has given the nod."

Mark watched as Sarah groaned, as Antony was her immediate

boss, meaning that she couldn't outright veto anything he'd approved. Still, she clearly wasn't about to let Adam run wild without a fight.

"Adam, this campaign is already walking a fine line," Sarah said, her voice steely. "If any part of this crosses into inappropriate territory—any part—I'll be the first one to shut it down, Antony or no Antony. And don't think for a second that I won't drag you down with it."

Adam's grin faltered for a split second before he recovered, adjusting his sunglasses and leaning against the table with a casual air. "Relax, Sarah. It's all under control. Trust me. The Babes are going to be the best thing this station has ever seen."

"Or the most embarrassing," Sarah shot back, narrowing her eyes. "Just make sure you're not the next front-page headline in Radio News Weekly."

She turned on her heel and strode out of the room, leaving a palpable tension in her wake. Mark exchanged a glance with Kevin, who raised an eyebrow as if to say "Told you so".

Adam, meanwhile, seemed unbothered, already rummaging through another box and muttering something about getting the branding just right.

"Looks like the circus is officially in town," Kevin murmured to Mark as they unpacked the uniforms. "You think she'll actually pull the plug on this if it goes south?"

Mark shrugged, carefully avoiding the pile of glittering outfits. "Depends on how much damage it does first. But if Adam keeps pushing his luck, I wouldn't bet against it."

"Speaking of bets," Kevin said with a grin, nodding towards the queue outside. "You still on for that fiver?"

Mark rolled his eyes but couldn't help smirking. "Yeah, why not? Might as well make this circus entertaining while it lasts."

As the first applicants were ushered into the conference room, the atmosphere shifted from chaotic to surreal. Adam greeted each hopeful with the enthusiasm of a game show host, peppering them with questions about their "passion for radio" and their ability to "represent the Brookes Vibes brand." Kevin and Mark sat awkwardly at the end of the panel, half-watching, half-trying not to burst out laughing at the absurdity of it all.

By the time the blonde in the bikini top finally stepped forward, Kevin leaned over and whispered, "Double or nothing she's the lead Babe by the end of the day."

Mark groaned but nodded. "You're on. But if this goes nuclear, you owe me more than a tenner."

Kevin smirked. "Deal. Let's see how far the 'future of radio branding' gets us."

"Hello, my name's Lisa and-"

"You're hired," Adam said without a single pause, cutting off Lisa mid-sentence. The room fell silent, save for the faint hum of the air conditioning. Kevin stifled a laugh, glancing at Mark, whose expression oscillated between incredulity and resignation. "Kevin, take Lisa to Studio 3 to get her new uniform and bring her back for the team photoshoot," Adam continued, completely oblivious to the stunned reactions around him. "Just make sure you take her particulars, bra size and that."

Kevin hesitated, then stood with a dramatic sigh. "Sure thing, boss," he said, casting a sideways glance at Mark. "Come on, Lisa. Let's get you kitted out for your exciting new career."

Mark chuckled at what Adam then said. "Adam, tell James that those two birds he pointed out to me are hired straight away, no interview."

Looking around at Antony, who was nodding like a Churchill dog, Mark realised that the situation had fully spiralled into a farce. He whispered to Kevin as he passed, "We're living in a sitcom, mate. This is beyond Radio Authority; this is Watchdog material."

Kevin smirked, shaking his head as he escorted Lisa out. "If it's a sitcom, we're the straight men, and Adam's the punchline."

Mark stood up and knew he had to find James Jenkins, one of the runners who seemed to be Adam's go-to errand boy for the day. The young lad had been roped into various ridiculous tasks, from tying balloons to the Babemobile to fetching coffee for the applicants. Mark spotted him loitering near the vending machines, fiddling with his pager—a relic of the GWR days that Adam had insisted was "retro cool."

"Oi, Jenkins," Mark called out, catching the lad's attention. "Your fearless leader wants you to hire two more 'birds.' No interview, straight into uniforms."

James blinked, clearly overwhelmed by the day's events. "Wait, what? Which ones?"

"Dunno. Apparently, Adam's already got them picked out. Something about the two you pointed out to him. Jot down their particulars and get them into uniform. He says that all Babes must have uniforms two cup sizes too small because, and I quote, 'it's all about impact.'"

James stared at Mark for a moment, mouth slightly agape. "You're joking, right?"

Mark raised his hands in mock surrender. "I wish I were, mate. But apparently, Adam thinks we're running some sort of FHM-sponsored circus. Just do what you've got to do and try not to lose your sanity in the process."

James groaned, rubbing his temples. "This place gets more ridiculous by the hour. Fine, I'll do it. But if anyone asks, I'm blaming you."

"Blame me all you want," Mark said with a chuckle, patting James on the shoulder. "Just try not to end up on the front page of The Daily Mail."

As James trudged off to carry out Adam's latest absurd directive, Mark leaned against the vending machine and let out a sigh. The whole situation was spiralling into an uncontrollable farce, and he couldn't help but feel like he was watching a slow-motion car crash. The mix of Adam's unchecked ego, Antony's blind approval, and Sarah's simmering frustration was a recipe for disaster, and Mark knew it was only a matter of time before the whole thing imploded.

****

CHAPTER 2 – Interviewed Without An Interview

Saturday 20th September 2003

Carly Hemsworth was your typical Oxford University student - broke, 19 and eager to make a quick few quid while balancing essays and late nights at the Bodleian. Being a regular listener of Brookes Vibes, the blonde girl knew that the opportunity to gain money and exposure by just chatting to students and handing out free merchandise sounded too good to pass up. After all, how hard could it be to don a uniform, smile for a few hours, and hit the town promoting Brookes Vibes?

Standing in the queue outside the Brookes Vibes studio, she had to chuckle as most of the queue was either blonde or brunette, leggy (like herself) and busty (like herself). The irony wasn't lost on her that the "Brookes Babes" seemed to be a very specific demographic, a fact she doubted was coincidental. Still, she reasoned, it wasn't her job to worry about the ethics of the campaign. She just wanted the money.

"Carly!" a squeal from behind her, and she chuckled, as her best friend and dormmate, Clarissa Stanhope, hurried up to join her. Clarissa was every bit Carly's opposite in appearance—shorter, with fiery red hair and a sprinkle of freckles—but just as sharp-witted and quick to laugh. The irony in that, like Carly, Clarissa was wearing hardly anything, despite Oxford being a more conservative city, wasn't lost on Carly. They both knew the unspoken rule of making it through something like this: you had to play the part, even if it made you cringe.

"Thought you'd chicken out," Carly teased, raising an eyebrow at Clarissa's outfit—a cropped denim jacket over a camisole and a mini skirt that would've made their college dean raise an eyebrow.

"And miss the chance to watch this circus up close?" Clarissa shot back, her grin wicked. "Besides, I need the cash more than you do. My overdraft is in freefall."

Carly laughed as they shuffled forward in the queue. "Same here. But you've got to admit, this is all a bit…" She gestured at the queue, where a group of girls in stilettos and heavy makeup giggled loudly, "… ridiculous."

"Oh, absolutely. But isn't that part of the fun?" Clarissa leaned closer and lowered her voice. "And let's be real— how hard can it be to hand out pens and smile? The whole 'Babes' thing is gross, sure, but if we're getting paid to wear a crop top and chat to people, I'm game."

Carly nodded, though a small part of her still felt uneasy. She had grown up listening to radio stations that felt like community hubs, places where people came together over shared music and chatter. This, on the other hand, felt… different. A little too glossy, a little too shallow. But it was a job, and jobs were hard to come by when you were 19 and broke.

"You see her by the kebab van?" Carly asked, pointing to a blonde who was obviously under 18 but wanted to pass herself off as older. The girl's glittery eyeshadow and platform heels screamed effort, though her nervous glances gave away her inexperience.

"Yeah," Clarissa replied, smirking. "You know my brother lives in Nottingham, and he says the Trent FM Black Thunders are just like the candidates here, all hairspray and heels, barely old enough to be out past curfew. He's one of the male Thunders at Trent... ironic, as he's got a marketing degree and the personality of a brick... and he says that hooking up with the female Thunders isn't just fine, but all but practically expected. He said one of the promotions assistants who're station based back when he started left after a messy break-up with a Thunder. Bloke named Adam something."

Carly had done some research on the management team of Brookes Vibes using the computers at the library, and the name "Adam Banks" had come up more than once. A former Trent FM promotions assistant turned self-proclaimed marketing guru, Adam was known for his wild ideas and a track record that veered between brilliant and borderline scandalous. She had to wonder if the Adam her friend's brother mentioned was the same one running this circus. If so, it explained a lot.

As the queue moved forward, Carly and Clarissa finally stepped inside the modest Brookes Vibes studio building. The faint smell of stale coffee and warm electronics filled the air, and the low hum of conversation buzzed around them. Carly glanced at the posters on the walls, a mix of cheesy slogans and event flyers promoting everything from local club nights to charity pub quizzes. The vibe was friendly but chaotic, and it was clear that this was a place where professionalism often played second fiddle to improvisation.

They were ushered into a waiting area by a harried-looking intern who barely glanced up from her clipboard. "You'll be called in one at a time. Just relax, and someone will come to get you," she said briskly before hurrying off to deal with some other part of the unfolding madness.

Carly sat down on a battered sofa, smoothing her skirt nervously. Clarissa plopped down beside her, already pulling out a packet of gum. "You nervous?" she asked, handing Carly a piece.

"A bit," Carly admitted, unwrapping the gum. "Not about the interview, though. More about what we're walking into. Did you see that guy in the leather jacket outside? Looked like he'd just walked off the set of a '90s boy band video."

Suddenly Carly felt a tap on a shoulder. Looking up, she saw one of her male friends, James Jenkins, a law student who she'd hooked up with a couple of times but had kept things casual. James was tall, with an easy smile and a knack for showing up at the most unexpected moments.

"Carly," he said, grinning down at her. "Didn't expect to see you here. Thought this wasn't your kind of thing."

"Desperate times," she replied with a shrug, gesturing to the scene around them. "What about you? Don't tell me you're trying out for the Brookes Babes too."

James laughed, sliding into the seat next to her. "Nope. I spend my weekends working here as a runner. Which reminds me, the marketing boss says you and Clarissa are hired."

Carly blinked, momentarily stunned. "Wait, what? We haven't even done the interview yet."

James smirked, leaning back in his seat. "Welcome to the world of radio promotions. Half the time, they've already made up their minds before you walk in the door. Adam spotted you two in the queue and decided on the spot."

Clarissa let out a low whistle, exchanging a bemused glance with Carly. "Well, that's one way to boost a girl's confidence."

"It's not exactly a compliment," James said, his tone laced with dry humour. "Adam's got a type, and you two apparently fit the bill. Don't get me wrong, you're both overqualified compared to most of the people who've applied today, but Adam's not exactly looking for talent here. Your uniform is in Studio 3, follow me."

Carly and Clarissa exchanged wary glances but got up to follow James through the maze of narrow corridors. The atmosphere buzzed with energy, a mix of excitement and chaos. They passed a makeshift recording studio where a DJ was enthusiastically promoting an upcoming club night, his voice echoing through the building.

"Does the boss need me to give him particulars or anything?" Carly asked, confused why she and Clarissa were still being hired without so much as a basic interview. The whole process felt rushed, chaotic, and slightly surreal.

James shook his head, leading them into Studio 3. "Not really. Adam's idea of recruitment is more about… well, appearances. If you look the part and aren't likely to trip over your own feet handing out flyers, you're in. He asked me your name as I mentioned I knew you two and got me to note down your dorm address for Payroll. Anyway, I've... well, been kind of tasked to keep you pair and some of the Babes comfortable."

Carly raised an eyebrow at James as they entered Studio 3. "Comfortable? What's that supposed to mean? Tea and biscuits while we wait to be paraded around Oxford in those awful uniforms?"

"Erm... I'm... to be your... basically a human dildo. Basically, it's going to be a stressful job for you ladies, and I'm to be the guy to... release that stress. After all, Carly, me and you both know you love a good shag when you're stressing. And Clarissa, you and Frank seem to love that one corner of the library where nobody goes."

Carly froze, her jaw tightening as she stared at James in disbelief. "Excuse me?" she said, her voice sharp enough to cut through the noise of the studio. Clarissa's expression mirrored her friend's, a mix of shock and rising anger. Suddenly James burst out laughing, something Carly never expected from the studious law student she thought she knew.

"Relax, I'm joking," James said, holding up his hands in mock surrender. "Honestly, Carly, you should see your face. You looked like you were about to throttle me. It's all pretty straightforward—Adam just asked me to show you two around, get you settled, and make sure you know where the snacks are. Sex is just optional."

Carly's glare could have cut through steel. "Very funny, James. You've missed your calling as a stand-up comedian," she said icily, crossing her arms. Clarissa, meanwhile, let out a sarcastic laugh, shaking her head.

"Optional, huh?" Clarissa said, raising an eyebrow. "Tell me, is this Adam bloke writing a handbook for how not to run a workplace, or is he just making it up as he goes along?"

"Well, him and half the senior bosses are formerly GWR Group, and the rumours are that most GWR stations, like Beacon, Trent, GWR, all those, are full of casual hook-ups, cocaine among some of the presenters, and promotions that skirt every Radio Authority regulation you can think of," James replied, his tone now half-serious. "Adam's just a product of that culture. He probably thinks this is all perfectly normal."

Carly and Clarissa exchanged a glance, their initial amusement at the absurdity of the situation giving way to a shared unease.

"Well," Carly said finally, "normal or not, we're not here for that. We're here for the job. So, let's skip the jokes and get on with it."

James held up his hands again, this time in genuine apology. "Fair enough. Sorry if I crossed a line—it's just... this place brings out the worst in people sometimes. Let me get the uniforms for you. Now, Carly, you're a 36DD, right?"

Carly's eyes widened in disbelief, and her hands clenched into fists at her sides. She stared at James, her voice laced with irritation. "What the hell kind of question is that?"

"Hey, I need to know so I can give you the correct uniform. After all, we've shagged, so I should know what you wear, right?" James said with a grin that was anything but charming.

Carly's fist clenched tighter, and she took a deliberate step closer to him. "James, if you think for a second that our... past gives you the right to talk to me like that, you're sorely mistaken. Now, why don't you just get the uniforms without the commentary, yeah?"

Clarissa, still standing a few paces back, couldn't suppress a smirk as James's grin faltered. "Oof. That's a solid 10 for the smackdown, Carly. Remind me never to cross you."

James quickly turned away, muttering something under his breath about "sensitive women" as he rummaged through a box in the corner. Carly exchanged a look with Clarissa, who raised her eyebrows in a silent, "What did we get ourselves into?"

Moments later, James handed them two sets of uniforms wrapped in plastic: bright pink crop tops with "Brookes Babes" scrawled in glittering letters, paired with matching miniskirts that looked like they had been designed for a Barbie doll. Carly held hers up, barely able to contain her disgust.

It was then that she noticed that the label of the top had a chest size which was 2 cups smaller than her actual size. Carly's irritation boiled over, and she held the top up for James to see, her expression incredulous. "This isn't even the right size! What, are we supposed to just squeeze into these and hope for the best? Or is this part of the whole 'image' thing Adam's got going?"

James shrugged, clearly unbothered by her frustration. "Look, I'm just doing what I was told. You're not the only ones who've complained about the sizing. Adam reckons it'll 'encourage a better fit for the branding.'" His air quotes around "better fit" made it clear even he thought the reasoning was ridiculous. "At least he hadn't got what he'd originally planned for the Babes... think tight fitting bodysuits in all black with "strategically placed cutouts." Apparently, it was vetoed by Sarah before the designs even made it to the printer."

Carly and Clarissa exchanged horrified looks. "Cutouts?" Carly repeated, her voice rising. "What is this, a bad Bond villain audition?"

Clarissa snorted, holding up her skirt with one hand. "Honestly, Carly, I'm starting to think we should've stayed in the library and lived off instant noodles instead of coming here."

"Too late now," Carly muttered, pinching the bridge of her nose and taking a deep breath. "Right, let's just put these on, get through today, and figure out if this is even worth it."

"Speak for yourself," Clarissa said, shooting a glance at the skimpy uniform. "If they expect me to go out in this without some serious concessions—like a jacket or at least a pair of tights—they're dreaming."

James, sensing the tension, held up his hands again. "Look, I get it. This isn't exactly ideal, but it's just how it is here. You want to talk to Adam about it? Be my guest. But trust me, he's not going to change his mind unless Sarah herself storms in. Oh, and as for your pay, it's a fiver an hour, cash in hand... and a twenty quid signing bonus."

Carly knew that the minimum wage was £3.80 for 18 to 21-year-olds, so the £5 hourly rate sounded like a small win despite the mounting indignities. The mention of a signing bonus meant that effectively it was a chance to get some decent food instead of Pot Noodles, ready meals and instant soup, especially as it was the start of the semester, and that her grant, which Carly was still waiting for, would be barely enough to cover rent and essentials.

"When do we get paid the bonus, and how often do we get paid for the shifts?" Carly asked, keeping her voice steady despite the simmering frustration underneath.

James glanced at his clipboard, avoiding eye contact. "The signing bonus is paid after your first event. The rest is weekly—cash in hand. Adam's idea to 'keep things simple,' though I think it's more to avoid paperwork."

Clarissa raised an eyebrow. "And by 'keep things simple,' you mean no contracts, no payslips, and no proof that we ever worked here if something goes wrong?"

James shrugged again, his trademark grin faltering under their scrutiny. "Look, it's not exactly the Ritz, but it's money. As a runner, I'm getting minimum wage, so you're doing better than me already. Plus, the tips from events can be decent if you're charming enough. Anyway, your first shift is tonight at The Bullingdon, promoting a Freshers' Week event," James said, flipping through his clipboard with a hint of discomfort. "Fox FM are there... y'know they're owned by Capital, right? Anyway, we're going to spoil their promo night by handing out flyers and offering freebies outside. Adam wants us to 'dominate the student market.'" His tone made it clear he was merely reciting orders rather than endorsing the plan.

Carly and Clarissa exchanged sceptical glances, their unease growing. "So, let me get this straight," Carly said, folding her arms. "We're supposed to stand outside, freezing our arses off in these outfits, trying to one-up a station that's got more budget, better branding, and, I'm guessing, a whole team of professionals?"

"Pretty much," James admitted, scratching the back of his neck. "And... well, part of the promotion involved you guys tying me to a lamppost and... well, pretending I'm a Fox listener."

Carly let out a sharp laugh, the sheer absurdity of James's words temporarily cutting through her growing frustration. "Tying you to a lamppost? What is this, a stag do gone wrong?"

Clarissa, however, looked more incredulous than amused. "Please tell me you're joking. Because if not, this might actually be the worst promotional strategy I've ever heard."

James held up his hands defensively. "Look, don't shoot the messenger, all right? Adam came up with the whole thing. Apparently, it's supposed to be a metaphor for how Brookes Vibes is 'unbinding' students from boring, corporate radio. Or something equally ridiculous. Personally, I think he just thought it would be funny."

Carly pinched the bridge of her nose, a habit she had when she was trying to process something particularly infuriating. "So let me get this straight. We're going to stand outside The Bullingdon in outfits designed for Barbie dolls, freeze to death, hand out cheap pens, and... tie you to a lamppost. And for all this, we get five quid an hour and the honour of representing Brookes Vibes?"

"Plus a twenty-quid bonus after your first event," James added, his attempt at optimism falling flat. "And don't forget the free condoms that you'll be getting... some for personal use and some to give out. Anyway, you've got 7 hours til you need to be back here ready to jump in the Babemobile."

Carly turned to Clarissa, her expression a mix of disbelief and resignation. "Well, Clarissa, this is it. Our illustrious careers in radio promotion are off to an unforgettable start."

Clarissa smirked, holding up her pink crop top with a flourish. "Unforgettable is one word for it. Completely ridiculous is another." She tossed the uniform over her shoulder and turned back to James. "So, James, aside from handing out pens and tying you to a lamppost, what else should we be prepared for tonight? Fire-eating? Juggling flaming torches? Wrestling a Fox FM mascot?"

James chuckled nervously, clearly unsure whether Clarissa was joking or genuinely expecting an answer. "Honestly, I wouldn't put it past Adam to suggest something like that. But as far as I know, it's just flyers, freebies, and 'engaging with the public.' Oh, and Adam mentioned something about a dance-off if we cross paths with the Fox FM team."

Clarissa's jaw dropped. "A dance-off? You're joking."

James shrugged. "I wish I were. He's convinced it'll be a great way to 'showcase the energy of Brookes Vibes.' His words, not mine."

Carly groaned, running a hand through her hair. "This keeps getting better and better. So not only do we have to freeze in these ridiculous outfits, but now we have to dance in them too? Fantastic."

Clarissa leaned in, whispering conspiratorially. "If we have to do a dance-off, I say we choreograph something so cringe-worthy that Adam regrets ever suggesting it."

Carly grinned despite herself. "Deal. If we're going down, we're going down in flames."

James checked his watch. "All right, ladies, I've got to get back to running errands. You've got a few hours to rest up, grab some food, and mentally prepare for tonight. Trust me, you'll need it." He paused at the door, smirking. "Oh, and if you happen to think of any creative insults for Fox FM, now's the time to workshop them. Adam loves a bit of 'friendly rivalry.'"

As James disappeared down the corridor, Carly turned to Clarissa with a rueful smile. "What have we gotten ourselves into?"

Clarissa shrugged, pulling her denim jacket tighter around her shoulders. "A fiver an hour, some free condoms, and a whole lot of embarrassment, apparently. But hey, at least it'll make a good story for the pub later."

Carly laughed, despite the sinking feeling in her stomach. "True. And who knows? Maybe we'll actually have some fun."

Clarissa raised an eyebrow. "Fun? Wearing this?" She held up the uniform again, letting the light catch the glittering "Brookes Babes" logo. "The only fun I'm having is watching Adam squirm when this all goes spectacularly wrong."

"Agreed," Carly said, grabbing her bag. "Now, let's get out of here before they come up with any more 'brilliant' ideas."

The two friends left Studio 3, their laughter echoing down the corridor. It was going to be a long night, but at least they had each other—and the promise of a few good pints at the end of it.

****

CHAPTER 3 – Fighting the Fox
Saturday 20th September 2003

By the time Carly and Clarissa arrived back at the Brookes Vibes studio that evening, the energy was electric, albeit slightly chaotic. Adam Banks was darting around the building like a man possessed, barking orders at interns, triple-checking the contents of the Babemobile, and loudly declaring that tonight was their moment to "put Brookes Vibes on the map."

Seeing James dressed as a typical Uni student, holding a Fox FM flyer in one hand and a faux-innocent expression on his face, Carly couldn't help but roll her eyes. "I can't believe we're really going to tie you to a lamppost," Carly said, shaking her head as she adjusted the hem of her glittery "Brookes Babes" crop top. She noticed James looking at her differently to the last times they'd hooked up, as if he was seeing her in a new light—not as the confident, sharp-witted Carly he knew, but as a part of Adam's chaotic circus. "Has the Fox FM crew been confirmed as going to be there tonight?" she added, trying to focus on anything other than her discomfort in the skimpy uniform.

"Yeah," Mark Harrison said, tightening a banner onto the Babemobile, chiming in with a smirk. "I know one of their street team... currently dating her, so I should know... anyway, she said that Fox FM have hired some blokes our age, 'fit ones', she said."

Carly let out a small laugh, adjusting her crop top again as she exchanged a glance with Clarissa. "Blokes our age, 'fit ones'? Sounds like Fox FM's street team might be more prepared for a nightclub than a promotional war."

Clarissa snorted, tugging at the hem of her own skirt. "If they're as 'fit' as they think, maybe we can use it to our advantage. Flirt a little, distract them, and grab the attention of the crowd while they're too busy trying to impress us. Hang on... is that a mattress in the Babemobile?"

"It's so I can try and shag some of the hunks," the same young looking person that Carly had seen in the queue earlier in the day said with a grin. "Hi, I'm Sally. Sally Clinton. I live just over the road and don't actually go to Brookes or Oxford Uni. I just thought it'd be fun to join in."

Carly and Clarissa exchanged incredulous looks. Clarissa was the first to speak. "You don't go to uni? How old are you, exactly?"

Sally chuckled. "16. Obviously the Fox FM hunks don't have to know—they'll probably see me and think that I'm 18 at least," Sally finished with a cheeky grin, flipping her hair over her shoulder. Carly and Clarissa exchanged uneasy glances, both clearly uncomfortable with the situation.

"Sally," Carly said, lowering her voice, "you know this is supposed to be an 18+ gig, right? Like, legally. If anyone finds out—"

"They won't," Sally interrupted breezily, leaning against the side of the Babemobile. "I mean, come on, my job is to distract the hunks while the rest of the Babes grab the attention of the crowd. Me and my mate, Kasey here, aren't even virgins so it's not as if we're naïve about what goes on in these kinds of gigs." She winked at Carly and Clarissa, clearly enjoying their shocked expressions. "I lost that on my birthday to my boyfriend, so I'm already aware of how to... please... a man."

Carly's jaw dropped at Sally's casual confession, and for a moment, she struggled to find the right words. Clarissa, however, recovered quicker, folding her arms and fixing Sally with a sharp glare.

"Right, first off, that's not something you should be bragging about to strangers," Clarissa said firmly, her voice laced with disbelief. "And second, do you even understand how much trouble Adam—and the rest of us—could get into if someone found out you're underage?"

Sally shrugged, her carefree attitude unshaken. "Relax. Nobody's gonna find out. Besides, everyone lies about their age to get into clubs and gigs. It's not a big deal. Anyway, I know Adam... his cousin is my uncle."

Carly exchanged a quick glance with Clarissa, her unease deepening. This wasn't just a chaotic gig anymore; it was a potential disaster waiting to happen. She lowered her voice, leaning in closer to Sally. "Look, I don't care who your uncle is, but you being here puts everyone at risk. If the Fox FM crew or anyone else gets wind of this, it's not just Adam who'll be in trouble—it's all of us. You're playing with fire, Sally."

Sally rolled her eyes, brushing off Carly's concerns with a dismissive wave. "You're overthinking it. I'll be fine.

Adam knows, and he said it's cool, so what's the big deal?"

Carly was about to respond when Adam himself strode over, clipboard in hand and an air of frantic determination. "Ladies! Ladies! Focus! Tonight is our night. We're here to dominate, not debate. Sally, stop distracting the Babes and get into position. And Carly, Clarissa, you're front and centre with the flyers and the freebies. This is the kind of high-energy branding that'll make Fox FM wish they stayed in bed."

Carly turned to Adam, her frustration boiling over. "Adam, do you even realise Sally's only sixteen? She shouldn't be here. If anyone finds out—"

"Shhh," Adam hissed, glancing around dramatically as though the walls themselves might be listening. "She's fine. She's mature for her age, and besides, she's not actually doing anything illegal. The station's legal team assured me that so long as she doesn't go into the club, but is outside handing out flyers, we're in the clear. What she gets up to with the Fox FM guys is on her and not the station. Anyway, I've been involved in things like this before at Trent, and it's all above board... after all, the Black Thunders up there are more than wild, they're practically a travelling circus. Nobody batted an eyelid then, so stop worrying and focus on the task at hand, yeah?"

Carly felt her stomach churn as Adam's nonchalance grated against her already frazzled nerves. Clarissa, ever the sharp-tongued one, stepped in before Carly could unleash her growing frustration.

"Right, so the plan is to tie James to a lamppost, hand out freebies, and distract the Fox FM crew with glitter and giggles. Got it," Clarissa said, her voice dripping with sarcasm. "Anything else, fearless leader?"

"Yeah... we need a couple of you to gyrate round him now and again. Mary, Ally... you up for it?"

Two blonde haired women who Carly recognised as going to the 'other' university in Oxford — Brookes — nodded as if they had been patted on the head and were the Churchill dogs Adam seemed to love managing. Carly exchanged a knowing look with Clarissa, her unease growing with every passing second. This wasn't just unprofessional; it was veering dangerously close to a full-blown farce.

"No," Carly said, as, in a way, even though she and James had a few one night stands, and they were close, she couldn't stand the thought of other women gyrating around him instead of her. She knew that it wasn't controlling or possessive, but rather a mix of protectiveness and sheer disbelief at the absurdity of the entire situation. "Clarissa and I'll step in instead."

Clarissa shot Carly a look of surprise. "What the heck?" she whispered, and Carly could see the confusion on her friend's face. Clarissa leaned in closer, her voice a hushed hiss. "Why are you volunteering us for that? I mean, I'd rather wrestle the Fox FM mascot than do whatever Adam thinks counts as 'gyrating.'"

"Because I don't want those Brookes slags doing it around James," Carly whispered back firmly, her voice low but laced with irritation. "They'll try and fuck him before the night is out, and there's only one... well, pussy... I want his cock touching."

Clarissa blinked, momentarily stunned by Carly's bluntness. Then, a slow grin spread across her face as she shook her head in disbelief. "You're unbelievable," she muttered under her breath. "Fine, but you owe me a pint for this—and not one of those watered-down ones at The Bullingdon. Look, do you fancy James or something?"

Carly hesitated, her cheeks flushing as she glanced at James, who was currently tying a Fox FM-branded scarf around his wrist for his lamppost "performance." She sighed, leaning closer to Clarissa. "It's not about fancying him. It's... complicated. We've hooked up a few times, yeah, but I don't want to see him used as part of Adam's ridiculous show—or worse, by those girls who think this is some kind of hen do."

Clarissa raised an eyebrow, a knowing smirk tugging at her lips. "So, it's about fancying him and not wanting competition, then?"

Carly rolled her eyes. "Clarissa, I'm just trying to keep this circus from turning into a complete disaster. If it means protecting James from whatever this is..." She gestured vaguely at the Babemobile, the flyers, and the ridiculous uniforms. "...then fine. But don't make it out to be something it's not."

"Sure, sure," Clarissa said with a grin, clearly unconvinced. "You just want to 'protect' him. Got it."

Before Carly could respond, Adam clapped his hands together, his voice booming over the chatter. "All right, team! Let's move out! Babemobile's loaded, everyone knows their roles, and tonight we're going to show Oxford who's boss. Carly, Clarissa, front and centre with James. Mary and Ally, you're on standby. Sally, for the love of God, please don't do anything that'll get us on the front page of the Oxford Mail."

Sally shot him a cheeky salute, clearly unfazed by his warning. "Relax, Adam. I've got this."

Carly watched as James got in via the side door of the front Babemobile where most of the promo stuff was, with everyone else apart from her and Clarissa going for the emptier Babemobile. Seeing James climb in, and not much space for 3 people to sit in the goods part of it, she knew what was coming.

"I guess I'll have to sit on your lap while Clarissa sits next to us?" She said to James with a raised eyebrow, trying to mask her embarrassment with a casual tone. James looked momentarily caught off guard, but then he grinned, patting his lap in mock invitation.

"Well, Carly, if you insist. Just don't crush me; I've got to survive the night to be tied to a lamppost, remember?"

Clarissa rolled her eyes as she climbed into the Babemobile. "Honestly, this is turning into a Carry On film. Let's just get this over with before Adam comes up with any more 'brilliant' ideas."

Climbing onto James's lap, she noticed he placed his arms around her chest, to protect her, but she could also feel a growing erection that her dolphin shorts were sitting on, his tight jeans leaving little to the imagination. Carly's face flushed a deep red, and she quickly glanced out of the window, avoiding eye contact with James.

"James," she hissed under her breath, leaning slightly closer to him to avoid Clarissa overhearing. "Seriously?"

James gave her a sheepish grin, clearly aware of what was happening but trying to play it cool. "What can I say, Carly? It's a tight space... literally. Anyway, we've shagged a few times last year, remember, so it's not as if this is entirely unfamiliar territory." His grin was teasing, but there was a flicker of nervousness in his eyes as he tried to gauge Carly's reaction. "Anyway, if you're wondering why I'm holding you, it's so you don't fall onto Clarissa. After all, we've got no seats back here, we're sitting on a mattress with a duvet on top, and we've got loads of boxes with us and a banner on top. Then there's the fact you volunteered to gyrate round me when we get to the Bullingdon, so I figured we're past the point of being shy."

Carly shot him a glare, though she couldn't help the small smile tugging at the corners of her lips. "You're impossible, you know that?" she muttered, shifting slightly to make herself more comfortable—though she realised too late that it only made things more awkward. "Anyway, those skanks who Adam was picking would have been fucking you right now. Your cock is only for 1 person, Jenkins, unless I say otherwise. Understand. If I catch any of those skanks trying to fuck you, I'll tear their limbs apart and feed them to the ducks in South Park Lake. There's only one person allowed, apart from me, to fuck you... and she's sitting in this van right now," she added, nodding toward Clarissa, whose expression was a mix of exasperation and amusement.

Clarissa raised an eyebrow. "I appreciate the vote of confidence, Carly, but I'll pass on your love triangle drama, thanks. I'm here to survive this nightmare and maybe grab a free kebab if I play my cards right. You two sort out your… dynamic."

James chuckled, his grin widening. "Dynamic, eh? Sounds like we're already a step ahead of Fox FM. They don't have this kind of team spirit, I bet."

"Team spirit?" Carly shot back, glaring at him while trying not to smile. "You're being tied to a lamppost in front of a crowd, and I'm gyrating around you in a glittery crop top. If that's team spirit, I think we need to reconsider our career choices."

The Babemobile suddenly slammed it's brakes as Adam, driving erratically, narrowly avoided colliding with a cyclist who darted into the road. Carly lurched forward, clutching onto James for balance as the boxes in the back shifted ominously. It was then she felt James's hand on her breasts, his quick stabilisation of her momentarily crossing a boundary that made her freeze. The conflict of her mind, where she, in part, wanted him to keep his hand there, and another part wanted to slap him, made her cheeks burn even brighter. The irony his erection was still hard, and she was partly enjoying it and partly furious at herself for even entertaining the thought in the middle of this chaotic promotional nightmare.

"James," she hissed again, her voice low but sharp. "Hands. Off."

Secretly, however, she wanted him to keep his hands there, and to maybe tease her nipples or whisper something flirtatious, but she quickly shook the thought from her mind. This was neither the time nor the place for mixed signals—not when they were en route to a night that already promised embarrassment on multiple levels.

It was then that Adam slammed the brakes on again, and Carly felt James's hand which was on her breasts accidentally slip into her braless top. The fact that the top was already two cup sizes too small, pushing her breasts up, made the situation even more mortifying. What made it worse that, and she knew that he wasn't aware of it, James had started teasing her nipples in the same way she liked when, the previous year the two had hooked up several times, he would tease her nipples and paint hickeys on her neck and breasts, the sensation of his touch igniting a rush of conflicting emotions in her. She could feel her core wetting, and that the scrap of fabric that was masquerading as her shorts wasn't going to hide it for long.

It was then she remembered that she was a squirter, and that the colour of the shorts was light enough that if she didn't regain control of the situation quickly, her arousal would become very visible.

And then it happened.

James had, unknowingly, teased her nipples to the point where he had made her core explode, and now her shorts were visibly damp, betraying her attempt to keep composure amidst the chaos.

"Looks like James got you going Carly?" Clarissa said with a grin which Carly knew was half teasing and half astonished at how chaotic the night was already shaping up to be. It was then that Carly felt another orgasm build and she clenched her fists tightly, trying to suppress the sensation. Carly inhaled sharply, shifting her position on James's lap to create a bit of distance between them. Her face burned with embarrassment as she avoided both James's teasing smirk and Clarissa's knowing glance.

"Clarissa, if you don't shut up, I swear I'll leave you to handle the Fox FM dance-off on your own," Carly muttered, half-serious, her voice low and tense.

Clarissa chuckled, leaning back against the van's side. "Relax, Carly. It's not like anyone's going to notice when we're out there freezing our bits off. Besides, isn't this kind of thing what Adam wanted? High-energy branding and all that?"

Carly shot her a glare. "This isn't branding, it's humiliation. And James—" she turned to him, her eyes narrowing. "—keep your hands where I can see them. Or so help me, I'll make sure you're tied to that lamppost with glitter glued to your eyebrows."

James held up his hands in mock surrender, though his grin remained firmly in place. "Hey, I'm just trying to survive the ride, same as you. If anything, you've been a great source of... entertainment." He winked, clearly enjoying her flustered state.

The Babemobile lurched to a stop outside The Bullingdon, and Adam's voice rang out from the driver's seat. "All right, team! Showtime! Grab the gear and let's get moving—Fox FM's not going to know what hit them!"

Carly climbed off James's lap as gracefully as she could, ignoring the dampness of her shorts and his lingering grin. Clarissa followed, her usual sarcastic quips momentarily replaced by a focused determination. The street outside was already bustling with students and revellers, and Carly could see the Fox FM team setting up across the way, their branded van gleaming under the streetlights.

"Let's just get this over with," Carly muttered, grabbing a box of flyers and a handful of freebies. As she stepped onto the pavement, she glanced back at James, who was busy adjusting his makeshift lamppost costume.

"James," she called over her shoulder, her tone softer this time. "Try not to embarrass yourself too much, yeah?"

He smirked, adjusting the Fox FM scarf around his neck. "Don't worry, Carly. If I go down, I'm taking you with me."

Carly rolled her eyes, though a small smile tugged at her lips. She had a feeling tonight was going to be unforgettable—for all the wrong reasons.

****

CHAPTER 4 – Adam

Tuesday 24th September 2003

If there was one thing Adam Banks knew from working with Trent FM's Black Thunders is that there were obvious couples, ones who had enough sexual tension and wouldn't admit their feelings to each other, and ones who would prefer casual hookups. James and Carly, he had concluded, were of the middle kind: the ones who had undeniable chemistry but hadn't yet figured out whether they were destined for something deeper or just casual fun. As Adam watched them during the Bullingdon promo event, he smirked to himself. It was all too familiar. He'd seen it a hundred times before—couples who danced around their feelings while everyone else could see what was obvious.

Looking at the pieces of paper on his desk, Adam smiled, as they were lecture schedules for each of the Babes that they had dropped off the previous evening, some of them being Brookes students and the others students at Oxford University. There was a simple reason he had asked for them, and James's as well, even though James was a runner and reported to the production side, not the promotions team: playing Cupid.

Adam knew that some of the staff in the station viewed his antics as chaotic or borderline unprofessional, but he knew he had a patron in the senior management team-the Board themselves.

The board of the parent company of Brookes Vibes, James knew, were made up of former GWR senior staff, and that it was an old boys club, where having a GWR owned station on your CV meant the interview questions wasn't the usual ones, but more along the lines of reminiscing about conquests, the Black Thunders and their infamous antics, and how many Radio Authority complaints could be dodged while still pulling off outrageous stunts. Adam had been part of this culture at Trent FM, and he thrived in it. Now, at Brookes Vibes, he wasn't just playing the game; he was orchestrating it. The board's trust in him was based on one thing: results. And if that meant turning the station's promotions team into a mix of chaos and spectacle, so be it.

"Hmmm... so Thursday afternoons, Saturdays and Sundays they're both free," he muttered, looking at the schedules for James and Carly. "Is Annabelle clear for Saturday too, I wonder."

Adam knew why he was looking for Anabelle Young's schedule, as she was a Brookes student who he could tell instantly was the kind of person whose flirtations made any bloke go gooey. The fact that, during her interview, she had all but said she'd sleep with him to get the job only confirmed Adam's suspicions that Anabelle wasn't just confident—she was strategic. But Adam, despite his reputation, had learned over the years to avoid mixing business with personal gratification. He had bigger plans, and Anabelle's flirtations were just another tool in his promotional arsenal.

Having already booked the Market Square area for a promotion on Saturday, he knew exactly what kind of method to promote Brookes Vibes, as well as get Carly and James together, could be done.

"Carrie? Be a dear and grab the Yellow Pages from the reception desk," Adam called out to the station's long-suffering admin assistant, Carrie Mason, who barely looked up from her computer as she responded with a flat, "Sure thing, Adam."

Adam leaned back in his chair, twirling a pen between his fingers as he reviewed his plan for Saturday. The Market Square promotion wasn't just about raising Brookes Vibes' profile—it was about creating moments. Adam had always believed that the key to a successful radio promotion was spectacle, the kind that got people talking long after the event ended. But this time, there was an extra layer to his scheme.

He knew that there was a supplier of mud pits for hire in the Yellow Pages, and he grinned as the idea solidified in his mind. A good old-fashioned mud wrestling competition would be the perfect attention-grabber. It was the kind of stunt that would generate buzz, draw a crowd, and—most importantly—give him a chance to play Cupid with James and Carly.

He knew that by getting James in some tight trunks and having Anabelle flirt with James while Carly looked on, the situation would certainly stoke Carly's jealousy. Adam wasn't blind to the subtle looks Carly gave James when she thought no one was watching, nor the protective way she volunteered to gyrate around him at The Bullingdon. He knew how to read people, and the tension between the two was practically a promotional asset in itself.

The fact that he knew that the mud pit would mean that fur would fly between Carly and Anabelle, and that the mostly male students who listened to Brookes Vibes who would attend the event would absolutely lap it up, made it all the more appealing to Adam. He wasn't just planning a promotion—he was crafting a spectacle that would cement Brookes Vibes as the talk of the town.

Carrie returned, plonking the hefty Yellow Pages onto his desk with a look that said she had better things to do. "Here's your bloody book. You do know the internet exists, right?"

Adam waved her off with a grin. "Oh, Carrie, sometimes the old ways are the best. There's something magical about flipping through the pages and finding exactly what you need. Anyway, the company I'm after isn't online, so this is the only way to get their details." He flipped through the Yellow Pages with practised ease, landing on the section for event rentals. His eyes scanned the listings until he found it.

Oxford Outdoor Events—Mud Pits, Foam Machines, and More!

"Bingo," Adam muttered, jotting down the phone number on a notepad. He picked up the receiver of his desk phone and dialled, his grin widening as he heard the cheerful voice on the other end.

"Oxford Outdoor Events, how can I help?"

"Hi Dave, it's Adam here at Vibes, how are you mate?"

Adam knew Dave Galloway from his time at Trent FM, when Dave had been a Black Thunders supplier for various chaotic stunts. Dave's voice on the other end was unmistakably cheerful, tinged with that can-do attitude Adam always appreciated.

"Adam! Long time, mate. Still cooking up those wild promotions, eh? What can I do for you?"

Adam leaned forward in his chair, a mischievous glint in his eye. "Dave, I need one of your finest mud pits. Big enough to draw a crowd, small enough to fit into Market Square, and messy enough to make it the talk of the town. You've got something like that in your arsenal, don't you?"

Hearing the hearty chuckle that came from Dave's end of the line, Adam knew he was speaking to the right man for the job. "A mud pit, eh? Classic move, Adam. You know I've got just the thing. How soon do you need it?"

"This Saturday," Adam replied without hesitation. "We're doing a promotion in Market Square, and I want this to be big. It's got to be the kind of thing people remember—and talk about—for weeks. I'll have your portable shower units if you've got one and some foam machines if you've got any."

Dave's laughter echoed through the receiver. "Adam, you've not changed a bit. Mud pits, foam machines, and showers? Sounds like you're planning an all-out spectacle. Let me check availability." There was a brief pause, the sound of pages flipping in the background. "You're in luck. I've got a pit available, complete with a pump system for refilling, and a couple of portable showers. Foam machines? I've got two on hand."

Adam leaned back, triumphant. "Perfect. Can you deliver them Friday afternoon? I'll need time to set everything up. Oh, and if you've got any extras—like, I don't know, inflatable barriers or a proper referee's whistle—throw them in. I want this to look professional."

"You're going all out, aren't you?" Dave replied with a grin evident in his tone. "You want the 'Deluxe Mud Wrestling Package'—that's what we call it."

Adam laughed. "Dave, mate, I'll take whatever you've got that'll make this the event of the year. Send over the invoice; I'll get it signed off today."

After wrapping up the call, Adam leaned back in his chair, spinning his pen with satisfaction. The pieces were falling into place. A mud pit in the middle of Market Square, foam for dramatic effect, and the added tension of Carly and Anabelle vying for James's attention—what could possibly go wrong?

Logging into the text messaging system that the DJs around the Home Counties Radio Group used to receive on-air text messages from listeners and to respond to them, he knew that there would be plenty of blackmail material, especially as it was the same software GWR used for their DJs to receive and respond to texts. Adam's mischievous grin widened as he saw some of the DJs offering to casually hook up with listeners, such as one from the Reading studio over at Buzz Beats.

Artie Tilsley: *Hey gorgeous, if you want to come down to the studio after my shift, I'll let you answer the phones.*

Adam knew that in GWR parlance, offering a listener to answer the phones was code for inviting them into the studio for something much less professional. The response from the listener, however, was even more gold.

07700 900503: *Be careful what you promise, babe. I've got plans for you that don't involve phones. xx*

The irony, Adam knew, was that the text system was used across all the stations in the Home Counties Radio Group, meaning any senior manager with access could pull up a transcript. While Artie from Buzz Beats was playing with fire, Adam couldn't help but appreciate the chaos. It reminded him why he loved this industry: the unpredictability, the borderline ridiculousness, and the way it all somehow came together.

Clicking the tab that the DJs could text each other to, the show ideas for the current CHR daytime show "20 Degrees Hotter" was like the wild west, with hosts suggesting the most random themes that the fixed playlists could run for their show. Adam knew that the same 20 songs each day was played on each of the 6 stations in the group, so the DJs tried to make their shows unique by adding themes. Adam scrolled through the suggestions, shaking his head and chuckling at some of the more outlandish ideas:

"Songs from Artists that Management Love"

"Artists who Love Penis"

"20 Degrees of the Same Thing"

"It's Kylie Time"

"Who's Ever Sang"

"Artists with Y in the Name"

Adam knew that half of the DJs were formerly Emap and GWR and brought their irreverent style to the table, making the corporate rigidity of the playlist feel almost absurd. Yet, he couldn't deny that the themes often added a spark of personality to the otherwise repetitive song rotations.

Artie Tilsley: *Has Lotus Notes gone down for anyone else? I don't want to phone Milton Keynes get the tech team try and pair me off with their skanky interns again.*

Harry Potter: *Yeah, I've just had one of them try and pair me off with their cousin who apparently 'loves radio guys.' Think I'll pass. You know it's the same tech lot who deal with GWR's systems, so expect a lot of "try turning it off and on again" before they offer any real help.*

Artie Tilsley: *Brilliant. GWR tech support and matchmaking service in one. Truly the pinnacle of efficiency.*

Adam chuckled to himself, the banter in the internal system always a source of amusement. He made a mental note to keep an eye on the messages—sometimes the best ideas (or the most incriminating dirt) came from the chatter between DJs. But for now, his focus was on the Saturday mud wrestling event.

****

"Adam, what's this invoice come into my inbox for trunks with "Hunk" on them?" Sarah Linton said as Adam walked into her office three hours later.

Adam walked into Sarah's office, his usual smirk firmly in place. He knew what this was about, and he was ready to sell it.

"Ah, the trunks," Adam said, dropping into the chair opposite Sarah's desk with a casual air. "I'm going to co-opt James into being the sole Vibes Hunk, a bit of eye candy for the ladies who listen to our station. The mud wrestling event needs a focal point, Sarah, and James is perfect for it. You've seen him—he's fit, he's charming, and let's be honest, he'll draw a crowd."

Sarah sighed, pinching the bridge of her nose. "Adam, this isn't Trent FM. We're trying to establish a respectable brand here, not turn Market Square into an episode of Gladiators. What exactly is your plan for this… spectacle?"

Adam leaned forward, his grin widening. "Simple. James is the eye candy for the young mums and female students who want a bit of a cheeky thrill, and Carly and Anabelle are the stars of the mud wrestling match. Carly's competitive streak and Anabelle's… let's call it flair for the dramatic will keep the crowd engaged. We'll have foam machines for effect, freebies for the students, and a DJ set up to keep the energy high. It's harmless fun, Sarah, and it'll make Brookes Vibes the talk of the town."

Sarah raised an eyebrow. "And you think this will boost our reputation? Because all I see is a potential Radio Authority complaint waiting to happen."

Adam waved a hand dismissively. "Come on, Sarah. This is what local radio thrives on—community engagement, a bit of chaos, and something memorable. No one remembers the safe promos. They remember the ones that push boundaries."

"And what happens if Carly or Anabelle refuses to participate? Or if James decides he doesn't want to prance around in a pair of trunks that say 'Hunk'?"

"They're broke Uni students. They'll do it for the money. Plus, I've already factored in the signing bonuses and shift payments. Carly and Anabelle both need the cash, and James? Well, he's already half in with the lamppost stunt. A bit of harmless fun in trunks won't push him over the edge." Adam leaned back in his chair, exuding confidence.

Sarah folded her arms, her expression sceptical. "And what if it all goes wrong? What's your plan then, Adam? Because I'll tell you now, the board might love a bit of boundary-pushing, but they'll drop you the second Radio Authority comes knocking."

Adam smirked, leaning forward again. "Sarah, you're worrying too much. Anyway, the stunts that various GWR stations pulled over the years set the blueprint for this. Do you think Radio Authority hasn't dealt with complaints about the Black Thunders or Beacon's infamous Bikini Babes campaigns? The key is plausible deniability and staying just on the right side of the line. Besides, I've done my homework—there's nothing illegal about a mud wrestling event in Market Square. The council's aware we're doing a promo event, so long as we keep it clean— figuratively, of course—we're golden."

Sarah sighed again, leaning back in her chair. "Fine, Adam. But if this goes sideways, it's your head on the block. And you're dealing with the fallout, not me. I don't want to see my inbox flooded with complaints from outraged parents or the university board."

Adam grinned, rising from his seat. "Trust me, Sarah, this is going to be legendary. You'll thank me when we're topping the student radio ratings and Fox FM is scrambling to keep up. Anyway, I need to hire some more Babes and get a third Babemobile."

Sarah growled at the mention of a third Babemobile. "You mean to say you want a third Ford Transit with more of your so-called Babes climbing out of it like a clown car? Adam, we're already stretching the budget with two of those gaudy monstrosities. What possible justification do you have for a third?"

"Erm... Artie needs a new girlfriend as he's using the SMS system to recruit potential hookups," Adam said, his grin widening as he played up the ridiculousness. "He's on the late shift before we hand over to the Mix Network, right?"

Sarah's face fell into her hands. "Adam, if you ever start a sentence with 'Artie needs a girlfriend' again, I might actually resign on the spot. And for the record, if Artie gets caught using the SMS system for 'recruitment,' he'll be doing a lot more than searching for a new girlfriend—he'll be looking for a new job."

Adam chuckled, his trademark smirk firmly in place. "Relax, Sarah. I'm just pointing out the colourful personalities we've got on the team. Anyway, Max over at Slough is just as "creative" with his SMS responses. It's all part of the 'charm' of radio, right?" Adam quipped with a wink, already halfway out the door.

"WHAT!" Sarah screamed, and Adam knew he had hit a nerve. He paused in the doorway, his smirk morphing into something a bit more cautious. Sarah was on her feet now, glaring at him with the full force of her authority.

"Adam, you better not be suggesting that half our staff, your clique of ex-GWR mates included, are using company systems to hook up with listeners."

"Hey, it's not like I'm doing it," Adam interrupted, raising his hands defensively, though the smirk lingering on his face didn't help his case. "I'm just saying, Sarah, this is the industry. People flirt; it's harmless. Anyway, you only run this station, not Reading, Cambridge, MK, Watford or Slough," Adam finished with a casual shrug, clearly underestimating the storm brewing in Sarah's eyes. She took a deep breath, visibly trying to keep her composure. "You're not a proper jock unless you've shagged a sales rep, a newsreader, a promo girl and a few listeners."

Sarah's frustration reached its peak, and she fixed Adam with a steely glare. "Adam, if that's your definition of professionalism, I'm surprised you've made it this far without being hauled into an HR tribunal. And for the record, if this station turns into a tabloid scandal, you'll be the one explaining it to the board."

Adam, ever the unflappable performer, grinned wider. "Relax, Sarah. That's why they pay me the big bucks—to walk the line and keep things interesting. Anyway, don't knock the promo game. It's what makes this industry tick."

"Tick?" Sarah snapped. "It's what makes Radio Authority tick—tick-tick-boom, Adam. And I swear, if one more ridiculous invoice or complaint lands on my desk because of your antics, you'll find yourself running promotions for a hospital radio station."

Adam chuckled, unfazed. "Hospital radio? They'd love me there. Imagine the bingo nights with foam machines and mud wrestling." He shot her a wink and strode out of the office before she could respond, leaving Sarah groaning into her hands.

****

CHAPTER 5 – The Library
Saturday 28th September 2003

It had only been a couple of days since the first semester of his second year studying law at Oxford had started, and James Jenkins already felt the pressure building. Between navigating his coursework, maintaining his position as a runner at Brookes Vibes, and fending off Adam Banks' increasingly absurd promotional schemes, the balance was proving tenuous. Yet, somehow, here he was, sitting in the Radcliffe Camera with a pile of legal textbooks and a mind that was anything but focused.

The scent of old paper and polished wood filled the air, the quiet hum of concentrated minds broken only by the occasional rustle of pages or the scratch of a pen. James had always loved the library—it was one of the few places where he could find some semblance of peace amidst the chaos of university life. But today, even the hallowed silence of the Radcliffe couldn't quiet his racing thoughts.

He tapped his pen against his notebook, glancing at the half-finished notes scrawled in his slanted handwriting. Torts, liability, negligence… The words swam before his eyes, refusing to stick. His mind kept drifting back to the weekend's events, the lamppost stunt, and the way Carly had been so fiercely protective of him. There was a fire in her that both intrigued and unsettled him, and he couldn't help but wonder what it all meant.

A soft thud broke his reverie as a book landed on the desk beside him. He looked up to see Carly herself, her blonde hair tied up in a loose bun, a wry smile playing on her lips.

"Fancy seeing you here," she whispered, sliding into the chair opposite him. "Didn't think the library was your scene, Jenkins."

James chuckled softly, leaning back in his chair. "What can I say? Even I need to hit the books sometimes. What brings you here, Hemsworth? Don't tell me you're taking up law as a side hustle. Or do you fancy another of our friends with benefits sessions?"

James knew that he and Carly had history with their relationship being friends with benefits, a few one night stands the previous year when one of the two had been stressed out and needed some light relief. Carly rolled her eyes at his cheeky grin, pulling a thick textbook from her bag and setting it on the table with a thud.

"Not everything is about you, Jenkins," she whispered back, though her teasing tone softened the words. "I'm here because my dorm is chaos, and I actually need to get some work done. Believe it or not, I do study occasionally."

James smirked, leaning forward on his elbows. "Let me guess—you're here to escape Clarissa blasting Destiny's Child and avoid Adam's latest attempt to recruit you for 'Brookes Babes: The Sequel.'"

"Yeah, he is a bit too much, isn't he?" Carly replied, rolling her eyes as she opened her textbook. "You know, I'm hoping my Sociology degree goes well this and next year, because I've decided, I want to join radio full time in a HR team and weed morons like Adam out of the industry. Imagine—radio that's actually professional and doesn't involve mud pits or glittery crop tops." She smirked, her voice dripping with sarcasm, though there was a flicker of genuine ambition in her eyes. "And maybe marry someone who isn't a total jerk like you, Jenkins."

James chuckled, as he knew that this was part of their mating ritual—the playful banter, the jabs that carried just enough truth to sting without wounding. He leaned back in his chair, studying her as she flipped through her book with the air of someone determined to focus but clearly distracted.

"Marry someone like me, you mean?" he teased, raising an eyebrow. "I mean, it makes sense. You'd never be bored."

Carly shot him a look, her lips curving into a sly smile. "Oh, please. You're exactly the kind of guy who'd leave his socks on the floor and expect his wife to laugh at your terrible jokes."

"And you're the kind of girl who'd complain about it but secretly find it endearing," James countered, his grin widening.

She rolled her eyes, though the faint pink creeping into her cheeks betrayed her amusement. "You've got a real high opinion of yourself, don't you?"

"Someone's got to," he said lightly, but his gaze softened as he added, "But seriously, Carly, I think you'd be great in HR. You've got the guts to call people out when they're being idiots, and God knows this industry could use a bit of that. Look, seriously, why did you apply for the Brookes Babe job when you could get a better job as an intern at a proper radio station? You're smart, capable, and clearly overqualified for this mess."

Carly looked up from her book, her expression shifting to something more thoughtful. "Honestly? I needed the money. The grant barely covers rent, let alone food, and Brookes Vibes was paying better than waiting tables at The Bullingdon. Plus," she paused, a hint of a smirk returning, "you can't deny it's been entertaining. Where else would I get to see you tied to a lamppost?"

James laughed softly, shaking his head. "Fair point. Although I'm not sure that's something I want immortalised in the annals of university history."

Carly's eyes twinkled with mischief. "Oh, don't worry. Anyway, why did you apply to be a runner and all round dogsbody when you've got your mock courts, your debates, and your fancy law lectures to keep you busy? Surely there's a more dignified part-time job out there for someone like you."

James shrugged, a faint smile tugging at the corners of his mouth. "Honestly? Same as you. Money's tight, and this gig lets me keep some semblance of control over my schedule. Plus," he added, leaning closer with a mock conspiratorial tone, "I get to see the madness up close. Where else would I witness someone like Adam Banks in his natural habitat?"

Carly laughed, covering her mouth to stifle the sound in the quiet library. "True. It's like watching a reality show, only with fewer scripted lines and more glitter."

James grinned, leaning back again. "And hey, being a runner means I get to bump into you more often. Can't say that's not a perk."

Carly raised an eyebrow, but her smirk gave her away. "Careful, Jenkins. Keep that up, and I might start thinking you enjoy my company."

"Guilty as charged," he said smoothly, his voice dropping just enough to make her cheeks flush again.

Suddenly James's Nokia 3310 bleeped, and he knew that it was likely Adam or someone from the Brookes Vibes team. Picking his phone from his pocket, he saw it wasn't either, but one of the Babes, a woman named Anabelle, a Brookes student who had flirted her way into his contacts and now seemed intent on texting him at every opportunity.

Anabelle: *Hey sxy, u up 4 a drink l8r? Heard ur free 2day xx*

James chuckled as, being on T-Mobile's Pay As You Go plan, he knew that text space was a premium, especially as the storage of them was limited on the 3310 was full. He sighed, shaking his head slightly as he read the text. Carly noticed the flicker of amusement on his face and raised an eyebrow.

"Who's that?" she asked, her tone casual but edged with curiosity.

James hesitated for a split second, then shrugged. "One of the Babes. Anabelle. She's, uh, keen on staying in touch."

Carly snorted, folding her arms as she leaned back in her chair. "Anabelle? The one who spends more time flirting than actually working? Let me guess—she's got you on speed dial for her latest 'fun night out.'"

"Something like that," James admitted, his grin sheepish as he slipped his phone back into his pocket. "She's harmless. Just… enthusiastic."

Carly tilted her head, her smirk widening. "Harmless, huh? So why didn't you text her back? Could it be that you're worried I might judge your taste in... extracurricular activities?"

"Nah, I don't want to waste 35p for sending a reply when I could just tell her no next time I see her," James said with a grin. "Besides, I'd rather not encourage her. She's got enough confidence without me adding fuel to the fire."

Carly chuckled, leaning her chin on her hand. "Smart move. Anabelle strikes me as the type who'd take a 'no' as a challenge anyway."

"Exactly," James said, shaking his head. "I've got enough on my plate without her adding to the chaos. Speaking of which, I should probably get back to this." He gestured to the pile of textbooks in front of him, though his expression made it clear his enthusiasm for studying was at an all-time low.

Carly glanced at the books, then back at him, a playful glint in her eye. "What are you working on?"

"Torts," James said with a groan. "Specifically negligence and liability. Exciting stuff."

"Ooh, sounds riveting," Carly teased. "Tell me, Jenkins, do you actually enjoy law, or are you just in it for the money?"

James paused, his expression softening as he considered the question. "I like it, mostly. It's challenging, and there's a lot of problem-solving involved, which I enjoy. Anyway, my Granddad's a partner in a London firm, so there's a bit of family expectation too."

Carly raised an eyebrow, leaning forward slightly. "Ah, family pressure. That explains a lot. So, you're planning to join the family firm, make a name for yourself, and spend your days in a fancy suit arguing cases in court?"

James laughed softly, shaking his head. "Something like that. Although, if I'm being honest, I'm not sure I want to follow in his footsteps exactly. The idea of working in a big firm has its perks, but it's also... a lot. You're on call 24/7, dealing with high-stakes cases, and there's barely any time for anything else. It's why I like working at Brookes Vibes—it's chaotic, but it's a different kind of chaos."

"Different how?" Carly asked, genuinely curious now.

"It's unpredictable," James replied, a small smile tugging at his lips. "Like Adam, for example. The guy's a walking disaster, but he knows how to keep things interesting. I only got a runner job there last year because they'd put a note on the student job board that made it sound like a professional entry-level gig. I had to go through 2 rounds of interviews by the boss there, Sarah, just to make sure I wasn't pranking them or applying on a dare. Before Adam came up with the Babes, I'd be spending my morning doing general things, grabbing cartridges, grabbing records, covering an early morning shift when a presenter was running late or calling in sick, and occasionally writing the odd promo script. It was mad, but it felt... real. Like I was actually part of something. You remember that one show last year, that Big Bam show on a Sunday, when The Legal Eagle was covering for Big Bam?"

Carly tilted her head, intrigued. "Oh yeah, I remember. That was the show where everything went wrong, right? The one where half the songs didn't play, and the poor guy was left filling the gaps with awkward banter about traffic updates on a Sunday morning?"

James grinned, nodding. "That's the one. It... well, was me. The whole thing was a shitshow... the one cartridge slot got jammed, and then the vinyl player decided to scratch itself out of commission midway through a track. Then the backup CD system just refused to read the discs. The whole studio felt cursed that morning. And then I had to invent traffic and bus delays just to fill the dead air. I remember making up a story about a bus breaking down on Woodstock Road, even though there wasn't a single person on the streets who would have noticed or cared."

Carly laughed, covering her mouth to stifle the sound in the quiet library. "You made up traffic delays? James, you're unbelievable."

"Hey, it was either that or dead air," James replied, his grin widening. "And let me tell you, dead air in radio is the kiss of death. I was doing whatever I could to keep the show afloat, even if it meant convincing listeners that Oxford was in the middle of a fictional traffic apocalypse.

It was that, Elton John's Greatest Hits or Ministry of Sound: The Annual II."

Carly shook her head, a broad grin on her face. "Ministry of Sound? God, James, that would have been a sight. Is it true Vibes lets the presenters just put whatever tracks they want?"

"Apart from the 20 Degrees Hotter CHR slots, yeah," James replied, chuckling. "The big bosses, as you know, are former GWR, and GWR at the moment is enforcing strict playlists at their stations. So, for our main chart shows, the playlist is locked in advance. But for the other slots? If the presenter's quick enough to grab the right records or CDs from the library, they can pretty much play whatever they want. Sarah's fine with that as she comes from Radio Oxford, good old Auntie Beeb, so she believes in letting the presenters have some creative freedom. But Adam? He's the wildcard. He's pushing for more of that GWR-style rigid playlist control, claiming it's 'what the kids want.' Honestly, I think he just likes the power trip of dictating what everyone plays. He's only the Promotions Coordinator but everyone knows he wants the big seat, and the bosses being ex GWR nod like donkeys whenever he pitches his "visionary ideas". Don't get me wrong, I like S Club and Steps as much as the next guy, but if I have to hear Tragedy on rotation one more time, I might start questioning my life choices."

"Hey, don't disrespect Steps!" Carly interjected with mock indignation, a playful smile tugging at her lips. "Tragedy is a classic, Jenkins. It's practically a cultural treasure."

James held his hands up in surrender, his grin broadening. "All right, all right. I'll give you that one. But admit it—if you had to hear it five times a day for a week straight, you'd be begging for some Oasis or Blur to cleanse your ears."

Carly tilted her head, pretending to consider. "Hmm, maybe. But then again, I wouldn't mind a bit of Spice Girls to break the monotony. Girl Power, you know?"

James chuckled, shaking his head. "You've got eclectic taste, Hemsworth. Spice Girls one minute, trying to dismantle the patriarchy the next. You're a walking contradiction. Hey, I'm on shift Sunday in the runner role, so do you fancy spending the day at the studio. It's an Adam Free Zone then, and maybe Bam'll let you spin a few tracks," he added, his grin mischievous. "Sarah won't mind as long as you're on the payroll, and you've got someone who's trained covering you."

Carly raised an eyebrow, a glint of intrigue in her eyes. "Are you trying to lure me into Brookes Vibes HQ on a Sunday, Jenkins? What's the catch?"

James shrugged, his expression feigning innocence. "No catch. Just thought you might enjoy the chaos-free version of Vibes. No mud pits, no glitter, just music and the occasional made-up traffic report. And hey, if you're good, I might even let you pick a track or two."

Carly laughed, leaning forward on her elbows. "You know what? I might just take you up on that. But if you play another Ministry of Sound compilation, I'm out."

"Deal," James said, grinning. "Although, you'll have to admit, there's something nostalgic about a bit of '90s house music to liven up a Sunday morning."

"Fine," Carly conceded with a smirk. "But only if I get to pick at least one Spice Girls track. Deal?"

"Deal," James agreed, reaching across the table to shake her hand. "Welcome to the world of radio, Hemsworth. Just don't let Adam find out—he'll probably try to make you the new face of Brookes Babes: DJ Edition."

As the two shook hands, James noticed Clarissa coming over with Tina, Emma and Hayley, three other members of the Brookes Babes, carrying coffee cups and wearing the unmistakable look of people about to stir some mischief. Clarissa, ever the ringleader, shot James and Carly a sly grin as she approached the table.

"Well, well, look who we've found having a study date," Clarissa teased, sliding into the seat next to Carly while the others clustered around. "Should we leave you two lovebirds to it, or is this a public performance?"

James rolled his eyes but smirked. "We're just studying, Clarissa. But by all means, feel free to narrate this like it's some grand romance novel."

"Just studying, my arse," Clarissa shot back, nudging Carly with her elbow. "Adam's phoned me. Em, Tina and I are doing a leaflet Saturday over at JR Hospital, and apparently you and Jenkins won't be there, but in the Market Square."

Carly groaned, sinking into her chair as if Clarissa's words physically weighed her down. "Market Square? What now? Another ridiculous Adam Banks masterpiece?"

Clarissa grinned, clearly enjoying Carly's frustration. "Apparently. Adam's decided you and Jenkins are the 'dream team' for high visibility. Something about your 'chemistry' and how it'll 'draw people in.'" She made exaggerated air quotes with her fingers, her tone dripping with sarcasm.

James shook his head, laughing under his breath. "Dream team? More like a disaster waiting to happen. What's the plan this time—tying us both to lampposts?"

"Close," Clarissa replied, smirking. "You're hosting some 'live engagement activity' in the square. One of the Brookes skanks are joining you. He says that you'll find out tomorrow."

Carly's groan was audible enough to draw a sharp glance from the librarian, who pointedly raised a finger to her lips. Carly mouthed a quick apology before turning her incredulous gaze back to Clarissa.

"'Live engagement activity'? That sounds like code for public humiliation," Carly whispered sharply. "And what's this about a Brookes skank joining us? Who's he dug up this time? Mary? Ally?"

Clarissa shrugged, sipping her coffee with a smug grin. "Didn't get details, just that Adam thinks it'll be 'a great opportunity to showcase the Babes' brand' or whatever nonsense he's cooked up. You'd better bring your A-game, Hemsworth."

Carly slumped back in her chair, rubbing her temples. "This isn't a radio job—it's a social experiment in how far Adam can push us before we all revolt."

James chuckled, clearly enjoying her misery a bit too much. "Come on, it might not be so bad. Market Square's not as public as The Bullingdon was, and at least this time I won't be tied to a lamppost."

Clarissa smirked, her gaze flicking between Carly and James. "No, but I wouldn't rule out glitter cannons or impromptu karaoke. Adam's got a way of turning even the simplest tasks into full-blown theatre."

James leaned forward, grinning at Carly. "Well, if it's going to be a disaster, at least we'll go down together. And who knows? Maybe this Brookes skank will take some of the attention off us."

Carly rolled her eyes, her voice heavy with sarcasm. "Oh, joy. That'll make it all worthwhile."

Just then, Tina, Emma, and Hayley pulled up chairs and plopped themselves down at the table, their voices barely hushed despite the library's sacred quiet. Tina, ever the optimist, grinned as she set down a latte. "Guys, you're overthinking it. Market Square could be fun! It's got foot traffic, atmosphere, and—"

"Pigeons," Carly cut in, her expression deadpan. "Lots and lots of pigeons. The perfect audience for Adam's nonsense."

Tina laughed, undeterred. "Hey, pigeons need entertainment too. And who knows? Maybe one of them will steal a flyer and become Brookes Vibes' most loyal listener."

Emma snorted into her coffee, trying to keep her laughter quiet. "Can't be worse than Adam's idea of 'branding.' Did I tell you he wanted us to wear feather boas at the hospital promo on Saturday? Something about 'bringing glamour to healthcare.'"

James arched an eyebrow. "Feather boas? Is he running a radio station or auditioning for a Vegas revue?"

Hayley chimed in, her tone sceptical but amused. "Knowing Adam, he'd probably love the Vegas vibe. I can already hear him pitching the 'Vibes Babes All-Stars' as a national brand."

Clarissa rolled her eyes, leaning back in her chair. "And we'd all quit before he could get the logo printed. Honestly, the guy's a walking HR nightmare."

Carly groaned, rubbing her temples again. "I can't believe we're stuck with him. If he says one more thing about 'chemistry' or 'visual engagement,' I might lose it."

James smirked, resting his chin on his hand. "Well, at least we've got each other, Hemsworth. If we're going to survive this circus, we might as well do it together."

Carly glanced at him, her frustration softening slightly as a small smile tugged at her lips. "Yeah, Jenkins. If I'm going down, I'm dragging you with me."

"Deal," James said with a grin. "But just so you know, if pigeons start attacking the glitter cannons, you're on your own."

The group burst into quiet laughter, earning another stern look from the librarian. Carly shook her head, her smile lingering as she looked around at her friends. For all the chaos Adam brought into their lives, moments like this—laughing together in the midst of the madness—made it almost worth it.

****

CHAPTER 6 – The Hunk
Saturday 28th September 2003

"Right, James," Adam began, clapping his hands together in a show of enthusiasm that made James instinctively flinch. "These are your trunks for the day." He held up a pair of black swim shorts with the word HUNK emblazoned in bold, glittering gold letters across the back.

Carly had to chuckle at how she and James had arrived at the Brookes Vibes HQ early, as James had told her that he wanted to show her something, only for Adam to grab the two and whisk them into the promotions office without so much as a greeting. Now, James was holding a pair of what could only be described as the most garish swim trunks ever created, his expression a mixture of horror and disbelief.

"You cannot be serious," James finally managed, staring at the offending garment as though it might bite him.

"Deadly serious, mate," Adam replied, his grin stretching from ear to ear. "You're the face—well, backside—of this promotion. The listeners are going to love it, and if we're lucky, it'll make the front page of the student papers. Just think of the exposure!"

"Exposure's the right word," Carly muttered under her breath, unable to resist. James shot her a withering look, which only made her laugh harder.

"Adam, there's no way I'm wearing these in public," James protested, thrusting the trunks back at him.

"James," Adam said, adopting a faux serious tone as he held up his hands, "think of this as a rite of passage. Every great radio personality has done something ridiculous in the name of promotion. Besides, the mud wrestling isn't about you; it's about the station. You're just the hook to get people in. Anyway, here's a pill or two to help enhance... something."

James blinked at Adam, unsure whether he'd misheard. "Pills? What are you on about?"

Adam smirked, waving his hand dismissively. "Relax, mate. It'll help you get a stiffy."

James's jaw practically hit the floor, and Carly doubled over in laughter, clutching her sides.

"Are you joking?" James finally spluttered, his face now a shade of crimson that matched the promotional flyers scattered across Adam's desk.

"Nope, we need your trunks look like you're packing a bit of extra muscle," Adam said with a wink, clearly relishing James's discomfort. "Trust me, it's all part of the showbiz magic. Everyone does it—ask any male model. Well, maybe not on their first gig, but you're a natural!"

Carly wiped tears of laughter from her eyes and managed to gasp, "Oh, James, please—please tell me you're not actually considering it!"

James, still holding the garish trunks at arm's length as if they might contaminate him, rounded on Adam. "There is no way I'm wearing these. Forget the pills—this whole thing is insane. Mud wrestling in Market Square? Do you even hear yourself?"

Adam leaned casually against his desk, clearly unbothered by James's protests. "It's called engagement, James. You want to stand out in this industry, right? Well, this is how you do it. You think Chris Moyles or Scott Mills got where they are by playing it safe? Nah, mate. They put themselves out there, did the mad stuff, and look at them now. You've got to embrace the chaos. Anyway, two Babes fighting over you in 12 degrees weather, its every blokes dream, right?"

Carly watched the door open, and Annabelle walk in, her manicured fingers tapping rhythmically on the frame before she entered fully, her breasts, which Carly could tell were fake and, thanks to the Babes uniform of a low-cut top, almost falling out of the plunging neckline. Her arrival drew an immediate reaction from Adam, whose grin widened as if he'd just found the final piece of his promotional puzzle. Carly, however, was unimpressed.

"Skank," she muttered, and she noticed James had heard her. He glanced sideways, suppressing a smirk, though his expression quickly sobered when Annabelle's gaze landed squarely on him. She sashayed into the room, her heels clicking audibly against the tiled floor, and leaned casually against the edge of Adam's desk, her overly bright smile aimed directly at James.

"Well, well," Annabelle purred, flicking her hair over her shoulder. "If it isn't our very own 'Hunk.'" She let the word linger, her gaze raking over James in a way that made him visibly uncomfortable.

"Annabelle, perfect timing!" Adam exclaimed, clapping his hands together again. "James was just about to try on his trunks for the big event. Weren't you, James?"

"I was just about to tell you no," James retorted, glaring at Adam. "In fact, I'm still telling you no."

Annabelle pouted dramatically, tilting her head as though James had just insulted her personally. "Oh, come on, James. Don't be such a spoilsport. It's all in good fun. And think of all the attention you'll get—girls swooning over you, guys wanting to be you…" She trailed off, her eyes sparkling with mischief.

Carly, who had been silently fuming, finally spoke up, her tone dripping with sarcasm. "Yes, James, think of all the attention. Who wouldn't want to be ogled in freezing temperatures while rolling around in a pit of mud?"

In a way, Carly knew that she really wanted to see James wearing nothing but the trunks, as she knew he had the body for it, as they had slept together the previous Uni year, and were friends with benefits, and that her crush on him was still as strong as ever, even though she knew they'd both tried to keep things casual. But seeing Annabelle fawning over him like that made Carly's blood boil. She wasn't sure if it was jealousy, protectiveness, or just sheer frustration with how ridiculous this whole situation was—but it was something.

James shot her a quick glance, clearly catching the edge in her tone, but before he could say anything, Adam interjected. "See? Even Carly agrees this is a golden opportunity, mate. You're overthinking it. Besides, the girls are going to be in the mud too—it's not like you're the only one taking one for the team here."

Annabelle's pout turned into a smug smile as she turned to Carly. "Oh, don't tell me you're jealous, Carly. It's just a bit of fun. Maybe you're worried James won't have eyes for anyone else once I'm done with him?"

Carly rolled her eyes, crossing her arms tightly over her chest. "Oh, please. If I wanted to roll around in mud to impress someone, I'd at least make sure it wasn't supervised by him," she said, jerking her thumb towards Adam.

Adam, unfazed, grinned. "Carly, I'm flattered you think I'd supervise. I'll be too busy managing the DJ set and hyping up the crowd. But don't worry, I'll make sure we've got plenty of towels for everyone once it's over."

James, still clutching the trunks, finally let out an exasperated sigh. "Fine. I'll do it. But I'm not taking any pills, and if this goes sideways, I'm holding you personally responsible, Adam."

****

An hour later, James was standing by the Babemobile, and Carly had to admit, after taking the pills, his erection was even bigger than what she remembered from their previous encounters. The swim trunks didn't leave much to the imagination, and James's discomfort was palpable. He kept shifting his weight from foot to foot, trying to look anywhere but at Carly or Annabelle, who were both dressed in their 'Babes' low cut tops and short skirts, the stockings and heels that completed their promotional outfits doing little to offer warmth in the crisp autumn air.

The Market Square was buzzing with a mix of curiosity and incredulity as students and locals gathered to witness the spectacle. Adam was in his element, darting between the DJ booth and the mud pit, his headset crackling as he barked orders at the production team. The foam machines were already churning out bubbles, and the portable showers stood at the ready, their sleek white enclosures gleaming under the weak September sun.

Carly watched as James adjusted his trunks for the hundredth time, clearly regretting every decision that had led him to this moment. She couldn't help but smirk. "Looking good, Hunk," she teased, her tone light but with just enough edge to let him know she was enjoying his discomfort.

"Remind me why I agreed to this," James muttered, glancing around as if searching for an escape route.

"Because you're a people pleaser," Carly replied sweetly, before adding under her breath, "and a pushover."

Annabelle, who had been standing nearby, sidled up to James and placed a perfectly manicured hand on his arm. "Relax, James," she cooed. "You look amazing. Everyone's going to love you. Fancy a quickie in the Babemobile before Big Bam starts his show?"

James stiffened (even more than the pills had managed), his face a mixture of horror and disbelief as he glanced between Annabelle and Carly. Carly's expression immediately darkened, her lips tightening into a thin line as she folded her arms.

"Annabelle, maybe save the seduction routine for someone who actually wants it," Carly snapped, her voice sharper than she intended. Pulling the buxom blonde aside, Carly knew that she was unofficially marking her territory, making Annabelle realise that James wasn't as available as she thought. "He's not interested, okay? And maybe tone it down—this is a mud wrestling event, not Blind Date."

Annabelle raised an eyebrow, her smug smile fading slightly as she sized Carly up. "Relax, Carly. It's just banter. Besides, isn't it up to James to decide who he's interested in?"

"He doesn't want some Brookes skank. He's mine, bitch, and if you so much as even think of touching him again, you'll be eating mud before we even start the wrestling." Carly's voice was low and laced with a cold determination that caught Annabelle off guard.

"Well, I don't see your name on his forehead," Annabelle shot back, crossing her arms and leaning in slightly, her voice a mocking whisper. "He's single, has fucking hot pecs, and is a law student. The perfect catch, wouldn't you say?"

Carly clenched her jaw, stepping closer until she was just inches from Annabelle. "Yeah, he is. Which is why you're not going anywhere near him. Let's keep this professional, shall we? Mud wrestling's messy enough without your drama adding to it."

Annabelle raised her hands in mock surrender, her smirk returning as she stepped back. "Alright, alright. Don't get your knickers in a twist, darling. I'll play nice. For now."

Carly knew Annabelle was pushing her buttons, but there was something about her that felt calculated. The woman oozed confidence, but Carly could sense it was a facade meant to provoke and dominate. Carly exhaled sharply, willing herself to focus on the ridiculous event ahead rather than Annabelle's antics. She turned on her heel and marched back towards James, who was now trying to adjust his trunks while also avoiding the gaze of a group of girls giggling nearby.

"Everything alright?" James asked, his tone tentative. He'd clearly noticed the tension between Carly and Annabelle.

"Peachy," Carly replied curtly, then softened her tone when she saw the genuine concern in his eyes. "Look, let's just get through this. Do your bit, flash that award-winning smile, and maybe we'll both survive the day without throttling Adam or Annabelle."

James chuckled despite himself. "That bad, huh?"

"Worse," Carly muttered, grabbing a handful of flyers from the table near the Babemobile. "But hey, at least you've got me to save you from the fangirls."

"Much appreciated," James said, offering her a grateful smile that made Carly's stomach flip. Damn him and his stupid charm.

As the event kicked off, Adam took to the microphone with his usual over-the-top enthusiasm, hyping up the crowd and introducing the day's main attraction: "The Battle of the Babes." The foam machines spewed bubbles into the air as music blasted from the speakers, and a cheer erupted from the crowd as Carly and Annabelle were introduced as the mud-wrestling contenders.

Carly took her place near the mud pit, her heart pounding as the cold air nipped at her exposed skin. She shot a quick glance at James, who was stationed nearby, handing out promotional merchandise and flashing awkward smiles at the growing crowd. He caught her eye and gave her a subtle thumbs-up, his expression equal parts encouragement and apology.

Annabelle, of course, played up her role, blowing kisses to the crowd and striking exaggerated poses. Carly rolled her eyes but forced a confident smile as she prepared to step into the mud.

And then Annabelle did it.

She kissed James and started stroking the bulge in his trunks.

In full public view.

The crowd gasped, a mix of laughter, shock, and wolf whistles rippling through Market Square. James froze, his eyes wide with a combination of embarrassment and disbelief, as Annabelle leaned in closer, her lips barely brushing his ear as she whispered something Carly couldn't hear.

Carly, however, had seen enough. Her blood boiled, and without thinking, she stormed over to where the pair stood. Ignoring the mud pit, the foam machines, and the gawking crowd, she grabbed Annabelle's arm and threw the Brookes student into the mud pit, head first, causing Annabelle to land with a resounding splash. The crowd erupted in cheers and laughter, their attention now firmly fixed on the unexpected drama unfolding before them. Annabelle flailed in the mud, sputtering indignantly as she tried to regain her balance, her carefully crafted image now a soggy, messy shadow of itself.

And then Carly jumped in behind her, and started grappling with Annabelle in the mud, her frustration boiling over into a flurry of half-hearted wrestling moves that were more about venting her anger than following any scripted promotional stunt. The crowd's cheers grew louder, a chaotic mix of amusement and shock as the two women splashed and grappled, their supposed "friendly competition" quickly devolving into a full-blown spectacle.

Ding Ding Ding

The sound of the wrestling bell signifying that the bout was commencing filled the air, but neither Carly nor Annabelle paid it much attention. The crowd's cheers and jeers reached a fever pitch as the two women continued their impromptu brawl. Annabelle, now thoroughly coated in mud, managed to grab a handful of Carly's hair, but Carly retaliated with a firm shove that sent Annabelle stumbling backward and landing on her backside with a wet splat.

Carly watched as Adam grabbed the mic, a grin on his face. "The following contest is scheduled for one fall, and it is for the Queen of the Babes title! Introducing, in the mud wrestling pit to my left, Carly 'The Crusher' Hemsworth, and to my right, Annabelle 'The Glamazon' Young!"

The crowd roared with laughter and applause, eating up the impromptu chaos. Adam, ever the performer, milked the moment for all it was worth, gesturing dramatically toward the mud pit.

Carly, now thoroughly coated in mud herself, turned to glare at Adam. "You're enjoying this way too much!" she shouted, wiping a streak of mud off her face.

Showbiz, darling!" Adam called back, throwing his arms wide as if to take credit for the entire spectacle.

Annabelle, still seated in the mud, finally found her footing and glared daggers at Carly. "You're going to regret that, Hemsworth," she hissed, lunging forward and grabbing Carly by the waist. The two tumbled into the mud again, a flurry of limbs and streaks of brown as the crowd egged them on.

"And the special guest referee is our own Brookes Hunk, James "The Legal Eagle" Jenkins!" Carly heard Adam announce, and then saw Anabelle stand up and pull James, who was at the side of the ring, into the mud, before groping his backside with the force of someone staking a claim. James stumbled, his expression a mixture of shock and mortification as he landed in the mud alongside Carly and Annabelle. The crowd roared with laughter, and several students scrambled to capture the moment on their early-model camera phones, knowing this spectacle would be the talk of the campus for weeks.

Carly, seething at Annabelle's brazenness, pushed herself upright and wiped mud from her face. "You've crossed the line, Annabelle," she said through gritted teeth.

Annabelle, ever smug, tossed her mud-slicked hair over her shoulder and smirked. "Oh, please, Carly. Don't act like you own him. He's fair game, and he doesn't seem to mind, does he? Look, he's that stiff that a whistle might go off in a second!"

James, still seated in the mud, was now beetroot red. "Can we not? Seriously, this is insane," he muttered, his voice just loud enough for Carly to hear. He looked to her, his eyes pleading for someone to restore order, but Carly's blood was boiling too much to think straight.

And then Annabelle grabbed a large amount of mud and, pulling Carly's top forward, placed the mud in-between the fabric and Carly's skin, letting it slap back into place. Carly gasped at the sudden coldness against her chest and felt her frustration boil over into pure fury. The crowd's cheers and whistles intensified, their phones now firmly pointed at the mud-covered spectacle.

"Right, that's it!" Carly shouted, lunging toward Annabelle with a renewed determination. She grabbed the other woman by the shoulders and sent her toppling backward into the mud again. This time, Annabelle let out a shriek that was more indignation than pain, flailing as she tried to regain her balance.

James, who had been awkwardly trying to extricate himself from the pit, ended up slipping again and landed face-first in the mud, drawing another wave of laughter and applause from the crowd.

"Ladies, please," he said, his voice muffled as he tried to push himself up. "Can we not make this any worse than it already is?"

But Carly wasn't listening. She knew Annabelle wasn't done and was preparing for another dirty move, both figuratively and literally. The mud had long since stopped being a prop for the event and was now the battlefield of a personal grudge match. Carly braced herself, her heart pounding with adrenaline and frustration as Annabelle lunged toward her again, mud flying in every direction.

"Careful, Hemsworth," Annabelle hissed, grabbing Carly's arm in a mock grapple. "Wouldn't want you to ruin that reputation of yours. Oh wait—you already have."

Carly smirked, adrenaline now fuelling her actions. "Better to ruin a reputation than never have one to begin with, Annabelle."

The crowd's roars intensified as the two wrestled again, their movements increasingly chaotic. Carly managed to slip behind Annabelle, grabbing her waist and flipping her onto her back with an unceremonious splash. The mud swallowed Annabelle's shriek, and Carly stood over her triumphantly, catching her breath as the crowd cheered.

Adam, who had been narrating the entire scene with gleeful commentary, grabbed his microphone and declared, "And the winner and new Brookes Vibe Queen of the Babes, Carly 'The Crusher' Hemsworth!"

The crowd erupted into cheers and laughter, their applause a mix of genuine amusement and disbelief at the spectacle they'd just witnessed. Adam, ever the opportunist, was already motioning to the DJ to crank up the music, and foam from the machines cascaded into the scene, adding a surreal touch to the muddy chaos.

James finally managed to haul himself out of the pit, his trunks clinging awkwardly to him, mud streaking every visible part of his body. He shook his head, muttering under his breath, "This is beyond ridiculous." He glanced at Carly, who was still standing triumphantly in the mud, her chest heaving from exertion but her face alight with victory.

"Nice moves, Hemsworth," he said, his tone half-teasing, half-admiring. "You didn't need to go so hard, though. It's just Annabelle."

Carly shot him a sidelong glance, her smirk softening slightly. "She deserved it, Jenkins. Nobody gets to mess with my... um, with us, without consequences."

James raised an eyebrow, a small smile tugging at the corners of his mouth. "Your... what? Come on, Carly, finish the sentence."

Carly turned away quickly, pretending to smooth the mud on her skirt as she avoided his gaze. "Don't push your luck, Jenkins. You're still in those trunks, and I'm tempted to leave you here to face the crowd alone."

James laughed, his good humour returning despite the absurdity of the situation. "Fair enough. But just so you know, you looked kind of badass out there. A muddy, furious badass, but still."

Carly's cheeks flushed, though she quickly blamed it on the cold as she climbed out of the pit and grabbed a towel from the stack by the Babemobile. Annabelle, meanwhile, was sulking in the mud, her perfectly styled hair now a matted mess and her makeup streaked beyond recognition.

Adam, ever the entertainer, leaned into the microphone and said, "Ladies and gentlemen, let's hear it for the Babes! And don't forget to tune into Brookes Vibes for all the latest chaos and entertainment. You won't want to miss it!"

As the crowd began to disperse, chattering excitedly about the day's events, Carly found herself standing next to James, both of them wrapped in oversized towels and dripping mud onto the pavement. The tension from earlier seemed to have melted away, leaving a comfortable silence between them.

"Thanks for not letting me drown out there," James said, glancing at her with a grin.

Carly rolled her eyes but smiled. "You're welcome. But next time, maybe don't let Adam talk you into being the 'Hunk.'"

James chuckled, running a hand through his mud-streaked hair. "Next time, I'm bringing backup. Preferably someone who can stop you from turning a mud wrestling match into a full-on battle royale."

****

CHAPTER 7 – Carly On Air
Saturday 28th September 2003

Turning up at the Brookes Vibes studios in Summertown at 8am on a Sunday morning was not exactly Carly's idea of fun, but James had promised her that he'd try and show her what the station was like when it was an Adam free zone. Summertown's quiet streets were still waking up as Carly trudged towards the unassuming building that housed Brookes Vibes. The station didn't exactly scream "professional radio" from the outside—it looked more like a converted office block than a hub of local entertainment. But for all its quirks and chaos, Carly couldn't deny there was something endearing about it.

James was already waiting for her outside, leaning against the doorframe with a steaming coffee in hand. He looked uncharacteristically relaxed in a hoodie and jeans, his usual air of cheeky confidence softened by the early hour.

"Morning, Hemsworth," he greeted her with a grin. "I see you've survived the ungodly hour. I was half expecting you to call in sick."

Carly rolled her eyes, though she couldn't help but smile. "Believe me, I considered it. But then I thought, 'What if Jenkins manages to screw something up without me there to witness it?' I couldn't risk missing that."

"Touché," James replied, pushing the door open and gesturing for her to follow him inside. "Welcome to the Adam-free zone. I promise, no glitter, no lampposts, just pure professionalism. And care to guess what..."

Carly looked at James with the same raised eyebrow she often used when he was about to exaggerate. "What? That you're secretly the best thing about this station?"

James smirked, stepping aside to let her in. "Close. But no, I was going to say… free biscuits. The hobnobs are top-tier. Nah, Big Bam's called in sick, so I'm covering his 9am show... or should I say we are."

Carly stopped mid-step, her eyes narrowing as she turned to face James. "We? What do you mean 'we'? I thought I was just here to watch you flounder."

James grinned, clearly revelling in her scepticism. "Oh, come on, Hemsworth. You've got opinions, wit, and enough sass to power the whole of Oxfordshire. What better way to show you the ropes than throwing you on air with me? It'll be fun. Plus, we'll be the first show out of the automation, so we've got only the entire county of Oxfordshire to wake up. You see, overnight, the bosses here have a deal with GWR so they can air the Mix Network's overnight shows, which means we're the first voices people hear when they switch on after a night of cheesy pop and overplayed dance remixes. We get to reset the vibe."

Carly's mouth fell open in a mix of amusement and disbelief. "You're joking, right? You seriously want me, a total amateur, to go live on air with you? I haven't got a clue what I'm doing, Jenkins!"

James waved a dismissive hand. "Details, details. You'll be fine. Just be yourself—our listeners love a bit of personality. Besides, it's a Sunday morning. Half the audience are either hungover, still asleep, or driving their kids to some sports match. Low stakes."

Carly shook her head, a reluctant smile tugging at her lips. "This is either going to be brilliant or a total train wreck. Fine, I'll do it—but only if you promise not to throw me under the bus when it all goes wrong. Anyway, why do they use the Mix Network? I thought this was an independent station, not some GWR clone."

James shrugged, leading Carly down the narrow hallway towards the studio. "Technically, it is independent, but the Group bosses here, the owners, are former GWR management, so they got a deal with their old mob, as y'know Fox FM... they're owned by Capital, so it's a chance to stick a few middle fingers up. Capital and GWR hate each other so much that even if the two ever married, they'd probably end up being bossed around by GWR and moving into Capital's London HQ while pretending it was their idea all along." James chuckled at his own analogy. "Basically, it's cheaper for them to air The Mix overnight than to staff it locally, plus the bosses, as I said, hate Capital with that much of a vengeance that they'd probably broadcast static before they'd air anything related to Fox FM. It's all politics and saving cash. But hey, it keeps the lights on."

Carly rolled her eyes as they reached the studio door. "Sounds like everything in this industry is about politics or money. No wonder you're all so chaotic. How do you know all this, besides being a runner. I thought you'd just be the tea boy."

James chuckled, holding the studio door open for Carly. "Oh, I'm definitely the tea boy, don't get me wrong. But when you spend enough time hanging around here, you pick up on the politics—especially when Sarah's on a rant about the bosses upstairs. Plus, I might have sat in on a few meetings where I was meant to be fetching coffee but ended up eavesdropping instead."

Carly stepped into the studio and immediately took in the slightly shabby yet oddly charming setup. The desk was cluttered with equipment, CDs, and a few empty coffee cups. The walls were adorned with posters of events from years gone by, and the faint hum of the air conditioning filled the small space.

"I know Studio 3 was all full of clothes and Babes uniforms when I first came here last week, but I didn't realise how messy the actual studio could be," Carly said, scanning the room with a mix of amusement and concern. "Are all radio studios like this, or is Brookes Vibes just special?"

James grinned, setting his coffee down on the desk. "A bit of both, honestly. This place has character, let's call it that. And as for Studio 3, well, Adam treats it like his personal dressing room for his latest schemes. Don't worry, though—this one's fully functional. Mostly."

"Mostly?" Carly raised an eyebrow, stepping gingerly over a tangled cable on the floor.

"Relax," James said, waving her over to the microphone. "Everything important works… usually. Here, sit down. I'll walk you through it before we go live."

Carly perched nervously on the edge of the chair James pulled out for her. He leaned over the desk, flipping switches and adjusting sliders with a casual confidence that made it all seem deceptively simple.

"Right," James began, pointing to a few key controls. "This is your microphone—obviously. Keep about a fist's distance from it, and don't shout unless you want to blow out the listeners' eardrums. This slider here controls your volume, and this one's for the music. See this big red button? That's the cough button. Hit that if you need to clear your throat or, y'know, swear at me mid-show."

Carly smirked, leaning forward to examine the controls. "Tempting. What else?"

"These," James said, gesturing to a stack of CDs and a playlist sheet, "are our songs for the hour. The first track's queued up and ready to go as soon as we're live. I'll handle the intro, but feel free to jump in whenever. The main thing is to relax and have fun. It's not rocket science—it's just radio. Just treat it as when we're in the dorms, chilling and talking rubbish about Adam's latest disasters or Clarissa's obsession with glitter. The audience loves a bit of personality, remember?"

Carly exhaled slowly, glancing at the microphone with a mix of curiosity and apprehension. "Right, so no pressure, then. Just an entire county listening to me make a fool of myself."

James grinned, nudging her shoulder playfully. "Exactly. But if it makes you feel better, remember most of them probably haven't had their coffee yet. Their expectations are low. Now, I'll introduce the show-most of the time we use nicknames or radio names here, as its more relatable and a bit of fun. Big Bam, for instance, is just a nickname—his real name's Brian."

Carly laughed at this, her nerves loosening slightly. "Brian? Big Bam sounds way cooler. So what's your radio name, Jenkins? Let me guess—something ridiculously suave like James 'The Charmer' Jenkins?"

James smirked, leaning back in his chair. "Sometimes I go by 'The Legal Eagle, JJ'," he said with a mock-serious tone, "because of my law degree. But honestly, it depends on my mood. On a lazy Sunday like this, I might just stick with James J."

Carly snorted, leaning back in her chair. "Legal Eagle, huh? Very professional. Well, since I'm being thrown into the deep end here, do I get a radio name too? Or am I just 'Carly the Reluctant Co-Host'?"

James tapped his chin, pretending to consider it seriously. "How about 'Carly the Crusher'? You've got the mud wrestling cred to back it up. Or... 'The Queen Babe'? After all, you did win the mud wrestling match yesterday. It's only fitting."

Carly groaned, though she couldn't help but laugh. "Please don't. I don't want to be known as 'The Queen Babe.' That's the last thing I need. How about just... Carly H? Simple, understated, and less likely to make me cringe."

James nodded, pretending to be impressed. "Carly H it is. Alright, we're going live in thirty seconds. Ready?"

Carly took a deep breath, her palms slightly clammy as she adjusted her position in the chair. "As I'll ever be. Just… don't let me mess this up, okay?"

James grinned, his hand hovering over the button to activate their mics. "You've got this, Hemsworth. Here we go."

The red "ON AIR" light flicked on, and the faint hum of the intro music filled the studio. James leaned into his microphone, his voice instantly adopting the smooth, lively tone of a seasoned presenter.

"Good morning, Oxfordshire! You're listening to Brookes Vibes, and this is the Sunday Wake-Up with me, James J, and I'm filling in for Big Bam who's not well... there again, when you spend your Saturday doing a live show at Oxford's Market Square and having to watch two of the Brookes Babes, our very own beautiful street team, going at it in a mud wrestling match for the title of Queen of the Brookes Bakes... well, let's just say, you'd probably call in sick too!" James paused, flashing Carly a playful grin as he gestured for her to speak. "But don't worry, folks, you're in good hands this morning. Joining me today is a very special guest. Say hello to the Queen herself, Carly H!"

Carly felt a wave of heat rush to her face as James's words sunk in. She leaned forward, her voice a little hesitant but steady enough to make her debut.

"Good morning, Oxfordshire," she said, her voice carrying just the right balance of sarcasm and charm. "And let me clarify something right off the bat—I didn't ask for the title of Queen of the Babes. That was all

Adam's doing, and, trust me, I've already regretted stepping into that mud pit. But since I'm here, I guess I'll do my best to keep this show from derailing entirely."

James chuckled, his grin widening. "See, folks, this is why I brought Carly H on board today. Wit, charm, and absolutely no tolerance for nonsense. Exactly what you need on a Sunday morning."

Carly smirked, relaxing slightly as the banter flowed naturally. "Or maybe you just needed someone to bail you out when you inevitably mess up the playlist."

"Touché," James replied, leaning back in his chair. "Speaking of the playlist, we've got a cracking line-up this morning to ease you into the day. But before we get to that, Carly, how about you share a little insight into what it's like being a Brookes Babe? The people need to know—was the mud wrestling as glamorous as it looked?"

Carly groaned dramatically, shaking her head. "Oh, absolutely. Nothing screams glamour like freezing mud, foam cannons, and Adam Banks narrating your every move. Honestly, James, the only thing missing was a tiara."

James laughed, clearly enjoying her dry humour. "A tiara would've been the cherry on top. But hey, at least you got to win the crowd over—and maybe scare Annabelle into rethinking her career choices."

James laughed, clearly enjoying her dry humour. "A tiara would've been the cherry on top. But hey, at least you got to win the crowd over—and maybe scare Annabelle into rethinking her career choices. Anyway, if you want to say hello to Carly, just give us a ring, our phone number is 01865 570248 or text Y6NW4 on 60777, that's 01865 570248 or text Y6NW4 on 60777, that's Y for Yellow, 6 for Six, N for November, W for Whiskey, 4 for Four. Standard text rates apply, and if you're lucky, Carly might even read your text live on air."

Carly shot James a mock glare, leaning closer to her mic. "Or, if you want to save yourself the effort, just send in a compliment for James here. He clearly needs the ego boost."

James smirked, leaning back in his chair with an air of exaggerated nonchalance. "See what I mean, Oxfordshire? Pure wit. Alright, let's kick things off with something upbeat to wake everyone up. Here's It Feels So Good by Sonique, because nothing says Sunday morning like a throwback banger. Stay tuned—you're in for a treat."

He slid the music fader up, and the opening beats of the track filled the studio. As the song played, James turned to Carly, his grin still firmly in place.

"See? That wasn't so bad, was it?" he asked, pulling off his headphones.

Carly exhaled, sitting back in her chair with a half-smile. "Not bad at all. But don't get too comfortable, Jenkins. I'm just warming up."

"Good. Right, what we do if a listener phones in is we record the call first, and then I'll edit it in Audacity before we air it," James continued, gesturing towards the small recording setup to his right. "It's quicker than you'd think, and it makes sure we don't accidentally put any dodgy stuff live on air. You wouldn't believe the things people try to say when they think no one's listening."

Carly raised an eyebrow, intrigued. "Like what? Give me an example."

James chuckled, leaning back in his chair. "Oh, where to begin? We've had prank calls, people confessing to things they probably shouldn't, and even one guy trying to propose to his girlfriend live on air—after a very boozy night out. That one ended with her saying no, by the way. Pretty awkward."

Carly winced. "Ouch. And you just… deal with that on the fly?"

"Pretty much," James said with a shrug. "You learn to think on your feet in this job. Texts usually come to my computer here, so I'll keep an eye on those while we're live, but calls? They're a whole different ballgame. Anyway, it's all part of the fun. Keeps you sharp."

Before Carly could respond, the red light above the door began to flash—a signal that someone was calling in. James grinned, sliding his chair over to the recording station and putting on his headphones.

"Right on cue," he said, motioning for Carly to join him. "You're about to witness the magic of local radio."

Carly hesitated but eventually leaned over his shoulder as James hit a button to answer the call.

"Good morning, Brookes Vibes! Who's this?" James said, his voice bright and professional.

A slightly groggy voice crackled through the speaker. "Uh, hi. This is Dan from Headington. Just wanted to say, uh… great show so far. That Carly girl's hilarious."

Carly raised an eyebrow, a smile tugging at her lips as she mouthed, "Carly girl?" at James, who stifled a laugh.

"Thanks, Dan," James replied smoothly. "Carly's making her radio debut today, so I'm sure she appreciates the love. Anything else you want to share with Oxfordshire this fine morning?"

"Yeah," Dan said, sounding a bit more awake now. "Can you ask Carly if she really body slammed that Annabelle girl into the mud yesterday? I heard it got pretty heated."

James leaned back, giving Carly a playful look as he gestured for her to respond. Carly hesitated for a moment before leaning into the mic.

"Well, Dan," she began, her voice steady but laced with dry humour, "let's just say things got… a bit out of hand. But to be clear, it wasn't a body slam—it was more of a gentle nudge. Annabelle just happens to be very dramatic."

James covered his mouth to stifle a laugh, nodding encouragingly as Carly continued.

"But," she added, "if you're asking whether I'd do it again… well, let's just say I wouldn't rule it out."

Dan let out a hearty laugh. "Fair enough! Keep up the good work, guys. You've made my morning."

"Thanks for calling, Dan," James said, wrapping up the call with a grin. "Alright, Oxfordshire, you heard it here first—Carly H isn't afraid to get her hands dirty. We'll be back with more banter and bangers after this."

He clicked off the call and leaned back in his chair, grinning at Carly. "See? You're a natural."

Carly shook her head, though she couldn't hide her smile. "A natural at dodging ridiculous questions, maybe. But I have to admit—it's kind of fun."

James chuckled, spinning his chair back to the control panel. "Told you. Stick with me, Hemsworth—you might just become a radio star yet."

The pair settled into an easy rhythm for the rest of the show, their banter flowing naturally as they fielded texts, queued up songs, and occasionally teased each other on air. At 11 o'clock, James said something after the news that made Carly curious.

"Right, Oxfordshire, we're going in-the-mix with some 90s club classics to get your Sunday grooving! From Sonique to Faithless, we're bringing back the beats that defined a generation. Don't touch that dial, because Carly H and I are about to take you on a trip down memory lane. First up, it's a classic bit of Faithless with their biggest classic, Insomnia."

As the unmistakable opening beats of Insomnia by Faithless filled the studio, Carly turned to James with a bemused expression. "In-the-mix? What does that even mean? Are you moonlighting as a DJ now?"

James grinned, spinning his chair to face her. "Not exactly, but this is the part of the show where we string a few tracks together like we're in a club. It's all preloaded and automated—no actual DJ skills required. But it gives us a chance to take a breather, check messages, and maybe sneak a bit of fun... if you catch my drift. That or grab a few biscuits from the kitchen."

Carly raised an eyebrow, crossing her arms as she leaned back in her chair. "Fun? What kind of 'fun' are we talking about, Jenkins? Because if this involves more glitter or mud, I'm out."

James chuckled, shaking his head. "Relax, Hemsworth. I was thinking more along the lines of a coffee break. We've got about half hour of non-stop music, then some ads, then another 20 minutes before we head into the last hour of the show. You see, at 1, Alfie over at Milton Keynes does the network wide show before we take Hit40UK from Capital. It's one of their syndicated shows which GWR, Capital and a few other groups have partnered to broadcast across their networks." James glanced at the schedule pinned to the wall.

"I thought Dr Fox only did Ten-17," Carly interjected, leaning forward, suddenly intrigued by the intricacies of radio politics. "I didn't know Hit40UK was a show that was on every network like that, and I didn't know Alfie Peacock was on various stations either. I know there's the Mix Network as Ten-17 mentions on Core Control that they use the same playlists as Mix Network stations. Is it all just one big syndication club?"

James chuckled, impressed by Carly's curiosity. "Pretty much, yeah. Alfie Peacock's show is part of that syndication deal. Basically, he records segments from his studio, and they send it out to every station in the network to make it sound live and local. It's the same with Hit40UK—It's a network show that comes out of Capital in London, and it's broadcast across multiple stations. It's cheaper and easier for the big groups, plus it ensures a consistent sound.

"The Mix Network is another layer of that," James said, grinning as he revealed the inner workings. "The Mix and the Mix Network are GWR's baby, and as the big bosses here are all GWR alumni, they're in bed with their old colleagues. They want their stations to sound just polished enough to compete with Capital and the rest but still local enough to keep listeners happy. It's all about striking that balance."

Carly nodded slowly, letting it sink in. "So, basically, radio's one big illusion of being local while actually being run by a handful of people behind the scenes?"

"Exactly," James said with a smirk. "Welcome to the magic of commercial radio. But don't get me wrong—it's not all bad. There's still room for creativity, even if it's tucked between networked shows and corporate playlists. It's all about how you use the time you've got."

Carly looked thoughtful for a moment, then grinned. "Well, if that's the case, maybe we should make the most of our time on air and really shake things up. You know, give Adam something to complain about tomorrow."

James laughed, spinning back to his desk as the next track faded in seamlessly. "Now you're getting it, Hemsworth. Stick with me, and we'll have this station buzzing before lunchtime."

****

CHAPTER 8 – Congratulations, Adam
Monday 30th September 2003

The conference room at the Home Counties Radio Group HQ in Milton Keynes was a peculiar mix of corporate sterility and chaotic creativity. Posters for past promotional stunts—everything from foam parties to charity fundraisers—lined the walls, and a faint smell of burnt coffee lingered in the air.

Adam Banks sat at the far end of the table, leaning back in his chair with a self-satisfied grin plastered across his face. In front of him was a stack of flyers from the weekend's mud wrestling event, complete with photos of Carly, Annabelle, and James mid-chaos, mud-streaked but grinning—or, in James's case, grimacing. The headline on the main Oxford local newspaper, the Oxford Gazette, screamed: **"MUD, FOAM, AND FIASCO: BROOKES VIBES TAKES OVER MARKET SQUARE!"**

Adam tapped the paper with a flourish, addressing the room like a victorious general. "Ladies and gentlemen, I present to you... a promotional masterpiece."

The gathered staff—mainly made up of the Group Directors, as well as the other Promotions Coordinators, all nodded like Churchill dogs, their heads bobbing in approval. The fact that most of them were former GWR Group, like Adam, or former Capital Radio Group, meant that Adam was preaching to the choir. The GWR and Capital Radio alumni in the room had cut their teeth on the kind of boundary-pushing, headline-grabbing stunts

Adam thrived on. This was their bread and butter, their version of "radio gold."

Antony Peckham, one of the senior management team, a former GWR Bristol station manager who was now the Group Director for Promotions, stood up and headed to Adam, shaking his hand as if he were the next coming of the promotional Messiah.

"Well done, Adam," Peckham said, his Bristolian accent lending a certain weight to his words. "This is exactly what we've been looking for—a proper spectacle. Got the listeners talking, the students involved and even managed a bit of press coverage. The Gazette calling it a 'fiasco' only adds to the charm, if you ask me."

"Here here," Colin McTaggert, a former Scottish Radio Holdings Legal Director who had joined the Home Counties Radio Group as Group Head of Legal Affairs, chimed in. "Any publicity is good publicity in this game, and if the Oxford Gazette are talking about Brookes Vibes in the same breath as mud wrestling and chaos, then we've clearly got people paying attention. Bloody well done, Adam."

Adam basked in the praise, leaning back further in his chair with a cocky grin. "Thanks, Colin, Antony. You know, I always say the best way to get people engaged is to give them something they'll never forget. Mud, foam, drama—it's all part of the Brookes Vibes DNA."

Not everyone in the room was quite so impressed. Sarah Linton, the station manager for Brookes Vibes, sat with her arms crossed and a sceptical expression on her face. A veteran of BBC Local Radio, Sarah had spent her career prioritising content over stunts, and while she couldn't deny the event had generated buzz, she wasn't sold on Adam's methods.

"Let's not pat ourselves on the back too quickly," Sarah interjected, her tone calm but firm. "Yes, the event got people talking, but it also brought some complaints. Oxford City Council have sent an email saying that-"

"Oh, come on, give it a rest," Brian Jones, the station manager for Reading's Buzz Beats, the sister station to Brookes Vibes and a former Capital Radio alumnus, interrupted, rolling his eyes as he leaned back in his chair. "Complaints are part of the game, Sarah. You think Capital or Fox are saints? They'd go further than what Adam pulled off and wouldn't bat an eyelid. It's about making noise, not keeping everyone happy. Which reminds me, Adam, send me the hiring guide on how you picked your babes, as I might get my promo coordinator to replicate it at Buzz Beats. Nothing wrong with a bit of healthy competition, eh?" Brian added with a wink.

"Let me guess, Adam," Samuel O'Leary, the promotions coordinator at Buzz Beats and a former 2-Ten FM Black Thunder, said. "You used the Black Thunders guide and just gave it a Brookes Vibes twist, didn't you? Mud wrestling and babes? It's got classic GWR written all over it."

Adam chuckled, giving a mock bow. "You know me too well, Sam. A bit of inspiration from the Thunders. Can't beat the old GWR magic when it works so well, can you?"

The room erupted in laughter, with the GWR veterans exchanging knowing nods. For them, Adam was a prodigy—a younger, brasher version of their former selves, unafraid to push the boundaries of decency in the name of engagement.

"What do you mean, GWR magic?" Perdita Holmes, a former Emap alumnus and the Group Director for Community Engagement, interjected with a sly smile. "You're all acting like GWR invented the wheel. At Emap, we perfected the art of blending stunts with actual substance. Mud wrestling is fun, sure, but if it doesn't translate into listener loyalty or advertising revenue, then it's just noise. Have you got any data to back up the impact of this little escapade, Adam?"

Adam, ever the charmer, flashed his trademark grin. "Perdita, darling, we've had a large increase of contact by MSN Messenger, so far, it looks like the engagement has been fantastic. Listeners are reaching out, we're seeing a spike in mentions across the student forums, and—this is the kicker—the Gazette article alone has driven traffic to our website up by 20% since Saturday. If that's not translating into loyalty, I don't know what is. Anyway, it's not long until RAJAR send out the diaries to the students, so if we've done our job right, Brookes Vibes will be top of mind when they fill those in."

"All hail the RAJARs," Liam Nielson, the MK Vibes promotions coordinator and former Beacon FM promotions team member, quipped with a grin, raising his coffee cup in a mock toast. "If you can get even half of the students to remember Brookes Vibes when those diaries land, Adam, you'll be a bloody legend. And let's face it—mud wrestling will be a lot more memorable than some dull vox pops or a random freebie giveaway."

"Exactly!" Adam shot back, pointing at Liam as if he'd just delivered the gospel truth. "People remember spectacle. They remember fun. And that's what Brookes Vibes is all about—giving them something to talk about long after the weekend's over. Look, if Capital or Fox try to copy us now, it'll look like they're playing catch-up. We've set the tone for the term."

The irony, Adam knew, in that he was only falling back on his GWR Group training, and that he was merely defaulting to the tricks that stations like GWR and Beacon FM had mastered years earlier. But the key was to make it look fresh and original to the audience—and, crucially, to the higher-ups in this room.

Sarah, however, wasn't entirely convinced. She leaned forward, her gaze steady as she addressed Adam. "Look, I'm not denying that the event generated buzz. But we need to think long-term here. Brookes Vibes has to be more than just mud pits and stunts. If we want listener loyalty, we need to balance the spectacle with substance. What happens when the novelty wears off? How do we keep them engaged without resorting to the next over-the-top gimmick?"

Adam's smile faltered slightly, though he quickly recovered. "I hear you, Sarah, and I get it. But let's not underestimate the power of a good spectacle. It's a hook—a way to get people through the door. Once they're here, we hit them with great music, relatable presenters, and a station that feels like it's theirs. Mud wrestling gets their attention, but it's the vibe we create that keeps them tuned in. Anyway, the Babemobile is out today on a promo run in Banbury as John, you wanted to borrow it for Banbury Beats, right?"

"Yeah, that's right," John Matthews, the station manager for Banbury Beats and a 100.7 Heart FM Chrysalis alumnus, replied, nodding. "The Babemobile is a solid hook, Adam, and our guys are hyped to try it out. We're targeting the shopping centre crowd today, giving out branded tote bags, pens, and, of course, flyers for our charity gig next month. Mud wrestling might not be our style, but a bit of flair goes a long way. Thanks for lending us a couple of Babes by the way, too. That Clarissa has got our newly hired Street Team boss all... well, hot under the collar. He's only 21 and he's got a lot to learn about separating work from, well, distractions." John chuckled, eliciting a ripple of laughter from the room.

Adam, basking in the room's supportive laughter, gave a mock bow. "Always happy to share the love, John. Clarissa's a pro—she knows how to bring the energy. Just make sure your new guy keeps it professional. I run a tight ship at Vibes, and I don't need any dramas bouncing back my way."

"Well, if Adam's spending promotions money for Brookes on the Babemobile and his Babes, then I'll be spending mine on the same," Liam said with a grin, leaning back in his chair. "I mean, as RAJAR diaries are coming up soon, and Adam's said it's got an increase in MSN activity and website hits, then I'm not going to let MK Vibes fall behind."

"Hear hear," Oliver Totney, the Cambridge Buzz promotions coordinator, chimed in with a smirk. "Let me know the specs and that of the vans-"

"They're your bog standard Ford Transit with a yellow paint job on the one and a black paint job on the other," Adam cut in, his tone self-assured as he leaned forward. "Nothing fancy about the vans themselves. It's the branding and what we do with them that makes the difference. You slap a big, bold station logo on the side, load up a sound system, and get your street team hyped to hand out freebies and chat to the punters—it's all about making noise and being visible. Oh, and put a mattress inside each one. For the flyers and all that, such as the branded condoms and stuff, I used the same contractors GWR use. Obviously, Ollie, Liam and Sam, you know who the usual suppliers are. If you don't, I can send you the contacts later."

Adam watched as the trio's eyes glazed over and began another round of nodding as if they were at a North Korean military parade. It was clear that Adam had them eating out of his hand. His confidence and ability to drop the right industry buzzwords at the perfect moments had secured his reputation as the golden boy of Home Counties Radio Group's promotional team.

"Oh, come on," Perdita groaned. "You GWR fanboys and your obsession with branded vans and gimmicks. Surely there's more to engaging an audience than sticking a logo on a Ford Transit and hoping for the best. How about we focus on creating content that actually connects with listeners instead of just throwing condoms at them in a shopping centre?"

The room fell silent for a beat, the tension thick as Perdita's words cut through the self-congratulatory air. Adam, never one to back down from a challenge, leaned forward with a grin that was equal parts charm and deflection.

"Perdita, I hear you loud and clear," he said smoothly. "But let's not pretend that stunts and branding don't work. They're a foot in the door—a way to get people curious. Once they're listening, then it's up to the content teams to keep them there. We're not just throwing things at the wall to see what sticks. It's a strategy, and so far, it's working."

"That's right," Sarah replied cautiously, her arms still crossed as she regarded Adam with a sceptical expression. "What's your grand idea now, Adam?"

Adam straightened up, his trademark grin widening as he addressed the room. "Simple. We take an extra GWR show, one that listeners in our areas can't get... Core Control. I mean, we're already syndicating the 10pm-6am shows on weekdays from GWR, and the Radio Authority has us at 12 hours weekdays, 8 hours Saturday, 4 hours Sunday for our localness requirements."

The GWR alumni in the room started clapping and nodding enthusiastically, their approval palpable.

"Hear, hear," John said, standing up. "It'll show the Capital lot who's really in control. Core Control is a brilliant choice—it's got the energy, the playlist, and the branding that'll keep us competitive in Capital territory. Plus, it's pure GWR gold, isn't it? Perfect for driving engagement without breaking the budget. If only the Radio Authority would let GWR take over Capital and let them show the London lot how to properly run a network." His words were met with laughter from the

GWR alumni, but Sarah and a few others remained unimpressed. "Anyway, students will listen to it, as we're aiming for the CHR demo, right? They won't care whether it's local or networked if it sounds slick and has all their favourite tracks on rotation."

"Exactly John," Antony said with a knowing nod. "Core Control is tailor-made for this. It's got the right blend of high-energy tracks and that polished feel that GWR does so well. The students won't even notice—or care—that it's not local. They'll just know it sounds good and keeps the vibe going. Peter, do you agree?"

Peter McAllister, the former Deputy CEO of GWR Group under Ralph Bernard and now the CEO of Home Counties Radio Group, adjusted his glasses and leaned forward. A former architect of GWR's famously efficient, albeit formulaic, network strategy, Peter commanded respect in the room. His calm demeanour contrasted sharply with the animated GWR alumni.

"I see the merit in what Adam's suggesting," Peter began, his measured tone silencing the room. "Core Control aligns with what GWR perfected—streamlined content, consistent branding, and maximum listener retention. I'll have a chat with Ralph and see if he'll let us syndicate Core Control while being outside of GWR ownership. If he approves, then Sarah, I expect you to have Brookes ready to align with the schedule seamlessly. The same goes for Ryan in London and David in Winchester. Good idea, Adam. It will save the Group money in the long run as we can consolidate resources while still delivering high-quality programming. If there's nothing else, then I have a tee time of 1pm over at the Woburn Golf Club, and

I'd rather not keep my playing partners waiting. Adam, Antony, Samuel, Liam, would you care to join me over at the Woburn Golf Club?" Peter McAllister asked, standing up and adjusting his blazer, signalling the meeting was drawing to a close. "We can discuss this Core Control and expansion of the Babes scheme plan further over 18 holes."

****

Sarah was furious as she sat with Perdita Holmes in the canteen at the Home Counties Radio Group headquarters, a plate of salad in front of Perdita and a cup of tea in front of Sarah. The fluorescent lights buzzed faintly, adding to the uncomfortable atmosphere. Sarah's expression was a storm of frustration as she stirred her tea with more vigour than necessary. Perdita, always one to read the room, set down her fork and gave Sarah a pointed look.

"Let me guess," Perdita began, leaning back in her chair. "You're fuming because once again, Adam's charm and GWR nostalgia have everyone eating out of his hand?"

Sarah sighed, her shoulders slumping as she set down her spoon. "Exactly. Every time he opens his mouth, it's like the second coming of Ralph Bernard. They all act as if his stunts are the golden standard for modern radio. Mud wrestling? Babemobiles? Branded condoms? It's like we're stuck in 1998. And now this talk of syndicating Core Control? It's infuriating, Perdita."

Perdita nodded, her lips curving into a wry smile. "I know what you mean. The GWR crowd practically drool over anything that resembles their glory days. But the truth is, Adam knows how to work the system. He plays into their

112

nostalgia and throws in just enough buzzwords—RAJAR, MSN, engagement—to make it sound like he's the saviour of commercial radio. And Peter McAllister? He's not going to resist anything that screams 'GWR efficiency.' You'd think Ralph Bernard is secretly financing the whole operation with the way they worship him."

"Yeah, I wouldn't be surprised. I mean, look at how it's a 6 station network, 3 on GWR turf and 3 on Capital turf. With the ones like yours that are on GWR turf, Peter is going all tippy toes, not wanting to step on GWR's toes too much, while with us on Capital territory, he's practically throwing down the gauntlet. It's exhausting," Sarah said, leaning back in her chair and rubbing her temples. "And did you notice how the GWR alumni of the promotions side either were or have worked with their Black Thunders street team? It's like they're trying to clone GWR's old tricks and pretending it's revolutionary. The Babemobile idea might work for a term, but what happens when the novelty wears off? Mud wrestling doesn't exactly scream long-term strategy, does it?"

Perdita smirked, folding her arms. "It's classic GWR thinking—throw money at spectacle, and if it works, ride it until the wheels fall off. Then repeat. To be fair, though, it does get results in the short term. The Babemobile, the branded condoms—it's all flash and no substance, but it gets people talking. And in their eyes, that's enough. They don't care if it's sustainable, as long as they can report a spike in engagement and show the board some nice graphs."

Sarah let out a frustrated laugh. "And the worst part? I'm not even sure they realise how transparent it is. Or maybe they just don't care. As long as the GWR crowd get their nostalgia fix, they'll keep patting Adam on the back and funding his ridiculous ideas."

"True," Perdita said, her tone thoughtful. "But we can't just sit back and let them turn every station into a clone of GWR circa 1999. There's got to be a way to push back without sounding like a pair of naysayers stuck in the mud—or foam, as it were."

Sarah leaned forward, her expression brightening slightly. "I've been thinking about that. What if we focus on building a proper community engagement strategy? Something that balances the flashy stunts with real, meaningful connections. We've got the student market, sure, but there's a whole other audience out there—local families, small businesses, people who want more than just giveaways and gimmicks. If we can tap into that, we might actually create something lasting."

Perdita's smile widened, and she nodded approvingly. "Now you're talking. Real community connections, local voices, events that actually matter to people—that's what radio should be about. And if we can prove that it works, we'll have a counterpoint to Adam's circus act. It won't be easy, though. The GWR boys will fight tooth and nail to keep their nostalgia machine running."

"I know," Sarah said, her jaw set with determination. "But if we don't do something, Brookes Vibes—and the rest of the stations—will just become another cookie-cutter network. We have to show that there's a different way. A better way."

Perdita raised her mug in a toast. "Here's to fighting the good fight, then. Let's show them what real radio looks like."

Sarah clinked her cup against Perdita's mug with a small, hopeful smile. "Let's do it. For the listeners, not the headlines."

As the two women sat in the fluorescent-lit canteen, plotting a more authentic future for their stations, the echoes of laughter and self-congratulation from the meeting room faded into the background. For Sarah and Perdita, the fight for real radio was just beginning.

****

CHAPTER 9 - Road Trip
Saturday 4th October 2003

James had to chuckle at himself for this. Even though he and Carly had been assigned to do a promo drop in the Blackbird Leys area of Oxford, it felt more like an awkward date than a professional outing. The Babemobile rattled along the streets with its garish branding turning heads and eliciting the occasional honk from passing cars. Carly sat in the passenger seat, arms crossed and looking out of the window with an expression that was equal parts boredom and mild irritation.

"You alright there, Carly?" James asked, casting her a sidelong glance as they pulled up at a red light. "You've been quiet since we left the studio. That's not like you."

She turned to him with a small shrug, her eyes scanning the chaos of the dashboard, cluttered with flyers, half-empty bottles of water, and a random mix CD that Adam had insisted would "set the vibe." "Just thinking," she said, her voice flat. "About why we're even doing this, to be honest. Blackbird Leys isn't exactly buzzing with students, is it?"

James chuckled, trying to lighten the mood. "Yeah, but Adam's convinced we're spreading 'brand awareness.' Apparently, if we blanket Oxford with enough free pens and condoms, Brookes Vibes will become a household name."

Carly snorted, finally cracking a small smile. "Right, because nothing says quality radio like a glow-in-the-dark condom with a logo on it. You know... I heard that Mary took the van to Thame yesterday with one of the engineers. Not an engineer as in a mechanic for the Babemobile, but one of the studio engineers... and they fucked."

James chuckled, as it was well known in the radio industry that sex between colleagues was less taboo and more an open secret. "Honestly, I'm not surprised," James said, shifting gears as the light turned green. "The Babemobile seems to double as a mobile dating service at this point. It's practically a legend at Brookes Vibes—and not for the right reasons."

Carly smirked, her mood visibly lifting. "Well, at least we're keeping it professional today. Unless, of course, you've got plans to ruin that reputation, Jenkins."

James raised an eyebrow, playing along. "As tempting as it is to sully the pristine name of the Babemobile, I think I'll pass.... unless you fancy... well, going on a date?"

James knew that he had a really bad crush on Carly, and that he suspected, despite their relationship being more fuck buddies, friends with benefits, Carly might feel the same. But the idea of turning their casual dynamic into something more serious left him second-guessing himself. Carly, ever perceptive, caught the flicker of hesitation in his tone.

"A date, huh?" Carly replied, raising an eyebrow as she leaned back in her seat, arms still crossed but with a hint of amusement tugging at the corners of her mouth. "I'm not sure the Babemobile screams romance, James. Unless, of course, you're planning to woo me with some glow-in-the-dark merch and a playlist of Adam's dodgy dance remixes."

"Well, after all, we're lightly loaded on promo stuff and Adam did give us the van for the day." James said with a grin, "And we're only going down the road to Blackbird Leys. We could do the leaflet and carrier bag drop, then go down to Reading or Windsor... or just find a random layby on the side of the A40 and blast Adam's terrible dance mix at full volume. Really set the mood, you know?" James teased, his grin widening. "Hell, Adam did tell us that he'll pay us for... expenses."

Carly laughed, her eyes lighting up with genuine amusement for the first time that day. "Oh, how generous of him. What's the budget? A tenner and a packet of crisps from the petrol station?"

James smirked as he turned the van onto a quieter residential road. "Nah, Adam said he's had his promo budget tripled. Anyway, after last Sunday, you're a DJ now, and there's an unwritten rule that you're not a proper jock unless you've shagged someone in sales, someone in promos and someone in news. Apparently it's the old GWR rule, or so the old hands say. We're ticking boxes here, Hemsworth."

Carly rolled her eyes, though she couldn't help but laugh at James's cheeky grin. "First of all, I'm not a proper jock. That was a one-time deal. Secondly, if that's the GWR standard, it's a miracle any work gets done at all. No wonder the industry's got a reputation for being a soap opera. Anyway, why not? I mean, we've already established that this whole promo gig is a bit of a joke, and you can't deny the mattress is there for... well, a reason."

James chuckled, shaking his head as he kept his eyes on the road. "You've got a point, but Adam's reason for having it probably involves more questionable judgement than romantic intentions. Besides," he added with a teasing grin, "I didn't take you for someone who'd want to partake in Adam's grand vision of the Babemobile's extracurricular uses."

"Desperate times," Carly said dryly, though there was a flicker of mischief in her eyes. "And let's be honest, it's not like you haven't thought about it. That... and... well, I've... erm... I want your cock."

James gripped the steering wheel a little tighter, caught off guard by Carly's sudden bluntness. A laugh escaped him, more from shock than humour. "Well, that escalated quickly," he said, glancing at her with a mix of amusement and curiosity. "Is this your way of saying you've been thinking about us?"

Carly smirked, leaning her head back against the seat as she crossed her legs. "What can I say? Spending half the day in this ridiculous van with you does things to a girl. Besides, let's not act like we don't have history. Or chemistry. Especially the other night when we were in the Magdalen library and our... hands... touched."

James felt the heat rise in his cheeks, his grip on the steering wheel tightening. He'd never been good at hiding his feelings when Carly teased him, and this time was no exception. "The library, huh?" he said, trying to keep his tone light, though his voice wavered slightly. "You mean when you 'accidentally' dropped your pen just so I'd lean over and—"

"Don't flatter yourself, Jenkins," Carly interrupted, her smirk widening. "It was hardly a grand romantic gesture. But you've got to admit, there's something about those quiet moments, isn't there? Just you, me, and a pile of overdue books. Very... intimate."

James chuckled, shaking his head as he turned onto the main road leading towards Blackbird Leys. "Intimate, sure. Except for the part where the librarian gave us the stink-eye for whispering too loudly."

"Details," Carly said with a dismissive wave of her hand. She shifted in her seat, her smirk softening into something more thoughtful. "Seriously, though... you've been a good distraction lately. With all the Adam chaos, the ridiculous stunts, and this so-called 'radio career,' it's nice to have someone who doesn't take it all too seriously."

James glanced at her, his expression softening. "Well, I aim to please. And for what it's worth, you're a pretty great distraction too. Even if you do spend half your time mocking me."

Carly laughed, the sound warm and genuine. "It's part of my charm. Besides, you make it so easy, Jenkins."

He took a moment to gather his thoughts, his hands gripping the steering wheel as he kept his eyes on the road. "Honestly, Carly? Yeah, I do. I mean, we've always had fun, but you're more than just... that. You're smart, hilarious, and, let's face it, you've got a knack for keeping me on my toes. You're not just some 'booty call.' You're someone I actually care about. Plus, I did notice when Annabelle tried to-"

James paused mid-sentence, his voice trailing off as he recalled the mud wrestling incident and how Annabelle had blatantly tried to stake her claim on him. Before he could say anything, Carly chuckled. "Let me guess, when Annabelle tried to hump you and I took her aside and explained that there's only one pussy your cock will ever get near in this lifetime, and it's mine," Carly finished with a wicked grin, cutting James off mid-thought. "That I told her the facts of life and that if she ever tried to touch you again, I'd personally throw her into the mud pit headfirst? Yeah, that wasn't exactly subtle, was it?"

James couldn't help but laugh, shaking his head as he glanced at her. "Not subtle at all, but effective. I think she got the message loud and clear."

Carly leaned back in her seat, smirking. "Good. She needed to know her place. And just to be clear, Jenkins, I wasn't just doing it out of jealousy as she's a Brookes skank, and skanks from Brookes don't get to claim my... friend," Carly said, her smirk softening into something more serious. "But yeah, maybe I was a little protective. You've got this habit of attracting the wrong kind of attention, and someone's got to keep the vultures at bay."

James raised an eyebrow, his lips twitching into a smile. "Oh, so now you're my bodyguard, are you? Should I be worried that you're going to tackle anyone who so much as looks at me funny?"

Only if they deserve it," Carly shot back, her tone teasing but with an undertone of sincerity. "Seriously, though, James... I know we've kept things casual, but I don't think I'd be throwing girls into mud pits if I didn't, you know, care."

The air in the van grew quieter for a moment, the playful banter replaced by an unspoken understanding. James glanced at Carly, her eyes fixed on the road ahead but her posture slightly tense, as if she wasn't entirely comfortable with the vulnerability of her admission.

"Fuck it, yes, Jenkins, I completely and totally want you as my one and only... pillow... it's a permanent job, and the pay is non-existent," Carly finished with a laugh, her tone lightening as she glanced at James with a cheeky grin. "But the perks? Saving on rent by moving into my digs, taking me out to meals now and again, and getting skanks like Annabelle from even thinking of shagging you."

James felt his chest tighten, a strange mix of relief and excitement washing over him. He let out a soft laugh, the tension in the Babemobile lifting slightly as he risked a glance at Carly. "You make a convincing offer, Hemsworth. Though I have to say, the job perks sound a bit skewed in your favour."

Carly smirked, brushing a strand of hair away from her face as she turned to look at him. "Oh, come on, Jenkins. You get exclusive rights to my sparkling wit, devastating charm, and occasional heroics, like saving you from the likes of Annabelle. Not to mention the added bonus of being seen with me. That's worth its weight in gold. That... and you get to go on dates with the Queen of the Brookes Babes."

James couldn't help but laugh at her self-assured tone, shaking his head as they turned into a car park at the community centre in Blackbird Leys, the first stop on their promo drop. "Alright, Your Majesty, you've convinced me. But if I'm dating the Queen of the Brookes Babes, I expect some royal treatment. You know, coffee runs, a back rub or two... maybe a playlist that doesn't include Adam's club classics."

Carly rolled her eyes, her grin widening as she unbuckled her seatbelt. "Careful, Jenkins, or I'll have you demoted to court jester. Now, grab the flyers and those pens and keyrings, and I'll put the CD in with the rest of the promo stash. Let's spread some Brookes Vibes love."

James chuckled as he noticed that Carly was wearing the crown that Adam had brought as well as the Brookes Babes uniform of a mini skirt and low cut top. She had paired it with her signature cheeky smirk, clearly enjoying the ridiculousness of how Adam had proclaimed that she was the Queen of the Brookes Babes for her "victory" in the mud wrestling match. As she adjusted the plastic crown and smoothed out her skirt, James couldn't help but admire her ability to turn even the most ridiculous situations into something undeniably her.

"You're really going all in with the theme, aren't you?" James teased as he grabbed a box of promo goodies from the back of the van. "All hail Queen Carly, ruler of keyrings, pens, and glow-in-the-dark condoms."

Carly struck a mock-regal pose, placing one hand on her hip and raising the other in a theatrical wave. "Bow before me, peasant. And hurry up with those boxes—I have a kingdom to run."

James rolled his eyes, though he couldn't suppress his grin as they approached the community centre. The car park was buzzing with families, students, and locals who'd likely been lured by the promise of free merchandise and music blaring from the Babemobile's speakers.

As they set up their table, Carly seamlessly shifted into her outgoing promo persona, engaging with the crowd and handing out goodies with a mixture of charm and wit. James worked alongside her, alternating between helping with the giveaways and occasionally glancing at her when she wasn't looking.

She really was something, he thought—effortlessly charismatic, sharp-tongued, and, despite her teasing, surprisingly warm.

"Enjoy your freebie, mate," Carly said to a bloke who looked a bit too old to be excited about a Brookes Vibes pen. She turned to James with a sly grin. "See? Already winning hearts and minds. This 'queen' thing suits me."

James chuckled, handing a keyring to a little girl who shyly reached out for it. "No arguments here. You've got the crowd eating out of the palm of your hand. Adam would be proud."

Carly scoffed, flipping her hair dramatically. "Adam's just jealous he doesn't have my natural star power. He can keep his dodgy dance remixes and foam machines. The people clearly know who the real icon of Brookes Vibes is."

James laughed, shaking his head as he watched her hand out another flyer with a wink and a laugh to an older woman who looked slightly baffled by the commotion.

"I've got to admit, Hemsworth, you've got a talent for this. You could probably sell sand to a desert dweller."

Carly turned to him, her hands on her hips and the plastic crown slightly askew. "Oh, Jenkins, flattery will get you everywhere. But don't think for a second that it means you're off the hook for loading the van back up later."

"Wouldn't dream of it, Your Majesty," James quipped, giving her a mock bow before grabbing another box of merchandise from the van.

The day rolled on with a mix of light-hearted banter, enthusiastic locals, and the occasional absurd moment—like when a kid accidentally spilled his fizzy drink all over the promo table, prompting James to leap into action with a handful of napkins while Carly joked about adding "spill containment expert" to his CV.

An hour later, they had emptied their stock of merch, and it was only 1pm, an hour and half into their shift. "Right, your Royal Highness, where shall we go? We've got 6 hours until we need to report back to Adam, and the van's loaded with plenty of fuel and... possibilities," James asked, leaning casually against the Babemobile, his tone teasing but his eyes warm with curiosity. "We're out of goodies, we've got no more promo spots to hit, so... fancy a shag in a A40 layby?"

Carly raised an eyebrow, crossing her arms as she leaned against the Babemobile in response. "Wow, Jenkins. Straight to the point, are we? No romantic detour through the Cotswolds first? No carefully curated playlist of sappy love songs? Just 'fancy a shag in a layby?' Very smooth."

James laughed, rubbing the back of his neck, though a blush crept up his cheeks. "Alright, maybe not my finest proposal. But you've got to admit, the Babemobile does scream 'class.' We'd really be leaning into its reputation. Anyway, the duvet covers are clean... as I kinda brought them from my digs."

Carly let out a genuine laugh, the kind that made James's cheeks flush even more. She tilted her head, considering his suggestion with mock seriousness, before finally replying, "Well, Jenkins, I must say you've outdone yourself. Nothing says romance quite like a layby, a branded van, and the lingering scent of promotional keyrings. But hey, if we're going to embrace the ridiculousness of our lives, we might as well go all in."

James raised an eyebrow, his grin widening. "So that's a yes?"

Carly rolled her eyes but couldn't hide her smirk. "Let's not get ahead of ourselves. As long as it's not got an audience, then the layby can be our kingdom for the afternoon. But you're still buying me a proper meal afterwards. None of that petrol station sandwich nonsense. I'm thinking pub lunch—chips, a pint, maybe even dessert if you're lucky."

James grinned, nodding as he opened the driver's side door of the Babemobile. "A royal feast for Her Majesty, of course. Anything else on the agenda, or is a muddy layby and a pub lunch the pinnacle of this grand adventure?"

Carly hopped into the passenger seat, adjusting her plastic crown with exaggerated grace. "Depends. Are you going to play that Adam-approved mix CD again, or can we finally listen to something decent?"

"Fox FM do you?" James said with a grin as he started the engine and tuned the radio to Oxford's Fox FM, a rival station that James knew would wind Carly up.

Carly groaned dramatically, throwing her head back against the seat. "Fox FM? Really, Jenkins? You're a traitor to Brookes Vibes. Adam would have a meltdown if he found out."

James smirked as a sugary pop track filled the Babemobile. "Come on, it's research. Know your competition and all that. Besides, it's better than listening to Adam's dodgy remixes on repeat."

"Barely," Carly muttered, though the hint of a smile betrayed her amusement. "Fine, but if they play anything by Steps, I'm jumping out at the next roundabout."

The two settled into a comfortable silence as the Babemobile rattled along the A40, the autumn countryside blurring past the windows. The occasional burst of static from the radio filled the gaps between Carly's playful jabs and James's quick comebacks.

After about twenty minutes, James pulled into a secluded layby surrounded by trees, the golden afternoon light filtering through the leaves. He turned off the engine, the sudden silence broken only by the distant hum of passing cars.

"Well, here we are," James said, turning to Carly with a lopsided grin. "Your kingdom awaits, Your Majesty."

Carly raised an eyebrow, her smirk returning. "Not bad, Jenkins. Secluded, scenic... and just the right amount of dodgy. You've really outdone yourself."

James laughed, leaning back in his seat. "What can I say? I aim to please."

Carly tilted her head, studying him for a moment before unbuckling her seatbelt and climbing into the back of the van. "Well, are you coming, or are you going to sit there admiring your own handiwork?" she teased, her voice light but with a subtle challenge in her tone.

James didn't need to be asked twice. Grinning, he followed her into the back of the van, where the duvet he'd stashed earlier was spread out over the floor.

Carly sat cross-legged on the makeshift bed, adjusting her crown with mock seriousness. "Right then, Jenkins. Let's see if this layby lives up to its reputation."

James laughed, sitting opposite her and leaning back against the van wall. "I think we've already established that the Babemobile has a reputation for... versatility. But I've got to admit, I didn't think we'd actually end up here."

Carly smirked, reaching over to flick his forehead lightly. "You underestimate me, Jenkins. I thrive on chaos. Now shut up and kiss me before I change my mind."

James didn't need further encouragement. As the golden light of the autumn afternoon bathed the layby in a warm glow, the two of them forgot about promo drops, rival stations, and the chaos of Brookes Vibes—at least for a little while.

****

CHAPTER 10 – Breakdown
Saturday 4th October 2003

"Hello, Adam, it's James," James said, leaning back in the driver's seat of the Babemobile, his mobile phone pressed against his ear. The van was still parked in the secluded layby, but now its engine refused to start, leaving James and Carly stranded. The air was filled with the faint smell of damp leaves and the occasional rustle of the wind through the surrounding trees.

"James? What's up?" Adam's voice crackled down the line, his tone distracted.

"The Babemobile won't start. We've tried everything—turning the key, checking the petrol gauge. Nada. Looks like we're stuck," James explained, trying to keep his tone neutral but feeling the frustration creeping in.

"Stuck?" Adam's voice sharpened, suddenly interested. "Where exactly are you?"

"Erm... High Wycombe... hang on, a Black Thunder car has pulled up in the layby as well," James replied, craning his neck to glance at the sleek, black promotional car pulling in next to them. Emblazoned with the iconic GWR Group branding, the Black Thunder vehicle looked far more polished than the well-worn Babemobile.

Carly peered out of her window, raising an eyebrow. "Well, this just got interesting. Think they've come to rescue us, or is this a turf war?"

James grinned, lowering his phone slightly as he gestured towards the Black Thunder team climbing out of their car.

Two sharply dressed promo staff—complete with matching branded jackets—got out of the front of the car and then promptly jumped in the back of their vehicle.

"It seems, Adam, the Thunders are jumping in the back passenger seats... and they've shut the doors," James said on the phone, sighing.

"Wait, what?" Adam's voice rose in alarm, clearly trying to process James's report before bursting out laughing. "Which station does it say on the car?"

James squinted at the side of the sleek vehicle, the bold GWR logo gleaming under the muted autumn sunlight. He leaned closer, his voice tinged with amusement. "It's got... Trent FM... all over it."

James squinted at the side of the sleek vehicle, the bold GWR logo gleaming under the muted autumn sunlight. He leaned closer, his voice tinged with amusement. "It's got... Trent FM... all over it."

The sound of Adam laughing like a maniac echoed down the line. "Trent FM? Oh, brilliant! Looks like the Black Thunder crew are up to their usual antics. They're probably 'taking a break'—if you catch my drift. You know, they'll happily let you join in the break if you ask... it's another unwritten rule that promo teams from rival stations have an unspoken truce when it comes to... er... sharing downtime in secluded spots. Just make sure they don't take any pictures. Can you imagine the headlines?"

James rolled his eyes, stifling a laugh as he glanced at Carly, who was clearly enjoying the absurdity of the situation. "Right, Adam. Well, unless the Black Thunder lot are secretly mechanics, I don't think they're going to be much help with our engine problem."

"Fair enough," Adam said, still chuckling. "I'll call the garage we use for the Babemobile and get them to send someone out. Just... try not to make things more chaotic than they already are. And don't let Trent FM's crew outshine you in the meantime, yeah? Last thing we need is them getting one over on us."

"Got it," James replied before hanging up. He turned to Carly with a resigned shrug. "Help's on the way. But in the meantime, I think we're stuck here with the Black Thunder crew for company."

Carly smirked, leaning back in her seat. "Oh, I don't know. I think this could be fun. Should we go say hello? See if they've got any better snacks than us? I'm down to trade some glow-in-the-dark condoms for a decent packet of crisps."

James grinned, already stepping out of the van. "Why not? Let's see if Trent FM's finest are as slick as they look."

The pair approached the Black Thunder car, knocking lightly on the window. The back door creaked open, revealing a flushed-looking couple who were clearly not expecting company. The fact they were wearing 2-Ten-branded jackets made the situation even more surreal. The two promo staffers looked at James and Carly like deer caught in headlights.

"Ah, you must be the lot that's making Fox FM's owners, Capital, look like a bunch of amateurs," James said, breaking the awkward silence with a cheeky grin. "Didn't mean to interrupt your... break, but we thought we'd introduce ourselves since we're all clearly enjoying the same scenic layby."

The woman in the backseat of the Black Thunder car, who had hastily zipped up her jacket, cleared her throat and tried to regain some semblance of professionalism. "Uh, yeah. Just, um, taking five. Long day of promo runs, you know how it is."

Carly raised an eyebrow, arms crossed but with a playful smirk on her face. "Oh, we know exactly how it is. Our boss... let's just say he's... a former Thunder boss... from Trent FM."

The couple in the Black Thunder car exchanged a quick glance, their expressions a mix of embarrassment and intrigue. The man leaned forward, rubbing the back of his neck awkwardly. "Small world, eh? Former Thunder boss, you say? So let me guess, your Babe is your local station's version of the Black Thunder girls?"

"Yep, most of the senior bosses at our station, Brookes Vibes in Oxford, are former GWR Group, so they've brought a bit of that Thunder magic with them," James said with a grin, gesturing to Carly. "And yep, you're looking at the Queen of the Brookes Babes herself."

Carly rolled her eyes but couldn't help smirking. "It's a title I wear with immense pride, obviously," she quipped, adjusting the mock plastic crown still perched on her head. "So, what's the deal with Trent FM's finest? You lot taking a break or planning your next big stunt?"

The woman in the backseat, clearly warming up to the banter, chuckled. "We're 2-Ten FM crew. We've been... busy... with our Chiltern promo colleagues. You know how it is—long hours, lots of travel, and sometimes you just need to... unwind." Her sly smile didn't leave much to the imagination. "Our bosses haven't changed the stickers from Trent to 2-Ten yet. Budget cuts, you know."

James laughed, shaking his head. "Classic. Seems like the only thing that changes faster than the station logos are the promo rules of engagement. So, does the Thunder crew get bonus points for creativity, or are you just killing time while waiting for the next gig?"

The man in the backseat grinned, shrugging as he stepped out to lean against the car. "Depends on who's asking. But between us, we've had some downtime waiting for a call to head to Reading. Figured we'd make the most of it." He glanced at the Babemobile, smirking. "Though I've got to admit, your ride's seen better days. What happened?"

James looked at the 2003 registered Transit and sighed. "Dunno. Fuel is three quarters full, and the engine just refuses to start. We've tried the usual—checking the oil, tapping the battery, even giving it a bit of encouragement, but it's dead as a doornail. Adam, our boss, has called a mechanic, though, so we're just stuck here waiting. We've only had it two weeks."

The man from the 2-Ten FM Black Thunder crew chuckled, shaking his head as he looked over the Babemobile. "Two weeks and it's already broken down? Sounds about right for a promo van. These things get put through hell."

Carly leaned against the Babemobile, smirking as she crossed her arms. "Yeah, well, it's not exactly a luxury ride. But it does the job—when it's not throwing a tantrum. And hey, at least it's got character. Your Thunder car looks like it just rolled off the showroom floor."

The woman from 2-Ten FM laughed, stepping out of the Black Thunder car and stretching. "Looks can be deceiving. Ours is just as temperamental. Yesterday, the AC broke halfway through a promo run, and now it smells like a gym bag in there. Trust me, appearances aren't everything."

James grinned, glancing between the two Thunder staff. "Good to know we're all in the same sinking ship. So, what's next for you lot? Heading to Reading to hand out more pens and keyrings?"

"Nah, we're done for the day, we've got a few hours until we've gotta be back at Reading. Thought we'd take it easy for a bit. Promo life isn't all glamour, you know," the man from the Thunder crew replied with a grin.

"Tell me about it. Carly and I are uni students, and I'm officially a runner, but I've been dragged into promo work as... well... the gaffer says that my 'pecs draw the female crowd something rotten', and that makes me a 'walking promo magnet,'" James finished with a self-deprecating chuckle, glancing at Carly, who smirked at the admission.

Carly added with mock seriousness, "Yeah, his pecs are apparently the real star of the show. I'm just here for moral support and to hand out the glow-in-the-dark condoms. It's a team effort."

The 2-Ten FM crew burst out laughing, the tension easing further as they leaned casually against their car. The man gave James an exaggerated once-over. "Well, I can see why your boss is cashing in on you. Those pecs probably have a bigger following than your station."

James feigned a modest shrug. "What can I say? It's a curse. But hey, if it gets people talking about Brookes Vibes, I'll take one for the team."

Carly rolled her eyes, though her grin remained. "Let's not inflate your ego too much, Jenkins. We still need to actually get listeners tuning in after they grab the freebies."

The 2-Ten FM woman, who introduced herself as Sophie, grinned and leaned closer conspiratorially. "Alright, let's settle this. Brookes Vibes versus 2-Ten FM: who's got the better promo stash? Show us what you've got."

James and Carly exchanged a glance before James went to the back of the Babemobile and swung open the doors, revealing nothing, as they had given all their promo stash at Blackbird Leys earlier in the day, and all they had was a few of the condoms that was meant for the evening promo drop that Clarissa and Mark Harrison would be doing around the clubs in Oxford.

Sophie raised an eyebrow, peering into the back of the Babemobile. "Well, well, what do we have here? A few glow-in-the-dark condoms and... nothing else? Is this what passes for promo gold at Brookes Vibes?" she teased, leaning back with an exaggerated sigh of disappointment.

James scratched the back of his neck, giving her a sheepish grin. "Our boss said 'take the van out, you've got til 7, here's a few bits for Blackbird Leys and do what you want for the rest of the day.' So, yeah… the stash didn't last long. Blackbird Leys cleaned us out. Turns out people really love a good keyring and shopping bags."

The two 2-Ten FM Thunders chuckled. "Sounds like a typical GWR promo run to me," Sophie said with a smirk, folding her arms. "Do one drop, then let the street team... fuck... in a random layby. Our Promo Coordinator is the same, he doesn't care what we get up to as long as we show up on time for the next gig and the van comes back in one piece. You mentioned your boss is a Trent FM alum, right? Sounds like they've brought the classic GWR ethos with them—work hard, play harder, and let chaos reign in between."

Carly laughed, leaning against the side of the Babemobile. "That sums it up. Adam's got this weird obsession with the old school GWR way of doing things. Half the time, it feels like we're starring in a low-budget reality show rather than working for a radio station."

"He's even managed to get the big bosses to persuade GWR to let them air Mix Network shows overnight, because we're in Fox FM territory and with Fox being Capital, they're the enemy. " James said, chuckling at how the GWR vs Capital rivalry manifested even in their promo strategies. "Adam says airing Mix Network shows is like flipping the bird at Fox FM, even if the listeners don't have a clue. It's petty, but that's radio politics for you."

The man from the 2-Ten FM crew, who introduced himself as Ryan, laughed and shook his head. "Classic GWR. They'll do anything to wind up Capital. Though, to be fair, airing Mix Network shows isn't the worst idea. It's polished, sounds good, and the audience loves it."

Sophie added with a grin, "And it keeps the bosses happy. Nothing like a bit of corporate one-upmanship to spice things up, eh? Meanwhile, the rest of us are out here bribing people with branded condoms and trying to keep the vans running. Anyway, how long have you two been promo guys?"

"Two weeks," James said with a shrug, "Technically I'm a runner and have been since last Uni year, as y'know, skint Uni student and all that, but Adam's decided to rope me into promo work because, apparently, my 'charisma' and 'pecs' are too valuable to waste behind the scenes. Carly's been a Babe the same, 2 weeks. Adam hired her... without even interviewing her."

Ryan laughed, leaning against the Black Thunder car and shaking his head. "Hired her without an interview? Sounds about right. Sophie here was hired without an interview because she fit three unofficial criteria... breasts, blonde and leggy."

Carly smirked, her eyes flicking between Ryan and Sophie as she crossed her arms. "Let me guess, the official criteria were just as ridiculous? Something like 'can hand out freebies' and 'doesn't mind working ungodly hours in questionable conditions'?"

Sophie chuckled, brushing a strand of her blonde hair over her shoulder. "Pretty much. Though, in my case, it was more about the 'can wear the branded crop top and smile through anything' vibe. They didn't even ask if I could drive the Thunder car until my first day. It seems to be a GWR hallmark—hire first, figure out the details later. Half the time, it feels like they're making it up as they go along."

James laughed, leaning against the side of the Babemobile as Carly smirked. "Sounds about right. Adam's entire management philosophy seems to be built on winging it. Not that I'm complaining—it's been a laugh so far."

Sophie's smirk grew as she looked between James and Carly, noting their relaxed banter and the subtle way they stood just a little too close. "So, what's the deal with you two? You seem… comfortable. Are you just colleagues, or is there something more going on?"

Carly rolled her eyes dramatically but didn't step away from James. "Oh, here we go. Why does everyone assume that just because we work together and banter a bit, there's something going on? We're perfectly capable of being professional." Her teasing tone didn't entirely hide the flicker of amusement in her eyes.

James, ever the cheeky one, couldn't resist playing along. "Professional, yes. Completely platonic? That's… negotiable."

Sophie and Ryan exchanged knowing looks, their laughter cutting through the autumn air. "Oh, you two are definitely more than colleagues," Ryan said, grinning. "Don't worry, though. It's practically a rite of passage in promo work. There's something about long hours, cramped vans, and ridiculous stunts that just... brings people together."

"Well, I suppose it all started last year at Uni... I get stressed easy," Carly said with a grin, and James knew that she was referring to how her "stress relief" tactics often involved cheeky flirting and playful antics to distract herself—and James had been her favourite target. He couldn't help but chuckle as Carly launched into her retelling, embellishing just enough to make the story even more entertaining.

"So, picture this," Carly began, her hands gesturing animatedly as Sophie and Ryan leaned in with amused expressions. "We're at the Uni library, late at night, and James here—ever the diligent law student—is buried in his books, totally oblivious to the world around him. Meanwhile, I'm trying to cram for a sociology exam but completely losing the will to live."

"Classic," Sophie interjected with a grin. "Library vibes. Go on."

Carly smirked, leaning slightly towards James as she continued. "So, I decide to distract myself by distracting him. I 'accidentally' drop my pen, and when he leans over to pick it up, I—very casually—spill my drink all over his notes. Total accident, of course."

"Total accident?" James cut in, raising an eyebrow. "You practically launched your coffee at me, Hemsworth."

Carly waved a dismissive hand, her grin widening. "Details. The point is, it got your attention. And, being the gentleman that you are, you offered to let me copy your notes while I dried mine off. One thing led to another, and before you know it, we're bantering about everything from essay deadlines to terrible Uni parties... and fucking."

Carly's grin grew cheekier as James shifted awkwardly, clearly debating how much of their history he was willing to share with the 2-Ten FM crew. Ryan and Sophie, however, were eating it up, their laughter punctuating the brisk autumn air.

"Wait," Ryan said, holding up a hand to pause Carly's retelling. "So, you're saying that your epic love story—or whatever this is—started because you threw coffee at him in a library? That's one way to break the ice."

"It wasn't love," Carly corrected, her tone playful but laced with just enough sincerity to keep James blushing. "It was more like… a mutually beneficial arrangement. James here was the reliable, studious type, and I was the chaotic distraction he didn't know he needed. Although... I may have... well, laid my claim to his arse."

James groaned, rubbing his forehead as Carly's cheeky grin only widened. "Oh, for the love of… must you always overshare, Hemsworth?"

Sophie and Ryan were practically in stitches, leaning against their car for support. "This is gold," Sophie managed between fits of laughter. "You two are like a walking sitcom. Promo life is chaotic enough, but you've really raised the bar."

James shook his head, though he couldn't hide his amusement. "You see what I have to deal with? This is my life now—an endless cycle of Carly's theatrics and questionable decisions."

"Oh, come on, Jenkins," Carly teased, nudging him with her elbow. "Admit it—you love it. Besides, I'm the one who keeps this whole promo operation interesting. Without me, you'd just be another boring law student handing out pens."

"And without me," James shot back, "you'd still be trying to figure out how to start the Babemobile, let alone fix it."

****

CHAPTER 11 – Love Is In The Air
Sunday 19ᵗʰ October 2003

It had been two weeks since James had confessed his feelings to Carly, and their relationship had gone from friends with benefits to dating with the speed of a rocket-fuelled Black Thunder car on a promo run. The shift had been surprisingly natural, their banter as sharp as ever but now punctuated by stolen kisses and moments of tenderness that neither had anticipated.

Of course, Carly knew that she wasn't the only Babe to find love, as her best friend, Clarissa, had started dating the station electrician, Mark Harrison, a 19 year old who was an Oxford native and had left school after his GCSEs with several failing grades. Mark was a bit rough around the edges but had a good heart, and Carly couldn't deny that he made Clarissa genuinely happy. The four of them had become something of a double act, often grabbing a drink after work or swapping stories about Adam's latest hare-brained schemes.

Sunday morning found James and Carly in the Brookes Vibes studio, as Big Bam was off sick again, and James had found himself roped into covering the Sunday Wake-Up Show. Carly, as usual, had tagged along, partly out of curiosity and partly because James had sweet-talked her into co-hosting with him again.

This time, though, she had decided that, instead of staying fully clothed, she was going to be topless for the whole show—at least in the confines of the studio, as in the building was only going to be her, James, Clarissa and Mark, and as she and Clarissa shared a dorm, James was now a regular guest of Carly's, and Mark and Clarissa were similarly inseparable. Carly's mischievous streak was in full force as she teased James with her plan on their way to the studio, leaving him simultaneously amused and slightly flustered.

The irony, Carly knew, that there was no management for the station present, and that she could effectively exploit the absence of authority for a bit of fun wasn't lost on her. James, always the pragmatist, had initially protested her topless idea with a mix of amusement and genuine concern.

"Carly, you do realise this is still a professional environment, right?" James had said, shooting her a sideways glance as they walked into the studio.

"Oh, relax, Jenkins," Carly had replied, her tone light but her grin wicked. "It's not like anyone can see me. Plus, you're always going on about how radio's all about the voice and personality, not appearances. Consider this a test of how true that really is."

She knew that, had she had the idea a month ago, she'd have slapped herself silly for even considering it, as she believed that as it was her body, and her choice if she wanted to share it, she would. But now, with James in her life as more than just a friend, she felt comfortable pushing the boundaries—especially when it meant watching him squirm with that adorable mixture of amusement and embarrassment.

By the time they reached the studio, Carly had already discarded her hoodie, leaving her in just her low-rise jeans and her bra, which she dramatically removed before settling into the co-host's chair. James groaned, running a hand through his hair as he took his place at the desk, trying to focus on the show instead of Carly's deliberate antics.

"You're impossible," James muttered, leaning into the microphone as he prepared to open the show.

"And you love it," Carly shot back, leaning closer to him with a playful smirk.

The red ON AIR light blinked to life, and James launched into his intro, his voice smooth and professional despite the chaos just out of frame.

"Good morning, Oxfordshire! You're tuned into Brookes Vibes, and this is the Sunday Wake-Up Show with me, James J, in for Big Bam who's got another hangover... yeah, the man's had more sick days than we've had promo stunts this month. But don't worry, I'm not alone—I've got the Queen herself, Carly H, digging into this Sunday madness again... and for the first track of today, she's picked something that was an epic failure, Carly, what is it?"

"Oh, something that's nul points," Carly chimed in, her tone dripping with mischief as she leaned closer to the mic, completely unbothered by her lack of attire. "Oh, come on Jenkins, don't frown, you have to admit, you loved Jemini when they got nul points in Eurovision. You sang that song for days after!"

James groaned dramatically, leaning back in his chair with an exaggerated sigh. "Ah, yes. Cry Baby. The anthem that united a nation… in cringing. Thanks for bringing that gem back to haunt me, Carly."

Carly chuckled, her grin widening. "You're welcome. And for anyone wondering why this track is even on our playlist today, it's because sometimes you need a reminder that life isn't always perfect—especially when you're working at Brookes Vibes. And for the song after that, I've gone even more random, and back to 2000, the Christmas pop hit that never was, 'Can We Fix It?' by Bob the Builder. James, don't even try to deny you had that as your ringtone for six months."

James let out a laugh, shaking his head as he leaned back towards the microphone. "Alright, alright, guilty as charged. Though I'd argue it wasn't a ringtone so much as a lifestyle choice. I mean, come on, it's Bob the Builder. Can we fix it? Yes, we can!" He shot Carly a playful glare, adding, "But I'll get my revenge later when I dig up some of your guilty pleasures, Hemsworth."

James let out a laugh, shaking his head as he leaned back towards the microphone. "Alright, alright, guilty as charged. Though I'd argue it wasn't a ringtone so much as a lifestyle choice. I mean, come on, it's Bob the Builder. Can we fix it? Yes, we can!" He shot Carly a playful glare, adding, "But I'll get my revenge later when I dig up some of your guilty pleasures, Hemsworth. Would anyone love a guess as to what it is? If so, just give us a ring, its 1865 570248 or text us, starting it with Y6NW4 on 60777. Standard rates apply. Let us know your guesses or just call in to remind Carly how bad her taste in music is!"

Carly leaned back in her chair, her arms crossed casually over her chest, her smirk never wavering. "Oh, please, Jenkins. If anyone's guilty of musical sins, it's you. Bob the Builder? That's a career low, even for you. But I'll take guesses, if only to prove that my guilty pleasures are leagues above yours."

James rolled his eyes, slipping on his headphones as he queued up the first track. The slightly off-key tones of Jemini's Cry Baby filled the studio, prompting an exaggerated groan from James.

"I can't believe you actually put this on," he muttered, his tone half-amused, half-mortified. "We're going to have complaints rolling in before the first chorus."

"Oh, relax," Carly teased, leaning closer to the microphone. "It's Sunday morning—everyone's either hungover or still in bed. Besides, if this is the worst thing we play today, I think we're doing alright."

While the track was playing, Carly noticed the phone line indicator signifying that a call was coming through, and she knew James would answer it and record it before airing it after Bob the Builder had finished playing.

"You can pick it up, Hemsworth," James said with a chuckle, and Carly felt like she was going to burst into laughter at his cheeky tone but managed to compose herself as she picked up the receiver, pressing the button to record.

"You're listening to Brookes Vibes, it's the Queen herself here, who's calling?" Carly said in her most cheerful tone, leaning into the moment with the same effortless charm that James admired and occasionally dreaded.

A groggy voice came through the line, clearly still waking up. "Uh, hi. It's Dan from Headington. Just wanted to say... this is either the best or worst playlist I've ever heard, and I can't decide which."

Carly smirked, shooting James a look as she replied, "Well, Dan, we aim to confuse, delight, and occasionally horrify. Got to keep Oxfordshire on its toes. Any guesses on my guilty pleasure track coming up?"

Dan chuckled, his voice gaining a bit more energy. "Alright, I'm going with... Steps. Tragedy, maybe? Or better yet, 5, 6, 7, **8**. It's got Carly H written all over it."

Carly burst out laughing, her tone light and teasing. "Oh, Dan, you wound me. Steps? Really? I mean, sure, I danced to it at school discos, but I'm far more sophisticated than that these days. Well... sort of."

James leaned over to add his two pence. "She's lying, Dan. I've seen her do the full routine to Tragedy. Twice. Sober."

Dan laughed harder. "You two are ridiculous. Keep it up. This is the best thing I've heard on the radio in ages. Oh, and tell James I forgive him for Bob the Builder—but only just."

Carly grinned, finishing the call. "Thanks for calling, Dan. We'll play your guess after Bob the Builder. Stay tuned—as the track will be revealed after the 10am news."

The absurdity of Jemini and Bob the Builder had set the tone for the morning show, and by the time Carly hung up on Dan, she was laughing so hard she had to wipe away tears, which, compared to the coldness of the studio, was refreshing.

"You know, James, I'm freezing my tits off," she said just as Bob the Builder was ending, unaware that James had turned up the faders so both his and her microphones were live. "Mark, stop shagging Clarrissa and see if the heating is working in here," she continued, her voice echoing into the studio monitors before her face turned crimson as she realised what she'd just said live on air.

James's eyes widened in horror and delight simultaneously. He slapped the off button on Carly's mic but couldn't stop the snort of laughter that escaped him. "Well, Oxfordshire," he said smoothly, his voice barely containing his amusement as he took over, "you just got a behind-the-scenes peek at what goes on in the glamorous world of Brookes Vibes. For the record, the heating is indeed questionable, but rest assured, we're all... fully clothed and professional. Moving swiftly on, just to warm Carly up, we've got a bit of Nelly "Hot in Herre" coming up next. Stick-"

"You called, your Highness," Clarissa and Mark said, walking in, both naked as the day they were born. James froze mid-sentence, his hand hovering over the next track button as the sight of his two colleagues in their birthday suits caught him entirely off guard. Carly's face was a mixture of shock and uncontrollable laughter as she leaned back in her chair, utterly delighted by the turn of events.

"Clarissa! Mark!" Carly managed between fits of laughter, pointing at the pair. "You do realise we're on air, right? This isn't some nudist colony!"

Clarissa, ever the bold one, shrugged nonchalantly. "It's a Sunday. No one's listening anyway. Besides, Carly, you're hardly one to talk, Miss Topless Queen."

Carly held up her hands in mock surrender, still laughing. "Fair play, fair play. But seriously, you two—put some clothes on before Adam hears about this. The last thing we need is another lecture on 'station professionalism.'"

Mark, grinning like a mischievous schoolboy, grabbed a promotional Brookes Vibes T-shirt from a nearby chair and threw it over his head. It barely reached his waist. "Happy now?"

"Marginally," James said dryly, "Anyway, we've got Dan in Headington on the line, Carly, how about you answer."

Carly watched as James pressed play on the pre-recorded call, letting it play out. Turning to Mark, Carly chuckled as she watched him inspect the electric heater that was in the corner of the studio.

"Well, Mark, you've certainly made an entrance. Fix that heater, and we might forgive the... wardrobe malfunction," Carly quipped, still trying to stifle her laughter.

"Well, Mark, you've certainly made an entrance. Fix that heater, and we might forgive the... wardrobe malfunction," Carly quipped, still trying to stifle her laughter. "Sorry to stop you and Clarissa having a...

private moment, but we're trying to keep things somewhat professional here—at least by Brookes Vibes standards."

Mark gave a sheepish grin, turning his attention to the heater. "Alright, alright. Heating first, nudity second. Got it." Clarissa smirked and perched on the arm of Carly's chair, still unapologetically casual about the whole situation.

As Dan's pre-recorded call wrapped up, James leaned back into the microphone. "That was Dan from Headington with some, uh, colourful guesses about Carly's guilty pleasure track. And if you're just tuning in, you've missed quite the morning already. It's only 15 minutes into the show and we've had all sorts of chaos. It's me, James J, with Queen Carly, in for Big Bam who's off sick... again... and here's Nelly with Hot in Herre."

James hit the play button, and the familiar beat of Nelly's track filled the studio. He leaned back in his chair, letting out a long sigh as the chaos settled momentarily. Carly, still trying to catch her breath from laughter, reached over and gave his arm a playful squeeze.

"You know," she said, grinning at him, "if Adam was listening right now, he'd either be laughing his head off or driving down here to fire all of us."

James smirked, glancing at the clock. "Let's hope he's too hungover to notice. Though I wouldn't put it past him to burst in here unannounced, demanding to know why we've turned the studio into some kind of... radio nudist colony."

Clarissa, now wrapped in a spare hoodie she'd found draped over the back of a chair, laughed and leaned into the conversation. "Oh, please. Adam loves this kind of stuff. He'd probably turn it into a promo campaign. 'Brookes Vibes: Bare it All!' It'd go perfectly with those glow-in-the-dark condoms."

"That reminds me, are you two using the dorm tonight?" Carly asked, curious as the quartet had started an arrangement to coordinate their personal lives to accommodate their growing relationships and the chaos of shared living. "Or is it James and me using it on the schedule tonight?"

Mark glanced up from fiddling with the electric heater, his expression a mix of concentration and amusement. "You and James have got the dorm tonight," he said, winking at Carly. "Clarissa and I are heading back to my mum's. She's cooking a roast, and apparently, Clarissa needs to 'eat something proper' for once... according to mum."

"Wow, that's gone serious. From dating to meeting his mum in a week and half, 'Riss," James said with a laugh, glancing between Clarissa and Mark. "Looks like someone's skipping a few chapters in the dating manual."

Clarissa smirked, leaning back in her chair. "Oh, don't act so surprised, Jenkins. Unlike you and Carly, some of us know how to fast-track a good thing when we see it. Besides, Mark's mum is a sweetheart—she's already trying to fatten me up like a Christmas turkey."

Mark chuckled, giving the heater one last test before it finally roared to life with a faint hum. "Heating's sorted. And yeah, mum's already decided she likes Clarissa more than me. She's been telling me to 'not mess this one up' since last weekend."

Carly burst out laughing, tossing her hair over her shoulder as she turned to Clarissa. "Wow, Riss, already a hit with the in-laws. Meanwhile, James still hasn't braved my mum yet. Maybe you should give him some pointers."

James rolled his eyes but couldn't hide the smirk tugging at his lips. "I'm not avoiding your mum, Carly. I'm just… strategically delaying the inevitable. Besides, it's only been two weeks. I need time to prepare my 'yes, I'll take good care of her' speech."

Clarissa grinned. "Smart move, Jenkins. Carly's mum can be a bit… intense. But don't worry—if you survive her interrogation, you're golden."

Carly shot James a teasing glance. "Oh, don't worry, my mum's bark is worse than her bite. She'll love you—once she gets over the fact that you're not a med student or a millionaire."

Mark leaned against the counter, crossing his arms as the four of them relaxed in the studio. "So, what's the plan for the rest of the day? Apart from causing chaos on air, obviously."

James gestured to the clock. "Well, we've got two more hours of this circus to keep Oxfordshire entertained. Then, Carly and I might actually go out for a proper meal— assuming we don't get called into another last-minute promo gig."

Carly raised an eyebrow, her smirk returning. "Proper meal? Does that mean something fancier than the kebab van outside the station?"

James laughed, shaking his head. "Hey, I can do fancy when the occasion calls for it. Don't knock the kebab van, though—it's practically a Brookes institution."

Clarissa rolled her eyes, nudging Mark. "Come on, let's leave these two lovebirds to their radio antics. We'll swing by later to check if they've turned the studio into a full-blown sitcom set."

Mark grinned, grabbing his hoodie from the back of a chair. "You two behave. Or don't—it's more fun that way. Either way, make sure the place is still standing when Adam checks in tomorrow."

As Clarissa and Mark left the studio, Carly leaned back in her chair, her gaze softening as she looked at James. "You know, for all the chaos and madness, this is actually kind of fun. Us. This. The whole ridiculousness of it."

James reached over, giving her hand a gentle squeeze. "Yeah, it is. Even with the questionable music choices and the nudist colony vibes, I wouldn't trade it for anything."

Carly smiled, her playful demeanour giving way to something more sincere. "Good. Because, Jenkins, you're stuck with me now. Glow-in-the-dark condoms, bad playlists, and all."

James chuckled, his heart swelling at the sight of her smile. "Wouldn't have it any other way, Hemsworth."

As the next track faded out, James leaned back into the microphone, his voice steady and warm. "Alright, Oxfordshire, that was Nelly with Hot in Herre. Coming up next, we've got some classic Britney, but first, let us know—what's the most chaotic thing you've ever done on a Sunday morning? Text us at 60777 or give us a call on 01865 570248. Standard rates apply, but the laughs are free."

Carly leaned into her mic, her grin audible in her voice. "And if you've got a story that can top our morning so far, we might even send you some glow-in-the-dark condoms. Because nothing says 'Brookes Vibes' like questionable promo merch."

The two of them shared a laugh as the phone lines lit up, their banter flowing as naturally as ever. Chaos, humour, and just a hint of romance—Sunday mornings at Brookes Vibes had never been so entertaining.

****

CHAPTER 12 – Fireworks in the Babes

Wednesday 5th November 2025

The tension over the past month between Annabelle and Carly had been heavily brewing, bubbling beneath the surface like a dodgy club PA system on the verge of blowing out. Ever since the mud wrestling incident, where Carly had quite literally thrown Annabelle into the sludge, things had been… strained.

At first, Annabelle had played it off like a joke, but as the weeks went on, it became obvious she was holding a grudge. She took every opportunity to undermine Carly in the group chat, subtly twisting words in meetings, and ensuring that Adam was always aware whenever Carly was slightly late, even if it was by thirty seconds. It was becoming a battle of wills, and while Carly wasn't usually one to rise to petty drama, even she had her limits.

"Fucking skank is shagging Adam," Carly said as she, James and a few of the other Oxford Uni friends of theirs sat in a club in the City Centre, a dozen bottles of WKD and cigarettes on the table, Carly's Essex twang falling out without her realising that her Queens English styled accent had dropped. She noticed James chuckling as she carried on her rant. "I mean, babes, she properly fancies herself, don't she? Walks around like she's Queen of the Babes just because she's flashing her tits at Adam. Like, congrats, love, you've unlocked the easiest achievement in radio—shagging the boss." Carly took a long drag from her cigarette, exhaling a plume of smoke before grabbing her bottle of blue WKD and taking a sip. "As if that's gonna get her anywhere. Adam will forget she exists the second some new blonde turns up."

Looking at Mark, she saw his face was blank, as if she had had spoken in Klingon and not English when she realised that she had accidentally dropped her Essex twang. James, however, was still grinning, shaking his head as he took a sip of his pint. "Oh, Hemsworth, you do get proper lairy after a few drinks, don't you?" he teased, nudging her playfully. "Next thing we know, you'll be throwing hands in the middle of Park End like it's a re-run of the mud wrestling."

Carly scoffed, flipping her hair over her shoulder. "Please, babes, I have class," she said, though the wicked smirk on her lips betrayed her true thoughts. "Besides, if I was gonna smack the cow, I'd do it where it really matters— live on air, during The Babes Takeover that we're doing on Boxing Day. Give the people what they want."

"Ratings gold," Mark deadpanned, still looking slightly lost as he swirled his Bacardi Breezer in one hand. "But seriously, are we sure she's actually shagging Adam, or is she just trying to make it look like she is? Because let's be real, mate's got the attention span of a Capital FM playlist."

Carly raised an eyebrow, taking another drag from her cigarette before exhaling slowly. "Oh, she's shagging him. I caught them leaving the production studio together on Monday looking all... flustered. Adam was trying to straighten his shirt, and Annabelle had that 'I've just been shagged in a broom cupboard' glow about her." She wrinkled her nose. "Honestly, I'd rather bleach my eyes than ever think about Adam's sex life again, but here we are."

Clarissa chuckled at that, and James nearly choked on his pint, coughing as he set it down on the table. "Well, that's an image I didn't need," he muttered, shaking his head in mock horror. "Adam's already unbearable on a normal day, can you imagine him after a shag? He'd be strutting around the office like he's won a bloody Sony Award."

Carly smirked, taking another sip of her WKD. "Oh, babes, he already thinks he's the second coming of Chris Tarrant. Can you imagine what Annabelle's been whispering in his ear? Probably got him convinced he's the best thing to ever happen to radio." She rolled her eyes. "She's playing the long game, you know. Mark my words, in a month she'll be 'accidentally' dropping hints about wanting to co-host The Babes Takeover when we do our Boxing Day special. She'll act all sweet, bat her lashes, and before you know it, Adam'll be rearranging the lineup so she can have a starring role. Fucking skank."

"You know, you're cute when you're planning to rip Annabelle a brand new one," James murmured, leaning in slightly as he smirked at Carly. "It's like watching a Bond villain plot world domination, only with more WKD and fewer laser sharks. Oh, it reminds me," James then said, reverting to his 'posh boy' voice that was expected of him when he was in lectures or at a family function, "My father is having a soirée this weekend at the Henley house. He insists that I bring my 'delightful young lady' along. That would be you, in case you were wondering. He thinks I'm 'courting', his words, not mine, a 'well-bred young woman from a respectable background.'"

Carly nearly choked on her WKD, setting the bottle down with a clatter. "Oh my God, Jenkins," she gasped between laughs, clutching her stomach. "Your dad actually thinks I'm some posh debutante? Does he even know I'm from Essex?"

James grinned, clearly enjoying her reaction. "Not yet," he admitted, swirling the last of his pint in his glass. "But I figured I'd let the shock settle in once you turn up and call him 'babes' while nursing a bottle of blue WKD in one hand and a ciggie in the other. Anyway, he's invited several of his friends from the club he attends in Mayfair, you know, the lot who have tons of money and think that 'working-class' means someone who owns fewer than three horses. One of them, ironically, is a businessman who owns several racehorses, and whose son is chums with Simon Cowell."

Carly snorted, shaking her head in amusement. "Oh, Jenkins, this is gonna be glorious. Your old man's expecting some prim and proper Chelsea girl, and instead, he's getting me—Queen of the Babes, straight out of Essex, raised on cheap vodka and '90s club classics."

James grinned, clearly relishing the thought of the chaos Carly would inevitably bring. "Oh, absolutely. I can already picture it—my dad introducing you to his snobby Mayfair mates, and you casually dropping 'skank' into the conversation while sipping a WKD. You'll be the highlight of the evening."

Clarissa, who had been quietly sipping her drink, let out a wicked chuckle. "Mate, I need to be a fly on the wall for that. Will there be any media moguls in attendance?

Maybe someone from The Sun? Because I swear this is front-page material."

Carly smirked, swirling the bottle of WKD in her hand. "You're just jealous that I'm about to infiltrate the high society of Henley-on-Thames like some sort of Essex Trojan horse. Imagine it—me, sitting in a posh drawing room, nodding along while some Tory bloke bangs on about fox hunting, all while secretly wondering if they've got any Lambrini hidden in the kitchen."

Mark chuckled, finally finding his voice. "I mean, if anyone could pull it off, it'd be you, Carly. But I give it twenty minutes before you say something that makes his dad's monocle fall into his gin and tonic."

James shook his head, still grinning. "Oh, trust me, I'll be timing it. My father's got this very specific expression when he hears something that offends his delicate sensibilities—he furrows his brow, presses his lips together, and blinks exactly three times. I bet he'll do it the second you say 'babes.' Mother, on the other hand, is more liberal, as she comes from a true upper-middle-class background rather than old money, and she knows... well, that we're shagging."

Carly nearly fell off her chair, gripping the edge of the table as she let out a sharp laugh. "Wait, wait, what? Your mum knows we're shagging? And you just... casually drop this into conversation between rounds of WKD and Adam slander?" She wiped a tear from her eye, still cackling. "Oh my God, Jenkins, you absolute weapon."

James smirked, ever the picture of smugness. "Oh, she's known since we were fuck buddies. Apparently women have this thing where they can tell when their sons have that look. You know, the 'oh, he's getting laid regularly' look. Apparently, I was walking around looking too smug for someone who was supposedly just 'mates' with a girl who calls him 'Jenkins' half the time and 'babes' the other half. To be fair, she'd rather I married for love than one of my father's rich bitch contract daughters of his golf buddies. So, Carly Hemsworth, you're already ahead of the game in her eyes."

Carly wiped away the last of her laughter, shaking her head as she took another sip of WKD. "Oh, Jenkins, I don't know whether to be flattered or absolutely mortified. Your mum must think I'm some sort of harlot, rocking up to ruin the family name."

James leaned in slightly, his smirk still firmly in place. "On the contrary, she's rather amused by you. Thinks you've 'breathed life' into me, whatever that means. Also, she called you 'refreshingly unpolished.' Which, in posh speak, is actually a compliment. My aunt, her sister, isn't often talked about in polite circles because she ran off with a 'rapscallion of a shoemaker who deflowered her and then left her to live in a semi-detached in Basingstoke.' Mother still talks to her as, y'know, sisters and all that."

Carly knew that James hardly talked about his family, apart from the fact that he was the son of a barrister, and his father was also the son of a barrister, and so on for generations, all the way back to some ancestor who had likely represented Henry VIII in a divorce settlement. James played it down, but it was clear he came from money—the kind of money that bought silence rather than attention.

Yet here he was, casually discussing his mother's amusement at her existence and his aunt's scandalous affair with a shoemaker as if it were just another Tuesday.

"Wait, wait, wait," Carly said, setting her bottle down as she wiped the last tears of laughter from her eyes. "So, your mum actually likes me?"

James took another sip of his pint, nodding with a smirk. "She does. Thinks you're 'spirited,' which in posh mum code is somewhere between 'I tolerate her' and 'I wish she'd marry my son immediately.' And, let's be honest, you're a damn sight better than the girls my dad's been trying to throw at me since I was sixteen."

Carly tilted her head, watching him with curiosity. "Oh yeah? And what's the usual Jenkins-approved type then? Let me guess—double-barrelled surname, rides horses, probably named something like Arabella or Clementine?"

James groaned, running a hand through his hair. "Mate, you have no idea. Arabella was a real one. So was Theodora. And Imogen, and Letitia—who, by the way, once told me that she 'wasn't sure about Essex' as a concept. I'm not even sure what she meant, but I'm fairly certain she thought it was some kind of disease. Funnily enough Imogen is... in our year and does Humanities."

Carly let out a wheezing laugh, nearly toppling over in her chair as she grabbed James' arm for balance. "Oh my God, Jenkins, please tell me you introduced me to her at some point! I would have paid money—actual money—to see her reaction."

"You bumped into her on Freshers Week last year, the blonde girl with the pigtails who had come in the limo," James said with a grin. "Like us, she's in Magdalen, but she's usually too busy swanning around with the polo crowd to mix with us mere mortals."

Carly clapped a hand over her mouth as the memory resurfaced. "Oh my days, I remember her! She looked at me like I was some kind of lost stray who'd accidentally wandered onto campus. I think she flinched when I spoke." Carly doubled over in laughter, shaking her head. "Jenkins, you absolute posh boy reject! You were meant to marry a horse girl and produce future barristers, not shack up with a Babe from Essex who calls her boss a 'skank' on a daily basis."

James smirked, leaning back in his seat. "What can I say? I have a rebellious streak. Besides, can you imagine me actually settling down with someone like Imogen? My entire life would be brunches and Tatler photo shoots. The only excitement I'd get is whether the housekeeper used the wrong silverware for the fish course. Anyway, one of our guests this weekend is, according to father, is the former owner of Arthur Prince... a bookmaker and turf accountant."

Carly nearly choked on her WKD for the third time that night, setting the bottle down with a thud. "Hold on, Arthur Prince as in the Arthur Prince? The bookie? The one my dad used to bang on about whenever he lost a tenner on the horses?"

James smirked, tilting his pint glass towards her in a mock toast. "That would be the one. Apparently, he sold off his share in the nineties, but Father says he still has 'considerable influence in certain circles.'" He leaned in slightly, lowering his voice. "Which, in rich people code, means he still makes a fortune off people who fancy themselves as the next John McCririck. His son, Ashley, works in radio as an assistant to Richard Park at Capital Radio."

Carly chuckled, as, with Brookes Vibes and its parent company, the Home Counties Radio Group, being a staunch pro-GWR, anti-Capital organisation, meeting someone with ties to the enemy felt like walking into a lion's den. "So, what you're saying is… I have an opportunity to infiltrate high society and possibly start a civil war between GWR and Capital all in one evening? Jenkins, babes, you're really spoiling me."

James grinned, leaning back in his chair. "You're forgetting the best part—you'll also get to witness my father's slow realisation that his son is not, in fact, marrying a polo-playing aristocrat, but rather, a chaos merchant from Essex who works in radio promotions and uses the word 'skank' more than 'please' and 'thank you'."

Carly let out a mock gasp, pressing a hand to her chest in faux horror. "Oh, the scandal! What will the Daily Mail say?" She laughed, shaking her head. "Nah, but for real, Jenkins, this is gonna be hilarious. Your old man's expecting some posh bird with pearls and a family crest, and instead, he's getting me, who's currently holding a bottle of WKD and deciding whether or not to knock Annabelle out with it."

As soon as Carly said that, the Oxford Brookes part of the Brookes Babes walked into the club, led by none other than Annabelle herself. Carly knew that they were slated to do a promo run in the various clubs, and that Annabelle's arrival was like a gust of cold air cutting through the humid warmth of the club. As a Babe herself, she knew that the mini-skirt and low cut, two sizes too small, crop top with 'Babe' on the breasts in bright pink lettering was part of the uniform, but on Annabelle, it just looked calculated. Like she was trying to prove a point.

"Look," Clarissa said with a chuckle. "It's the Skank Patrol, with the Head Skank leading her Brookes Skank Brigade."

Carly exhaled sharply, gripping her bottle of WKD like it was a weapon of war. Annabelle had arrived, flanked by a group of Brookes Babes who, while technically part of the same promo team, had long since picked their sides in the brewing Cold War between Carly and Annabelle.

James glanced at Carly, his smirk still present but his eyes sharp. "Now, Hemsworth, do try and keep it civil. The last thing we need is you getting banned from Park End for committing grievous bodily harm with a bottle of cheap alcopop."

Carly smirked, but her eyes were locked on Annabelle. "Oh, don't worry, Jenkins. If I do it right, there'll be no evidence."

****

As Carly and James were walking back to their dorm near Magdalen Bridge, Carly was still fuming from the sight of Annabelle parading around Park End like she owned the place. The whole night, the tension had simmered just beneath the surface, a barely contained storm waiting to explode.

James, ever the peacemaker, had kept an arm slung lazily around her shoulders, steering her away from trouble while occasionally murmuring, "Not worth it, Hemsworth," into her ear. But Carly knew he was enjoying the drama just as much as she was—he was just more discreet about it.

As they reached the entrance to their dorm, Carly finally broke the silence, her voice sharp with lingering frustration.

"I swear, if that slag smirks at me one more time, I'm gonna launch her off the fucking Carfax Tower."

James snorted, fishing his keys out of his jacket pocket. "I'd pay good money to see that, but unfortunately, Oxford Council frowns upon yeeting promotional staff off historical landmarks. Bad for tourism, apparently. Anyway, I'm fucking horny."

Carly let out a sharp laugh, rolling her eyes as she swiped James' keys from his hand and unlocked the door. "Jenkins, babes, I swear to God, if you think you're gonna distract me with sex right now—"

James grinned, leaning against the doorframe with his usual air of smugness. "It's worked before."

Carly shot him a look before stepping inside, kicking off her heels with an irritated huff. "Yeah, well, tonight I'm fuelled by WKD, spite, and the absolute urge to ruin Annabelle's entire existence. You can't just shag the rage out of me."

James shut the door behind them, his smirk deepening. "No, but it'd be a fun experiment."

Carly exhaled, running a hand through her tousled hair. "You're such a posh prick sometimes, you know that?"

James stepped forward, sliding his arms around her waist, his lips brushing against her ear. "And yet, you're obsessed with me."

Carly bit her lip, suppressing the shiver that ran through her. He was infuriating, but he wasn't wrong. James Jenkins was a smug, overprivileged tosser—her smug, overprivileged tosser.

****

CHAPTER 13 – Meeting the Parents
Saturday 8th November 2025

The ride in the car that James's father had hired to take them to Henley was, to Carly's surprise, rather comfortable. It wasn't the stuffy, old-money affair she had pictured in her head—no vintage Rolls-Royce with a tweed-clad chauffeur, no cigar smoke curling through the air. Instead, it was a sleek, black Mercedes driven by a polite but silent man in his forties, who barely acknowledged their conversation beyond the occasional nod.

James, of course, had made the entire thing seem painfully casual. He sat next to her, legs crossed, looking effortlessly posh in his tailored navy blazer and crisp white shirt, an image of easy elegance that only someone who had grown up in privilege could pull off. He had told her not to stress about tonight, that his parents were 'more tolerable than most of the Henley lot'—which, in James-speak, meant they were only moderately insufferable.

Or in Essex English, to Carly, that meant they were still posh as fuck, just slightly less likely to ask if she "rode horses" or "summered in the Côte d'Azur."

Carly chuckled, as despite James wearing a tight-fitted pair of trousers, his erection was highly noticeable. As their journey was nearly an hour, a thought crossed her mind—she could definitely use this to her advantage.

Reaching her hand onto James's lap, she slowly inched her way towards the bulge that had been taunting her for the last ten minutes. Carly smirked, glancing up at James with an expression of pure mischief as she slowly traced a finger along the fabric of his trousers.

James cleared his throat sharply, shifting slightly in his seat as he shot her a warning look. "Hemsworth," he murmured under his breath, his voice tight, "we are in a chauffeured car on our way to my father's house. Now is not the time... unless... my bedroom at home is... spacious."

Carly's smirk widened, her fingers now resting lightly over the ever-growing evidence of James's predicament. "Oh, Jenkins, you say that like it's going to stop me," she whispered back, leaning in just enough so that her breath brushed against his ear. "Besides, we've got a good twenty minutes left before we get there... I reckon that's just enough time to make you squirm."

James sucked in a sharp breath, shifting uncomfortably in his seat as his gaze flicked to the rear-view mirror. The driver remained stoically focused on the road ahead, either oblivious or deliberately ignoring what was happening in the back of his boss's expensive car.

"You're evil," James muttered, his jaw tightening as he gripped Carly's wrist and gently pried her hand away from his lap. "And don't think I won't be getting you back for this later."

Carly leaned back, her smirk never faltering as she folded her arms across her chest. "I look forward to it, babes."

James exhaled, closing his eyes for a brief moment before composing himself, slipping seamlessly back into his usual smooth, untouchable posh-boy demeanour. The car turned down a winding country road, flanked by towering trees and high hedges, leading to what Carly assumed would be some sprawling estate with an unnecessarily large driveway.

She wasn't wrong.

As they rounded the final bend, a grand Georgian-style manor came into view, its pristine stone façade glowing under the dimming autumn sunlight. The gravel driveway was already occupied by a number of high-end cars—sleek Aston Martins, polished Bentleys, even a classic Jaguar parked near the front steps, as if someone had placed it there purely for aesthetic purposes.

Carly let out a low whistle. "Bloody hell, Jenkins. Your family doesn't do things by halves, do they?"

James chuckled, running a hand through his hair as the car rolled to a smooth stop outside the grand entrance. "Welcome to Henley, babes. Try not to cause too much of a scandal in the first five minutes."

Carly smirked, straightening her shoulders as the driver stepped out to open the door for them. "Oh, don't worry, Jenkins. I'll at least wait ten."

Stepping outside the car, Carly decided that, until she was comfortable round James's parents, she'd adopt her regular Oxford University persona, the one that she had started the previous year, her first year at the University, of someone who was just like the other students—polished, articulate, and effortlessly fitting into the world of privilege she had accidentally walked into. Her Essex twang had already faded into the background, replaced with the more refined, neutral accent she had carefully curated over the past year.

"Thank you, Carson," James said, and Carly chuckled at how her boyfriend had somehow made thanking a chauffeur sound like an aristocratic ritual. The driver—Carson, apparently—gave a polite nod before stepping back into the car and pulling away, leaving Carly standing on the pristine gravel with her head held high and a mischievous glint in her eye.

The grand entrance of the Jenkins estate loomed before her, all towering pillars, ivy-covered walls, and the kind of over-the-top elegance that screamed old money. Carly had seen stately homes before, but there was something particularly intimidating about this one—probably because, unlike a National Trust property, she couldn't just pay £12 for a ticket and wander around making sarcastic comments about the wallpaper.

"You think this is bad, you might want to look at the Monaco villa," James murmured, placing a gentle hand on the small of Carly's back as he guided her towards the grand wooden doors. "Father prefers the English countryside, but Mother enjoys... escaping the English weather when she can. Don't be surprised if she invites you for a winter getaway."

Carly nearly laughed at the casual way James spoke about a Monaco villa like it was just a casual weekend retreat. "Oh, Jenkins, you do realise I come from a place where a week in Marbella is considered the height of luxury, yeah?" she whispered. "This is next-level posh."

James smirked, pressing the doorbell. "I'm aware. Which is why this is going to be brilliant."

The door was opened by a middle-aged butler who looked as though he'd been personally trained by the Queen herself. He stepped aside with a stiff nod. "Mr James. Welcome."

"Thank you, Albert, how is Mrs Unwin?" James asked, and Carly noticed that James's tone had softened slightly—still polished and effortless, but with genuine warmth.

Albert, the butler, gave a measured nod. "Mrs Unwin is doing well, sir. She's in the kitchen preparing for tonight's dinner. She asked me to let you know that she's set aside your favourite lemon drizzle cake."

James smiled. "Ah, excellent. You know I can't come home without sampling Mrs Unwin's baking." He gestured towards Carly. "Albert, this is Carly Hemsworth."

Albert turned his gaze towards Carly, his expression perfectly neutral but his eyes subtly appraising. Carly met his gaze with a polite, well-practised smile, the one she reserved for Oxford professors who assumed she was less intelligent than she was.

"Miss Hemsworth," Albert said with a small nod of approval. "A pleasure."

Carly resisted the urge to curtsy—mostly because she wasn't sure if Albert would take it as a joke or an insult.

"Likewise," she replied smoothly, her clipped Oxford accent still firmly in place.

"JAMMMMIIIIIEEEEEE!" a screech from inside the house and Carly noticed James shudder at the high-pitched, unmistakably posh voice that echoed through the grand entrance hall. Carly barely had time to register what was happening before a blonde whirlwind in a silk dress came flying down the staircase towards them.

The fact that the blonde looked in her teens and her dress was that low cut that James groaned as the blonde figure flung herself at him, arms wrapping around his neck in an overly enthusiastic embrace. Carly took a step back, arching an eyebrow as she took in the girl properly.

She was young—probably seventeen or eighteen at most—but carried herself with the kind of entitlement that only came from a lifetime of privilege. Her platinum blonde hair was styled in loose waves, her expensive silk dress clinging to her slim frame in a way that was just a little too suggestive for a family gathering.

"Arabella," James muttered, gently prying her arms off him. "Didn't realise you'd be here."

Arabella. Oh, brilliant. One of the horse girls. Carly had heard about James's childhood 'friendships'—or more accurately, the parade of wealthy daughters his father had paraded in front of him in the hopes of orchestrating a lucrative marriage. Arabella was clearly one of them.

"Oh, darling, I wouldn't miss it!" Arabella trilled, her cut-glass accent making her sound like she'd stepped straight out of a BBC period drama. "Who's this... peasant?"

Carly had to physically restrain herself from bursting out laughing. *Peasant? Oh, babes, you've just made my night,* she thought as Arabella started caressing James's body.

"Arabella," he said smoothly, "this is Carly Hemsworth. My girlfriend." He let the words hang in the air, deliberately, as if to let them sink into Arabella's overprivileged little head. "Carly, this is Arabella Johnstone-Carter, daughter of the Baron of Chipping Norton."

Carly tilted her head slightly, giving Arabella a look of carefully curated politeness, the kind of smile she reserved for the aggressively posh girls at Oxford who eyed her with thinly veiled suspicion. "Charmed," she said smoothly, stretching the vowels in just the right way to match the accent she'd picked up since starting university.

Arabella, however, wasn't playing along. She looked Carly up and down, her painted lips pursing ever so slightly as though she'd just bitten into something sour. "Hemsworth, you say?" she drawled, barely masking her distaste. "Can't say I've ever heard of the family."

Carly smirked, because of course that would be Arabella's first response. She leaned in slightly, just enough to make it feel like a private little secret between them. "That's because we don't have a family crest, babes," she murmured, just loud enough for James to hear and smirk.

James, sensing an oncoming war, stepped in. "Arabella, aren't you supposed to be entertaining Father's business guests?" he asked, all smoothly, albeit with some disinterest. "I'm sure Lord Patterson would love to hear about your latest equestrian ventures, same with Mr

Tabor—after all, he owns several horses and has had a colt, Entrepreneur, which went on to win the 2,000 Guineas at Newmarket."

Arabella visibly bristled at the suggestion that she should toddle off and talk about horses with the older guests. Carly could see the barely concealed irritation flicker across her carefully made-up face. Clearly, Arabella had expected to be the centre of attention tonight, and James had just effortlessly redirected her elsewhere.

"Oh, Jamie," Arabella purred, placing a delicate hand on James's forearm, the kind of touch that was meant to look casual but was entirely calculated. "You know Daddy's already spoken to Mr Tabor—besides, they're all boring old men who only care about racing stats. Anyway, I spoke to Mr Tabor's son... seems he's... not interested in me."

James barely suppressed a smirk as he gently removed Arabella's hand from his forearm, his tone laced with polite disinterest. "That's a shame, Arabella. Perhaps you should try charming him again—Tabor money doesn't exactly grow on trees. Anyway, he's only 7 years older than us, so he's not entirely out of reach, is he?"

Arabella's expression soured further, but before she could retort, a new voice interrupted, cool and clipped.

"Arabella, dear, stop terrorising our guests and come and greet Lord Harrison properly."

Carly turned her head just in time to see a tall, impeccably dressed woman descending the grand staircase with all the grace of a seasoned aristocrat. She was stunning in that understated, old-money way—polished but not flashy, confident without a hint of desperation. Her honey-blonde hair was styled in an elegant chignon, and her piercing blue eyes flicked between Arabella, James, and Carly with mild curiosity.

James hugged the woman when she came close to him, and Carly noticed that she shared the same eyes as James. This was his mother.

"Mother," James greeted smoothly, pressing a kiss to her cheek before stepping back. "Carly, this is my mother, Alexandra Jenkins. Mother, this is Carly Hemsworth, my girlfriend."

Alexandra Jenkins gave Carly a long, assessing look, the kind that only women of her standing could manage—a mixture of polite curiosity and silent judgement, wrapped in a silk glove of civility. But to Carly's surprise, the older woman's lips curved into something resembling genuine amusement.

And then she laughed.

"James, keep the stuffy shit up around your father, but when it's just me in the room-oh, Arabella, your father is asking for you, by the way," Alexandra said with a graceful wave of her hand, dismissing Arabella as effortlessly as one might swat away an irritating fly.

Arabella hesitated for a fraction of a second, her lips pressing into a thin line as if she wanted to argue, but the sharpness in Alexandra's gaze made it clear that defying her was not an option. With a huff that was far too dramatic for someone of her supposed social standing,

Arabella turned on her heel and sauntered off towards the drawing room, throwing one last scowl over her shoulder at Carly before disappearing into the crowd.

"Where was I? Oh, yes, James, drop the posh act when it's just me in the room. We both know that you're like your aunt, and not one of your father's golf club Tories. Honestly, darling, you do this whole 'upper-class heir' performance so well, but you're fooling no one who's known you since you were in nappies. You know, your father is getting Ashley Tabor to give you a job at Capital once you've finished at Oxford in a year and half. Something to do with his connections with Richard Park and all that."

Carly chuckled, because Brookes Vibes, being owned by a group of former GWR executives, was staunchly anti-Capital. On the other hand, Carly knew that she, herself, wanted to get into HR with the Sociology degree that she was studying, and that she knew James wanted to get into Media Law, and that by going to a big group like Capital, GWR or Chrysalis, he would be setting himself up for a lucrative career, but at what cost?

James let out a short laugh, shaking his head. "Mother, you do realise that my current employer would consider that treason, right? The Brookes Vibes lot would rather see me rot than work for Capital."

Alexandra waved a hand dismissively. "Oh, please, James. We both know that radio politics are nothing more than a playground for overgrown children in cheap suits. You don't need to pledge allegiance to one side or another—you need to think about what will set you up for the future." She turned to Carly with a measured smile.

"And what about you, Miss Hemsworth? Are you planning to spend your career handing out glow-in-the-dark condoms on behalf of regional radio stations, or do you have bigger ambitions?"

Carly felt James stiffen beside her, but she met Alexandra's gaze evenly. She wasn't intimidated by posh women with sharp tongues—if anything, it was a sport back home in Essex to see who could come out on top in a verbal sparring match.

"I'm studying Sociology, actually," Carly said smoothly, keeping her Oxford accent firmly in place. "HR is the plan—radio's a bit of fun for now, but I'd rather be in a position where I can make actual decisions, not just be the girl with the free merch. Which reminds me, James... I had a letter this morning... you know my lecturers told me there was a chance for me to do an internship with a major media firm... I've been shortlisted."

James turned to Carly, eyebrows raised in genuine surprise. "Wait, you didn't tell me that."

Carly smirked, taking a sip of the champagne that had magically appeared in her hand—because of course, this kind of house had staff floating around with trays of alcohol at all times. "Well, babes, I thought I'd wait for the right moment. No better time than when your mother's questioning my entire life plan."

Alexandra's lips curved into something between approval and intrigue. "And which firm is this?"

Carly took a deliberate pause, just to enjoy the tension. "H Bauer Publishing. The publishing company that makes Bella, Take a Break and TV Choice."

Carly watched as James chuckled, and saw the glint in his mother's eyes that suggested a mix of amusement and interest.

"I know, Carly, love. I asked mother to pull a few strings and see if you'd be considered," James admitted, his smirk widening as Carly's eyes narrowed in suspicion.

"You what?" she demanded, setting her champagne flute down with a little too much force on the nearby mahogany side table.

James shrugged, looking far too pleased with himself. "Look, it's a competitive internship, and I know you'd get shortlisted anyway, but a gentle nudge in the right direction never hurts. You deserve a shot at it."

Carly exhaled sharply, torn between wanting to be annoyed at James for meddling and wanting to snog the smug expression off his face. "You absolute posh prick, Jenkins," she muttered, but there was no real heat behind it.

Alexandra let out a soft laugh, swirling the champagne in her glass before taking a slow sip. "Ah, young love. So full of deception and well-placed manipulation." She turned to Carly, a knowing glint in her eye. "You *do* realise that means you now owe him one, don't you?"

Carly shot James a look of pure suspicion. "Yeah, and what exactly *do* you want in return, Jenkins?"

James smirked, leaning in slightly, his lips close to her ear. "Oh, Hemsworth, I've already got you, so there's no need to bargain for anything else," he murmured, his voice dripping with smug satisfaction. "But if you're offering, I'm sure I can think of a few things."

Carly rolled her eyes but couldn't suppress the smirk tugging at her lips. "Oh, piss off, Jenkins. Just because you've got a trust fund and a blazer that costs more than my first car doesn't mean you can manipulate my career choices."

Alexandra chuckled into her champagne. "Oh, I do like you, Miss Hemsworth. You keep James on his toes—he needs that." She set her glass down on a nearby tray with effortless grace before glancing towards the large double doors leading into the dining room. "Now, if you'll excuse me, I need to ensure my husband isn't about to ambush you both with some tedious monologue about the integrity of media law."

Carly and James exchanged a glance as Alexandra swept off with the kind of regal poise that only women of her stature could pull off. Carly exhaled, her shoulders dropping slightly now that the first round of scrutiny was over. "Well, she didn't throw me out or call me a commoner, so I suppose that's a win."

James smirked, resting a hand on the small of her back. "She likes you, Hemsworth. Trust me, if she didn't, you'd know. She'd have already found some excuse to 'redirect' you to another part of the house while Father grilled me on why I was 'slumming it' with an Essex girl."

Carly scoffed, taking another sip of champagne. "Charming. So, when do I get to meet His Lordship, then? Is he going to do the whole 'stare disapprovingly over his spectacles' routine, or is he the type to pretend I don't exist?"

James let out a slow breath, his smirk fading slightly. "Oh, he'll acknowledge you—mainly because he won't want to appear rude in front of his peers—but don't expect warmth. He's… efficient with his words. Think Daily Telegraph editorial, but in human form."

Carly raised an eyebrow. "Brilliant. Can't wait to be treated like a potential PR disaster."

Before James could respond, a deep voice from behind them cut through the hum of conversation. "James. You remember Micheal Tabor and his son, Ashley, don't you?"

James turned smoothly, the smirk that had been playing on his lips sharpening into something more refined—more polished. This was Jenkins, heir to the family name mode, the carefully curated version of himself that he slipped into when dealing with the men who ran the world.

Carly, however, recognised the subtle shift. It was the same voice he used when he had to deal with Oxford's elite, the same effortless I belong here posture that he had mastered long before she had stumbled into his orbit. She was still adapting to this world, but she was nothing if not quick on her feet.

James's father, Lord Henry Jenkins, stood tall and imposing, his silver hair neatly combed back, his navy dinner jacket perfectly tailored to his lean frame. His gaze was as sharp as a freshly pressed newspaper column, the kind of stare that made lesser men stumble over their words.

Beside him stood two other figures—one that even Carly, with her admittedly minimal knowledge of horse racing, recognised immediately.

Michael Tabor. The legendary businessman, bookie, and thoroughbred owner. The man whose name had been muttered by every punter in Essex whenever they lost money on the horses. And next to him, his son, Ashley Tabor, a name that carried weight in the radio industry. He wasn't just someone in media—he was Capital Radio. One of the men who ran the biggest commercial radio brand in the country.

And here she was, stood in front of him, a Brookes Babe working for a radio group that actively loathed Capital.

Well, shit.

James extended his hand towards Tabor Senior first, his smile easy and charming. "Mr Tabor, good to see you again," he said, his voice rich with well-practised politeness. "It's been a while."

Michael Tabor nodded, shaking James's hand firmly. "Indeed, lad. Last time I saw you, you were still knee-high, chasing after that pony of your aunt's. You ever get into racing like your father, or are you still keeping your head buried in books?"

James chuckled. "Oh, I leave the betting to the experts. I prefer my investments to be slightly less unpredictable. I'm following in the family footsteps and studying to become a lawyer."

Ashley Tabor, standing slightly behind his father, gave James a measured look before glancing towards Carly with mild curiosity. "And this must be Carly Hemsworth," he said smoothly, his voice carrying the kind of careful neutrality that suggested he already knew exactly who she was.

Carly straightened slightly, shifting back into her well-practised Oxford accent. She had learned long ago that first impressions mattered in these circles, and she wasn't about to let James's family—or Capital's golden boy—catch her off guard. "That's me," she said with a polite but confident smile, extending a hand. "Pleasure to meet you, Mr Tabor."

Ashley shook her hand, his grip firm but not overbearing. "Likewise," he said, his tone unreadable. "Anyway, I must get off, Simon is working on a new project for ITV, and I'm part of his team that are handling the media partnerships for it. It's a potential replacement next year for Pop Idol."

Carly barely resisted the urge to let out a low whistle. Simon, as in Simon Cowell? That was next-level industry power. Even James, with all his natural charm and privilege, couldn't quite mask the flicker of intrigue that crossed his face.

Ashley seemed to notice, the corner of his mouth twitching slightly. "Yes, well, nothing's set in stone yet.

But these things move fast, and Simon has his way of making things happen." He turned his attention back to James. "Your father mentioned you're interested in media law. If you're looking for experience, you should consider working with us at Capital, once you graduate. A good legal mind with industry understanding is invaluable. Let me know and I'll get Richard to schedule a meeting with you."

Carly couldn't help but smirk. If James accepted that offer, he'd officially be committing the biggest act of betrayal in Brookes Vibes history. She could already picture Adam's face turning puce with rage at the idea of one of his own defecting to the enemy.

James, however, played it cool, nodding smoothly. "That's very generous, Ashley. I'll certainly keep it in mind."

Lord Henry Jenkins, who had been silently watching the exchange, finally spoke, his voice clipped and authoritative. "James, I assume you'll give it serious consideration. There's no better place to establish yourself in media law than working within one of the largest commercial radio groups in the country. A legal mind with industry knowledge is invaluable."

Carly barely held back a snort. He'd just parroted Ashley word for word. It was almost comical how men like this all spoke in carefully rehearsed soundbites.

James, to his credit, simply inclined his head. "Of course, Father."

Lord Jenkins turned his gaze towards Carly then, and she felt the full force of his scrutiny. She had to remind herself that she'd faced scarier people—Oxford examiners, pissed-off Brookes Vibes promo managers, and the wrath of a nightclub bouncer after sneaking WKDs into a VIP booth.

"You're in promotions," he stated rather than asked.

Carly gave a pleasant, if slightly knowing smile. "For now, yes. I'm studying sociology with an aim to go into HR. Radio's fun, but I'd rather be behind the scenes, making things happen."

He studied her for a long moment before giving the smallest nod of approval. "A sensible ambition."

Translation: 'At least you're not just another girl using my son to climb the social ladder.'

"Thank you," she said smoothly, glancing at James, whose lips twitched ever so slightly. He knew exactly what she was doing—matching his father's tone, playing the game.

Ashley, clearly intrigued, sipped from his whisky glass and regarded her with mild amusement. "Well, Carly, if you're interested in the HR side of media, you should consider applying at Capital when you graduate. We're always looking for people who understand both sides of the industry—talent and business."

Carly raised an eyebrow, her smirk returning. "That's a very kind offer, Mr Tabor, but I imagine my current employer would have a heart attack at the idea."

Ashley chuckled, clearly entertained by her response. "Ah yes, Brookes Vibes. I've heard they're… quite passionate in their allegiances. A group of Ralph Bernard acolytes if memory serves me."

Carly chuckled, swirling the last sip of her champagne in her glass. "Oh, you could say that, yeah. Passionate is a nice way of putting it. I think fanatical might be a better term. If I so much as breathe the words 'Capital Radio' in the office, I'll probably be excommunicated."

****

CHAPTER 14 – Annabelle's Power Play

Saturday 29th November 2003

Carly had never been one for office politics, but when it came to Annabelle Young, she was starting to reconsider.

For weeks, the tension between them had been growing, simmering beneath the surface of every team meeting, promo run, and passive-aggressive email conversation between the Oxford and the Brookes university students.

And then it all came to a head earlier that day.

Annabelle had, while she, Carly, Clarissa and James had been on a promo run on loan to the Banbury Beats station, pulled the ultimate power move.

She had dragged James into the Babemobile and tried to sleep with him. In broad daylight in Banbury town centre.

James had tried to resist, tried to extricate himself from the situation with some semblance of dignity, but Annabelle wasn't one to take no for an answer—especially when she was playing a game she was determined to win.

Carly had found out in the worst way possible.

She and Clarissa had been handing out promo flyers outside a café, chatting away about the upcoming Brookes Vibes Christmas party, when Mark had come jogging up to them, slightly out of breath, eyes wide with alarm.

"You need to get to the Babemobile. Now," he had panted, hands on his knees.

Carly had shared a look with Clarissa before setting off at a determined pace, her boots clicking against the pavement. She knew Annabelle had been up to something all afternoon—she'd been smug, smirking every time Carly so much as glanced in her direction.

And now, as Carly stormed towards the van, she realised why.

She flung the door open without thinking, her stomach already twisted in knots, and found Annabelle naked as the day she was born, and James's erection in Anabelle's quim, him trying to force her off while Annabelle was bouncing on top of him like a jockey on a racehorse.

For a second, the whole world seemed to slow down.

The sound of the bustling Banbury high street faded into nothing. Carly's brain refused to process what she was seeing—Annabelle, stark naked, riding James like her life depended on it, her manicured nails digging into his shoulders, her head thrown back in mock ecstasy.

James, for his part, looked like he was having the worst day of his life. His hands were on Annabelle's hips, but not in a way that suggested enthusiasm—more like he was actively trying to push her off him while she clung on like a stubborn limpet.

"Carly—" James started, his voice sharp with panic, but it was too late.

Carly saw red.

Without thinking, she lunged forward, grabbing Annabelle by the hair and yanking her backwards with a force that sent her sprawling onto the floor of the van. Annabelle let out a yelp, scrambling to cover herself with one of the discarded promo t-shirts that had been lying around.

"What the fuck do you think you're doing?" Carly spat, her Essex accent making a full comeback in her fury. "You desperate, slimy little rat!"

Annabelle, ever the actress, plastered an expression of faux innocence across her face. "Oh, Carly," she panted, adjusting the shirt over her chest like she was the victim here. "I thought you knew about our little arrangement. James and I have been... reconnecting." She smirked, knowing exactly what she was doing. "He's been struggling, poor thing, and I thought I'd offer some... stress relief."

Seeing red, Carly dragged Annabelle out of the Ford Transit, off the mattress, onto the ground, and, seeing the ironically placed mud pit that Adam had hired, decided that Annabelle needed a lesson in humility.

With a sharp shove, Carly sent Annabelle stumbling backwards into the thick, sludgy mud that had been left behind from the morning's promo stunt. Annabelle let out a high-pitched shriek as she landed on her arse, her bare legs coated in filth, her perfectly curled blonde hair now streaked with brown.

Clarissa, who had just arrived at the scene, burst out laughing. "Oh my God, Carly, you legend!" she cackled, clutching her stomach.

James, who had managed to yank his jeans back up with lightning speed, ran a hand through his dishevelled hair, looking as though he'd rather be anywhere else in the world. "Carly, for fuck's sake—"

"Oh, don't you Carly me, Jenkins!" she snapped, rounding on him. "What the fuck was that? You think I'm some sort of mug? Letting her climb on you like you're some kind of fairground ride?"

James groaned, rubbing his temples. "I wasn't letting her do anything, Carly! You think I wanted this? She just—" He gestured helplessly towards the still-spluttering Annabelle, who was now frantically trying to wipe mud from her face while looking around for help. "She jumped on me! I literally told her to get off—what part of that wasn't clear?!"

James groaned, rubbing his temples. "I wasn't letting her do anything, Carly! You think I wanted this? She just—" He gestured helplessly towards the still-spluttering Annabelle, who was now frantically trying to wipe mud from her face while looking around for help. "She jumped on me! I literally told her to get off—what part of that wasn't clear?! Look, if I wasn't serious about you, do you think I would have taken you to meet my bloody parents?"

Carly's glare didn't soften, though the mention of their recent trip to Henley did briefly flash through her mind. James had been serious about her, hadn't he? He wouldn't have put her through that whole ordeal with his aristocratic father and his laid back but posh mother if he didn't actually care. But that didn't erase the fact that Annabelle had been naked on top of him like some desperate homewrecker from Hollyoaks.

Annabelle, still sitting in the mud with a face like a slapped arse, flipped her wet hair over her shoulder, her smirk returning despite her absolute state. "Oh, please," she scoffed. "Carly, babes, don't act like you're shocked. Did you really think he was gonna settle for a girl from Essex when he could have me? I mean, look at him—look at me." She gestured to her mud-covered body, as if that somehow strengthened her case.

Slap.

Carly's hand acted without thinking, the crack of palm against cheek ringing out loud and clear over the stunned silence that had fallen over the promo team. Annabelle's head snapped to the side, her smirk vanishing in an instant.

The next thing Carly knew, however, was the pull of two people grabbing her and dragging her off Annabelle, the click of handcuffs, the cold bite of steel wrapped around her wrists. A sharp voice cut through the stunned silence.

"All right, that's enough! You're coming with us."

Carly blinked, her breath still coming fast as she processed what was happening. Two police officers— both looking unimpressed, both wearing the telltale fluorescent yellow vests—were now holding onto her arms, firmly but not aggressively. One of them, a stocky bloke in his forties with a gruff Midlands accent, was already pulling her towards the waiting panda car.

James was the first to snap out of his shock. "Wait— what? Officer, this isn't—" He ran a hand through his already-messy hair, looking half-dressed and entirely panicked.

"She attacked me!" Annabelle shrieked from the mud, her posh accent wobbling with faux distress. "Did you see that? She assaulted me! I want her charged!"

"Oh, she's not the only one being arrested," another police officer said, and Carly noticed a grin on her face as she pulled her handcuffs out and tried to grab Annabelle, who was resisting as if her life depended on it.

"Oh, no fucking way!" Annabelle shrieked, scrambling to her feet, slipping on the mud as she tried to dodge the officer's grasp. "I'm the victim here! She attacked me! Arrest her, not me!"

The officer, a woman in her early thirties with sharp eyes and an even sharper smirk, didn't look the least bit impressed. "You were stark naked in a public place in the middle of Banbury town centre, miss. That's an indecent exposure charge. Now, are you gonna come quietly, or are we adding resisting arrest to the list?"

Carly, despite the situation, felt a surge of vindictive satisfaction as Annabelle let out an outraged squawk, flailing uselessly as the officer snapped the cuffs around her wrists.

****

Carly was sat in the interview room, two Police Constables on the opposite side of the table, both looking as though they had seen it all before. The room smelled of cheap coffee and disinfectant, and the fluorescent light overhead cast an unforgiving glow over everything. Carly was still buzzing from adrenaline, her hands itching from where the handcuffs had bitten into her skin.

"Now, Miss Hemsworth, we can do this the easy-"

Before the PC could continue, a knock on the door of the interview room door interrupted the moment. The officer closest to the door exchanged a glance with his colleague before sighing and getting up to answer it.

Carly sat back in her chair, arms crossed, still simmering with fury but also aware of the ridiculousness of the situation. She had been arrested for slapping Annabelle Young—something that, in her opinion, should have been rewarded rather than punished. And now she was in some grimy interview room in a Banbury police station, probably about to be cautioned for common assault.

The door swung open, and Carly's eyes widened as a middle aged man walked in, a three piece suit, briefcase in hand, a face which Carly knew smelt 'QC and Police's Worst Nightmare' all over it.

"Erm, Mick, we need to suspend the interview," a PC who had escorted the man into the room announced, clearly uneasy. "This is Charles Carrington-Smythe the Third, Miss Hemsworth's... legal representation. You might want to watch this guy, Mick... he's already had the Super on the phone to the Chief Constable, and I think he's just threatened to sue the entire force if we don't wrap this up properly."

Carly blinked, her brain trying to process the whirlwind of events. Who the fuck was Charles Carrington-Smythe

the Third? And more importantly—how the hell had she managed to get a lawyer who sounded like he belonged in the House of Lords?

The middle-aged man in the three-piece suit strode into the room with the kind of confidence that only came with money, power, and an entire legal education built on tearing apart cases like this for fun. He barely acknowledged the officers as he placed his briefcase on the table and took a seat beside Carly.

"Miss Hemsworth," he said smoothly, flipping open a sleek black notebook. "You are under no obligation to answer any further questions, and I strongly advise you do not until we have formally established the complete incompetence of these proceedings."

Carly stared at him. "Who—?"

"James called me," Charles interrupted, not even looking up as he jotted something down in his notebook. "Or, more accurately, James's mother called me. She's, to put it in parlance your generation would use, an 'old Oxford chum'."

Carly's brain stalled. James's mother had called in legal reinforcements? And not just any solicitor, but this guy—Charles Carrington-Smythe III, who looked like he exclusively represented politicians, oil barons, and people with double-barrelled surnames.

Carly wasn't sure whether she wanted to groan or burst out laughing.

James's mother. Of course.

The same woman who had coolly dismissed Arabella with a flick of her hand at the Henley soirée was now responsible for summoning what looked like a walking, talking Daily Telegraph op-ed in the form of her new legal representative.

She turned her head slightly, sizing up Charles Carrington-Smythe III. He had the look of a man who thrived on the misery of anyone unfortunate enough to sit across from him in a courtroom. His suit was immaculate, his cufflinks probably worth more than her dad's entire car, and his neatly combed hair suggested he'd been born in a law library and raised on a diet of legal loopholes and old-money privilege.

Carly slumped back in her chair, crossing her arms. "James called you?"

Charles finally looked up from his notes, adjusting his glasses with the kind of patience usually reserved for dealing with toddlers or politicians. "Technically, James called his mother, who then called me. Because, and I quote, 'This situation is a ludicrous waste of taxpayer resources, and my son's girlfriend should not have to spend the night in a holding cell because she smacked an insufferable brat who had it coming.'"

Carly blinked. "She said that?"

A small, knowing smirk crossed Charles's face. "Well, perhaps I paraphrased slightly, but the general sentiment was there. His father, on the other hand, was more of a 'let her see the Magistrate without any assistance and see if she can handle herself' approach. Fortunately, your boyfriend's mother is significantly more pragmatic."

Carly exhaled, still processing the sheer absurdity of the situation. Here she was, sitting in a police station in Banbury, fresh from slapping Annabelle Young into a puddle of mud, and now she had a high-profile lawyer parachuted in by James's posh mother like she was some kind of diplomatic incident.

Charles leaned forward, fixing the officers with a look so cold it could have frozen a courtroom. "Now, gentlemen, I am entitled under English law to confer with my client in private, so unless you want a highly publicised lawsuit accusing the Banbury constabulary of wrongful arrest, I suggest you step outside and let me speak with Miss Hemsworth alone."

The officer named Mick exchanged a look with his colleague, both clearly weighing up whether it was worth dealing with a man who had The Third in his name and the confidence of someone who had destroyed careers in court. Mick exhaled sharply, then stood. "Right. We'll give you ten minutes."

The officers left the room, and as soon as the door clicked shut, Carly let out a sharp breath and turned to Charles. "Okay, seriously. Who are you?"

Charles Carrington-Smythe III adjusted his tie and folded his hands on the table like he was about to cross-examine her. "I'm a barrister, Miss Hemsworth. I've handled legal matters for some of the most influential families in the country. That, and James's mother's second cousin once removed. Which reminds me, James has asked me to arrange for your... opponent... to face a sexual assault charge."

Carly blinked.

She had been expecting a lecture. Maybe some drawn-out, posh legalese about keeping her temper in check. Possibly even a warning about how assault charges weren't a good look for an aspiring HR professional.

But this?

She had to have misheard him.

"Wait... what?" she said, leaning forward, her brain struggling to process the words that had just come out of Charles Carrington-Smythe III mouth.

The barrister merely adjusted his glasses and continued, completely unfazed. "James, as you may have gathered, is rather furious about today's events. And unlike yourself, who opted for immediate and physical retaliation, he has decided to take the legal approach. He wishes to press charges against Miss Young for sexual assault. The fact there's evidence on Miss Young that he fought her off, and that she had forced herself on him despite his clear refusals, means this case has strong merit. Given that this happened in a public vehicle, in a town centre, and that there were witnesses—including yourself—Annabelle Young could very well find herself in serious legal trouble."

Carly gawked at him, her mind racing. "Wait—James actually wants to press charges?"

Charles nodded, his expression impassive. "Yes. He has already given his statement to the officers. As I understand it, he is rather keen to ensure Miss Young faces appropriate consequences for her actions. And I must say, in my professional experience, cases such as this often result in—"

"Bloody hell," Carly muttered, rubbing a hand over her face. She'd been so caught up in her own fury that she hadn't even thought about James being the one to turn the tables legally.

"Now," Charles continued, "as for your own situation, I am having my team prepare a statement which you will read. Until then, I will be asking for police bail on the grounds that this was a provoked altercation in response to an ongoing pattern of harassment. Given the context, and the fact that Miss Young has now been arrested on separate charges, I anticipate we can resolve this swiftly without a formal caution on your record."

Carly exhaled, trying to wrap her head around everything. It wasn't every day you ended up in police custody, only to find yourself represented by a high-powered barrister with a double-barrelled surname and connections to your boyfriend's aristocratic mother.

Still, one thing was clear—James was done playing nice.

She leaned forward, folding her arms on the table. "So, let me get this straight. I get a slap on the wrist, Annabelle gets an indecent exposure charge, and James is taking her to court for sexual assault?"

Charles inclined his head slightly. "That would be the summary, yes."

Carly let out a low whistle. "Bloody hell. That's not just a power move, that's a full-blown declaration of war."

Charles gave her a measured look. "Miss Hemsworth, if there is one thing you should know about people like James's family, it's this: when they choose to engage in a battle, they do not intend to lose."

Carly's stomach twisted, though not with nerves—more with the sudden realisation that Annabelle Young had no idea what she'd just stepped into. This wasn't just a catfight in a promo van anymore.

This was about to get serious.

****

CHAPTER 15 – Forensically Deconstructing The Chaos
Wednesday 5ᵗʰ December 2025

Adam Banks was sat in the boardroom of the Home Counties Radio Group in Milton Keynes, his face a mixture of grimness and happiness, with the former GWR executives like Peter McAllister, Antony Peckham, and some of the others were all nodding like donkeys, as Adam gave his report, saying how Ralph Bernard, the current GWR executive chairman, would have loved the chaos that had unfolded in Banbury.

"It was classic radio," Adam continued, leaning back in his chair, arms folded with that infuriatingly smug look on his face. "Promo teams causing absolute carnage in town centres, getting the name out there. The Babes have never had this much attention—TV, tabloids, even that tosser on Capital's breakfast show was talking about us. It's exposure, gentlemen."

Peter McAllister, the group's managing director and one of the many ex-GWR bigwigs now running the Home Counties Radio Group, tapped his pen against the conference table. "Yes, Adam, it's exposure. Ralph and I had a conversation last night. He says that you're proving that the GWR way is the way we should keep up."

"Hear hear," Nathan Law, the newly installed Group Head of Compliance, a former Beacon FM compliance officer, said with a grin. "Ralph would be proud of our efforts and the way we're reviving the golden age of radio promotions. But—" Nathan's grin faded slightly as he glanced down at the file in front of him, the words BANBURY POLICE INCIDENT REPORT stamped across the top in bold. "—we do need to address the, uh, legal side of things."

Antony Peckham, another GWR relic and the group's Head of Promotions, cleared his throat. "Look, let's not get bogged down in minor details. The Babes Takeover is still scheduled for Boxing Day. If anything, this whole fiasco has boosted interest. The amount of media coverage we've had? You can't buy that. Capital might be laughing at us now, but trust me, they're taking notes. We're dominating student radio right now."

Peter McAllister nodded but didn't look entirely convinced. "That's all well and good, but I've just spent an hour on the phone with our insurance underwriters, and they are not impressed. We've got two members of our promo team arrested—arrested, for God's sake. Indecent exposure and assault, in a branded promo van. Do you have any idea how bad that looks?"

Adam scoffed. "Do you have any idea how brilliant it looks? That's rock and roll, Pete. It's rebellious, it's sexy, it's radio. This is exactly the kind of thing that made GWR great. You think Chris Tarrant built Capital's brand by playing it safe? Hell no! He pulled stunts like this every other weekend back in the '80s! And need I remind you—" Adam gestured towards the file with a smirk. "—Annabelle Young, the so-called victim in all this, is now facing a potential sexual assault charge herself. Our lad James did us all a favour by putting her in the firing line. The scandal is eating itself."

Colin McTaggert, a former Scottish Radio Holdings Legal Director who had joined the Home Counties Radio Group as Group Head of Legal Affairs, who Adam knew, despite being on the outside of the GWR Mafia, as it was often nicknamed, would fall in line with the rest of them, finally spoke up, adjusting his tie as he leaned forward. "Aye, well, let's not get ahead of ourselves, gentlemen. James Jenkins pressing charges complicates things. We're now dealing with potential legal battles involving one of our own, which is not ideal. If this were just a slap and a bit of mud-wrestling, we could laugh it off and spin it as student antics. But sexual assault? That's a minefield."

"Well," Samuel O'Leary, the promotions coordinator at Buzz Beats and a former 2-Ten FM Black Thunder, said, "why don't we pay him off, get him to drop the charges? Slip him a bit of cash, a few perks, maybe even a fast-track to presenting if that's what he wants. Let's be real, James Jenkins is an Oxford boy. He's not exactly struggling, but everyone's got a price."

Adam chuckled, as it was well known in the GWR that covering things up, turning a blind eye and throwing money at problems was part of the playbook. It was exactly how they'd handled countless other scandals over the years—dodgy competitions, rigged giveaways, dodgy record label "arrangements" that ensured certain tracks got played more than others. What was one more cover-up?

After all, if the rumours coming out of the Watershed, GWR's old Bristol headquarters, were to be believed, there were plenty of skeletons in GWR's closet, and this was tame by comparison.

But before Adam could respond, Perdita Holmes, the Home Counties Radio Group's Director for Community Engagement—and one of the only women in the room—leaned forward, fixing the men with a sharp glare. "Are you all actually hearing yourselves?" she snapped. "A payoff? To cover up a sexual assault allegation? Christ almighty, it's like I've walked into a scene from Yes, Minister, except somehow with less ethics."

Of course, Adam knew, that Perdita would open her mouth, being a former Emap alumnus, meaning that she wasn't entirely indoctrinated into the GWR way of doing things. EMAP had been many things—chaotic, commercially aggressive, and occasionally reckless—but they weren't this brazen about dodgy dealings. Adam knew she'd always been a thorn in the side of the old GWR boys, but right now, she was particularly irritating.

"Perdita," Adam said smoothly, leaning forward with his best let's-be-reasonable smile, "we're not covering anything up. We're just ensuring that things don't escalate needlessly. James pressing charges complicates everything. We need to think about the station's reputation."

"The station's reputation?" Perdita shot back, unimpressed. "Or your ego? Because let's be clear, Banks—this isn't about Brookes Vibes. This is about you. You want this to be a win, not because it helps the company, but because it keeps your 'Brookes Babes' nonsense afloat. You don't care what happens to James, or Carly, or anyone else, as long as you can keep playing at being the king of student radio."

Antony sighed dramatically. "Oh, for God's sake, Perdita. This isn't some grand ethical crisis. It's just a bit of promo fun that went slightly out of hand."

"Oh, come on, give it a rest," Brian Jones, the station manager for Reading's Buzz Beats, the sister station to Brookes Vibes and a former Capital Radio alumnus, interrupted, rolling his eyes as he leaned back in his chair. "Complaints are part of the game, Perdita. Although, I did hear something from my old friends at Capital which might put a spanner in any pay off..."

Adam narrowed his eyes, shifting slightly in his chair as Brian leaned forward with a knowing smirk. The room, which had been a mixture of smug bravado and casual corporate corruption, suddenly tensed ever so slightly.

"Go on, then," Adam drawled, drumming his fingers against the table. "What have Capital got to do with this?"

Brian tilted his head, enjoying the moment. He might have defected to the Home Counties Radio Group, but he still had plenty of mates at Leicester Square, and when it came to media politics, information was currency. And right now, he was holding the winning hand.

"You know Richard Park's minion, Ashley Tabor? A jumped-up cockwomble who's a nepotism poster child?"

Adam exhaled sharply, folding his arms. "Yes, Brian, we all know Ashley bloody Tabor. What's your point?"

Brian's grin widened. "Well, word from Leicester Square is that his old man is a business pal and club chum with

Lord Jenkins, the father of James Jenkins... and that young Tabor is keeping an eye on young Jenkins's career here."

Adam's smirk twitched ever so slightly, though he masked it with a casual chuckle. "Oh, so what? Jenkins is a posh boy, we all knew that. His dad's probably got connections everywhere."

Brian shook his head, clearly enjoying dragging this out. "Ah, but here's the kicker—Ashley Tabor's been sniffing around for legal talent for Capital's expanding empire, and guess who's suddenly been earmarked as a 'potential future media lawyer'?"

The room fell silent. Adam's fingers stilled against the table.

Peter, who had been absentmindedly tapping his pen, suddenly sat up straighter. "You're telling me... Capital has their eye on James Jenkins?"

Brian nodded, leaning back like a man who knew he had just dropped a grenade into the middle of the boardroom. "Yep. And more to the point—James's dad, Lord Henry Jenkins, likes Capital. Word is, he thinks GWR—sorry, us, the Home Counties Radio Group—are a bunch of 'lads playing radio' and that Capital is 'proper media.' He's already been having quiet words with Ashley's old man, seeing if James can be fast-tracked into a legal role over there once he finishes at Oxford. There is a way to ensure he plays ball, however. Adam knows who his Achillies heel is."

Adam chuckled, as he knew that James and Carly were officially dating, and had been for two months, meaning that he had the perfect leverage. James Jenkins might be a polished, Oxford-educated future media lawyer, but he had one very obvious weakness—Carly Hemsworth.

"Ah, Miss Hemsworth, the 'Queen of the Brookes Babes'," Adam said with a smirk, tapping his pen against the table rhythmically. "She's the key to all of this, isn't she? James might have all the privilege in the world, but he's head over heels for our feisty Essex princess. And if there's one thing I know about men who think they're too smart for this game—it's that love makes them stupid."

Perdita's expression hardened. "You are *not* seriously considering using Carly to manipulate James into dropping the charges, are you?" she demanded, her voice laced with disgust.

Adam shrugged, his smirk widening. "Oh, Perdita, don't be so dramatic. It's not manipulation—it's strategy. If James wants to play the big man and drag this into the courts, then we remind him what he has to lose. Carly likes being Queen of the Brookes Babes. She enjoys the power, the attention, the perks. And let's not pretend she wouldn't hate being pushed out by Annabelle's lot, especially now that Annabelle's been publicly humiliated."

"That's an extremely dangerous game to play, Adam," Peter said, rubbing his chin thoughtfully. "You're assuming Carly will just fall in line—that she'll pressure James into doing what we want. But what if she goes the other way? What if she doubles down and decides that she and James are better off without us?"

Antony waved a dismissive hand. "Oh, come off it, Pete. Hemsworth loves the attention. Do you really think she wants to go back to being just another sociology student? She thrives on the chaos, the drama, the power. And James? He's just along for the ride. The way I see it, we give Carly a choice—either she helps smooth this over, or we make things very difficult for her."

Perdita clenched her jaw. "And by that, you mean what, exactly? Threaten her? Give her the boot?"

Adam chuckled. "No, no, nothing that crude, Perdita. We just… shift the narrative. Make her irrelevant. We know she's the glue holding the Brookes Babes together right now—without her, James has no reason to care about this station, and without James, there's no legal case. So, we sideline her. Let Annabelle's faction of the Babes gain more influence. Slowly ease Carly out of the spotlight, give her less high-profile gigs. Maybe even start whispering a few things in the right ears about how her behaviour is 'problematic'—"

"That's disgusting," Perdita snapped, slamming her hand against the table. "She's a student, Adam. She's a twenty-year-old girl, not some pawn in your stupid little radio war. Anyway, remember who James is connected to— Ashley Tabor, and by association, Richard Park. That means that if James and Carly decide to turn against us, we're not just dealing with some legal squabble in Oxford. We're dealing with Capital. And you know Richard Park wouldn't hesitate to turn this into a national scandal if it meant taking down a rival group. Anyway, my sources at Emap tell me that Carly has a summer internship in HR at H Bauer Publishing."

Adam's smirk faltered—just slightly, but enough that Perdita caught it and knew she'd hit a nerve.

H Bauer Publishing. That was interesting.

He leaned back in his chair, carefully masking his irritation. "Well, well, well," he drawled, "seems our dear Miss Hemsworth is already looking for her exit strategy. And here I was thinking she was one of us."

Perdita scoffed. "Oh, please. She was never one of you. She was always going to be smarter than this nonsense. You lot treat radio like a lads' club, but Carly's actually thinking ahead. She's got a future outside of this circus."

"Sir," a secretary said, walking to Peter with an envelope. "This has come in the post just now, marked Private and Confidential."

Peter frowned, taking the envelope from the secretary with a murmur of thanks. The entire boardroom fell silent as he carefully tore it open, sliding out a crisp, neatly typed letter. His eyes scanned the contents, and as he read, his expression hardened.

"What is it?" Brian asked, already leaning forward with interest.

Peter didn't answer immediately. Instead, he exhaled sharply through his nose and set the letter down on the table. "It's from Charles Carrington-Smythe the Third."

A ripple of tension spread through the room. Even Adam, as smug and untouchable as he often acted, knew better than to ignore that name.

"What does it say?" Nathan asked, already anticipating the worst.

"Well, gentlemen, ladies… we're now the subject of a buyout offer… from Lord Henry Jenkins and Michael Tabor."

The words hung in the air, heavy and suffocating.

For the first time since Adam Banks had walked into this boardroom, the smirk was gone from his face.

Peter leaned back in his chair, rubbing his temple as if he could physically push away the headache forming. "It seems James Jenkins' father and Ashley Tabor's father have decided that they don't like the way we run things. And now, they want to take Brookes Vibes—and the rest of the Home Counties Radio Group—off our hands."

The silence stretched. Even Antony, usually the first to bluster about the legacy of GWR and how they'd outmanoeuvre Capital, looked rattled.

Perdita let out a low whistle. "Well, Adam," she said, voice dripping with satisfaction. "You wanted a power move? Congratulations. You just got one."

Adam clenched his jaw, but before he could snap back, Brian picked up the letter, scanning the legal jargon with the eye of a man who had spent enough years in commercial radio to know what was really being said.

"This isn't just a takeover bid," he muttered, flipping the pages. "This is hostile. They're citing 'concerns over leadership', 'excessive risk-taking in promotional campaigns', and 'lack of corporate governance'."

Perdita snorted. "I wonder where they got that impression from."

Adam's chair scraped back as he stood, slamming his palms against the table. "This is a fucking joke. You're telling me that some posh bastard, whose son has spent the last two months rolling around in the back of our promo van, wants to take our station away from us because we were too wild?" He let out a sharp laugh, shaking his head. "Come on, this is a bluff. They don't want Brookes Vibes—they want to scare us. They want James to look like a hero, coming in to clean up the mess his horrible working-class boss made. And they're using their fucking media connections to do it."

"Adam, sit down," Peter said sharply, voice edged with authority. "This is serious."

"Yeah, I can see that," Adam shot back. "But we're not rolling over and letting these pricks buy us out, are we?"

Peter exhaled. "That depends."

The room turned to him.

"On what?" Antony asked, his voice suddenly wary.

"What Ralph says. I mean, he is a shareholder of the Home Counties Radio Group, and he might have an opinion on whether or not we should be selling out. Anyway, the offer is from Tabor Senior, not mini-Richard Park."

Adam folded his arms across his chest, his jaw tightening as he tried to process the sheer audacity of what was unfolding. A hostile takeover? By James Jenkins' father and Michael bloody Tabor? He had expected some legal noise after Banbury, but this? This was a calculated power play of the highest order.

Perdita leaned back in her chair, the smirk still playing on her lips. "Oh, come on, Adam. You didn't think James Jenkins was just some 'promo van lackey', did you? His family own half of bloody Oxfordshire. You really thought he'd let his girlfriend get stitched up without calling in the cavalry? Out of interest, is it a firm advising them, or a speculative bid, Peter?"

Peter flipped to the final page of the letter, his brows furrowing as he scanned the final lines. "It's not just a speculative bid—it's formal. They've got Rothschilds advising them."

vote to sell out, if it meant getting rid of him, especially if James Jenkins' family was involved. This wasn't just some PR clean-up—this was a full-blown corporate coup.

Adam exhaled sharply, his mind racing. He had been playing at being the king of Brookes Vibes, lording over his promo empire with an iron grip, but now the game had changed. The people he had been treating as pawns— Carly, James, Annabelle—had turned out to have connections he hadn't accounted for.

Lord Henry Jenkins. Michael Tabor. Rothschilds.

This was an entirely different level of power.

Peter rubbed his chin thoughtfully before speaking again. "Look, we have a decision to make, and we have to make it fast. If they're making an offer, it means they've done their due diligence, they've lined up their chess pieces, and they think they can push us out. The question is, do we fight back, or do we cut our losses before this turns into a media circus that even *Private Eye* won't be able to ignore?"

Antony Peckham, who had been uncharacteristically quiet, finally spoke, his voice lower than usual. "We need to talk to Ralph. If we lose his support, we're finished. He's the last stronghold of the GWR way, and if he decides to cash out rather than back us, we might as well pack our bags."

Adam gritted his teeth, knowing they were right. For all his bravado, for all his talk about radio being about chaos, disruption, and raw energy, he had never actually gone up against men like this. Ralph Bernard had once held GWR together with sheer force of will, but even he had been smart enough to know when to bow out.

Would he side with them? Or would he see the writing on the wall and take the money?

Perdita, still smirking, tapped her fingers against the table. "Oh, and one more thing, Adam. You might want to rethink that little plan you had for Carly. Because if James gets even the slightest hint that you're trying to sideline or manipulate his girlfriend, I reckon he'll go full scorched-earth on you."

Adam clenched his fists under the table, his nails digging into his palms as he tried to keep his expression composed. This was supposed to be his moment—his triumph, proving that the Brookes Babes brand was an unstoppable force in student radio. Instead, the boardroom had turned into a war zone, and he was one move away from being checkmated.

He forced out a chuckle, though it lacked his usual arrogance. "So, what's the play here? We just roll over and let James bloody Jenkins and his aristocratic daddy waltz in and take over?"

Peter McAllister rubbed his temples. "It's not that simple, Adam. We need to assess our position. Right now, Brookes Vibes is making waves, yes—but we've also got a PR nightmare on our hands. Two of our promo team were arrested in a branded van. James pressing charges against Annabelle takes this beyond your usual 'cheeky radio hijinks.' This is a legal liability. And if James's father and Michael Tabor want to buy us out, it means they see an opportunity where we see a mess."

Adam gritted his teeth. "James isn't some power player. He's just a runner who got lucky because his dad has a title."

"Oh, come off it, Banks," Perdita scoffed, leaning back in her chair, arms folded. "James Jenkins is an Oxford law student with the best legal education money can buy, a direct pipeline to Capital Radio through the Tabor family, and a barrister cousin who could probably dismantle this entire organisation in a single afternoon. He is not just a 'runner'. He's dangerous."

Brian Jones smirked. "She's right. And let's not forget— he's dating Carly Hemsworth, who just so happens to be the most influential Brookes Babe, the one with the actual student following. If she walks, the entire brand falls apart."

Adam scoffed. "Carly loves this gig too much to walk."

"Does she?" Peter arched an eyebrow. "Because from what I hear, she's got an HR internship lined up at H Bauer Publishing for the summer. You might think she's your loyal queen, but she's already looking for her exit strategy."

That stung. Adam had always assumed Carly needed Brookes Vibes. She thrived in the chaos, enjoyed the power. She was his star—the glue that held the Babes together. But if she already had one foot out the door…

"Look," Antony Peckham said, cutting through the noise. "Ralph Bernard is the key. If Ralph backs us, we stand a chance of fighting this off. But if he decides to sell, then we need to start negotiating our positions."

A silence settled over the room. Even Adam knew what that meant.

If the Home Counties Radio Group were sold to James's father and Michael Tabor, Adam's days were numbered. He wouldn't be allowed to stay on—not after the stunt he had pulled in Banbury. He'd built the Brookes Babes brand around himself, but if James's family got their way, he'd be gone.

That thought chilled him.

****

CHAPTER 16 – Torn Loyalties
Mid-December 2003

The tension at Brookes Vibes had been simmering beneath the surface for weeks, but now it was finally spilling over. The Babes were no longer one united force of promo girls causing chaos across Oxford—there were factions.

And the split? Split right down the lines of the Oxford Brookes students like Annabelle Young, Lara Knight, Mary Thimbleson, Ally Perkins and their half of the team, versus the Oxford University students, like Carly, Clarissa, Tina Mackenzie, Emma Wright, and Hayley Lancashire, as well as unaligned Babes such as Sally Clinton, who had recently celebrated her 17th birthday and was, despite being under 18, a requirement of the job to attend club nights and bar promos. Sally had been keeping her head down, trying not to get dragged into the war between Carly and Annabelle, but it was becoming impossible to stay neutral when the entire team were being forced to pick sides.

Carly had known that Annabelle would try to claw her way back into power, but she hadn't expected Adam Banks to so brazenly back her. Then again, she should have. Adam thrived on chaos—he didn't care who was running the Brookes Babes, as long as they were making noise, getting attention, and ensuring that the station stayed in the headlines. And Annabelle, desperate for redemption after the Banbury incident, was more than happy to be his willing puppet.

And then there was James.

While publicly he was keeping his head down, refusing to get involved in the internal feuds of the Brookes Babes, Carly knew he was struggling. He wanted no part in the politics of promo teams, but he was inextricably linked to it now.

All because Annabelle had near enough raped him, and he was dating Carly, meaning that he was now a central figure in the Brookes Babes' cold war, whether he liked it or not. And Adam Banks knew it.

"Well, looks like the cat is amongst the pigeons," Carly said, as she and James were sat in their dorm, packing as the duo had managed to obtain a flat in Summertown that a quartet of freshers who had dropped out had left the rent paid on until the end of the academic year. It was a win for Carly and James—no more cramming into halls, no more dealing with shared kitchens full of unwashed dishes, and, most importantly, no more dorm-mates overhearing the endless radio station drama.

The irony that James wasn't meant to even be living in the same dorm as Carly, as he had a different room, the duo having only became a couple during the first few weeks of the term, meant that their cohabitation had been entirely unofficial. They'd somehow managed to make it work, sneaking between rooms when necessary, but now, with their own flat, they could finally live without having to worry about nosy hallmates or college wardens.

James zipped up his duffel bag, sighing as he ran a hand through his hair. "You know, I was hoping this whole thing would die down before Christmas," he muttered, his voice laced with exhaustion. "But no, instead, we've got a full-blown civil war in the promo team, and Adam's basically declared Annabelle his new queen."

Carly scoffed, tossing a pile of clothes into her suitcase. "Adam doesn't actually care about Annabelle—she's just the easiest way for him to keep stirring the pot. She'll do whatever he tells her, because she's desperate to be on top again." She shot James a look. "And let's be honest, he knows you're the real problem."

James arched a brow. "Oh, cheers, Hemsworth. Nice to know I'm the problem."

"You are the problem," Carly said, smirking slightly. "Because you're the only one who can properly take him down. If you go through with the lawsuit against Annabelle, Adam knows it'll make him look bad for backing her. That, and your dad and Michael Tabor are sniffing around Home Counties Radio Group, looking to take it over. Adam's not just trying to win the promo team war—he's trying to hold onto his job."

James exhaled, dragging a hand through his already-messy hair. "Christ. I didn't ask to be the poster boy for radio station politics. I just wanted a bloody part-time job and maybe some fun along the way. Now I've got Adam Banks playing Machiavelli, my father trying to buy my employer out from under him, and Annabelle going full psycho because she can't handle rejection."

Carly zipped up her suitcase with an aggressive yank. "Welcome to my world, babe."

There was a knock at the door before James could reply. Carly glanced at him before calling out, "Who is it?"

Clarissa's voice came through the door, slightly breathless. "It's me. You might want to open up—shit's about to get messy."

James and Carly exchanged a look before James strode over and pulled the door open. Clarissa stepped inside, closing it firmly behind her. She looked flustered, her scarf slightly askew, cheeks flushed as if she'd been speed-walking across campus.

"Alright, what now?" Carly asked, crossing her arms. "Has Annabelle declared herself Supreme Leader of the Babes yet?"

Clarissa snorted but shook her head. "No, but the skank patrol are on campus."

James groaned, rubbing his temples. "For the love of God, I swear this promo team has more drama than The Bold and the Beautiful."

Clarissa rolled her eyes, throwing her bag onto Carly's bed. "You joke, but I just ran into Lara and Ally outside the SU, and they're definitely up to something. They were whispering to each other like they were planning a bloody military coup. Oh, and you know you were meant to be lead on the Babes Takeover on Boxing Day..."

Carly groaned as Clarissa flopped onto Carly's bed, stretching her legs out with an exasperated sigh. "Well, guess what? Adam's just announced that Annabelle is now leading it instead."

"WHAT! She knows I was going to have this dolt here tied up in the studio and the new webcam aimed at him while me, you and the other girls tormented him live on air has been completely ruined," Carly exclaimed with a mixture of disbelief and frustration. "That was going to be our show! Our way of making sure Brookes Vibes had the biggest student radio stunt of the year! And now she's just waltzing in and taking over like she owns the place?"

Clarissa groaned, propping herself up on her elbows. "Oh, it gets better. Not only has Annabelle taken your spot as lead, but Adam is apparently reviewing everyone's roles in the Babes. He's calling it a 'performance review,' but we all know what that means—he's looking for an excuse to push you out."

Carly ran a hand down her face. "Unbelievable. He's actually going for it. I knew he'd try something after Banbury, but I didn't think he'd move this fast."

James, who had been leaning against the desk, now pushed himself upright, his brows furrowed in irritation. "This isn't just about promo team politics anymore, is it?" His voice was steady, but there was a sharp edge beneath it. "Adam's playing a bigger game here."

Clarissa nodded. "He's terrified of your dad and Michael Tabor swooping in and taking Brookes Vibes away from him. And let's be honest—he probably realises that *you* going after Annabelle is bad PR for him, too. He's trying to isolate Carly, push her out before she becomes a liability for him."

Before Carly could say anything, James had pulled his new Sony Ericsson T610 from his pocket and started scrolling through his contacts. His jaw was set, his usually relaxed demeanour replaced with something far more serious.

"Who are you calling?" Carly asked, watching him with a mix of curiosity and concern.

James didn't look up as he hit dial. "My father. I'm going to have him press the Chief Constable of Thames Valley Police for an update on Annabelle's pending charges. And while I'm at it, I'll have him apply for a civil injunction under the Protection from Harassment Act 1997 against Annabelle for you."

Carly knew, from James's legal studies, that the Protection from Harassment Act 1997 was no joke. It wasn't just a slap-on-the-wrist restraining order—it was a legal move that could seriously impact Annabelle's ability to keep her role within Brookes Vibes. If granted, it would mean she couldn't contact Carly directly or indirectly, attend any events Carly was at, or even be in the same building as her without risking legal consequences.

It was, in effect, using a nuclear warhead on a problem that Adam Banks had been trying to pretend didn't exist.

Clarissa let out a low whistle. "Bloody hell, Jenkins. Didn't realise you were going full scorched earth."

James shrugged, still holding the phone to his ear. "I tried playing nice. I tried ignoring it. But if Adam and Annabelle think they can screw Carly over and act like Banbury never happened, they're about to find out what happens when you push a Jenkins too far. Carly's my future wife, damnit, and it's my job to... erm... I mean..."

Carly watched as James rubbed his hand on the back of his neck, realising exactly what he had just said, and just as Tina, Hayley and Emma walked into the room, the three of them immediately catching onto James's slip-up.

"Sheesh, Jenkins," Tina said with a grin, exchanging looks with Hayley and Emma. "Going straight to the wife card already? You planning to propose over Christmas dinner or something?"

James, still holding his phone to his ear, turned slightly pink, clearing his throat as he avoided Carly's gaze. "I meant potential future wife. You know… possibly… in the far-off future…"

Carly, who had been fuming about Adam and Annabelle only moments before, now found herself smirking despite the situation. "Uh-huh. Sure, babe. 'Cause that totally sounded like an accidental slip and not a declaration."

James shot her a look before quickly shifting his attention back to the phone as his father's voice came through the other end. "Yes, it's me. I need an update on the Thames Valley Police case regarding Annabelle Young."

Tina flopped onto Carly's bed next to Clarissa, grinning. "Bloody hell, we've gone from dodgy promo wars to full-blown legal battles and wedding bells in one conversation. Anyway, Carly, what's with the cases?"

Carly glanced at the half-packed suitcase beside her and let out a sigh. "Me and James managed to nab a flat in Summertown—some freshers dropped out, and their rent's already covered until the end of the year. It'll give Clarissa and Mark some alone space to be a shag pad.

After all, it saves this place being on a rota where I have to spend the night in James's dorm and dodge the wardens."

Clarissa smirked. "Oh, babe, don't worry about me. I'll just take over your bed and tell them I'm the new Queen of the Babes. Annabelle would have a meltdown."

James, who was still on the phone, shot Clarissa an amused look before holding up a finger, signalling for quiet. "Yes, father, that's correct. The Protection from Harassment Act, and if necessary, a Non-Molestation Order, given Annabelle's behaviour."

Carly chuckled, as she could probably imagine Lord Jenkins going absolutely ballistic on the other end of the line, barking orders to his legal team and making sure that every possible legal measure was being taken to shut Annabelle Young down.

James paced the small dorm room, his Sony Ericsson T610 pressed tightly to his ear, his jaw tense as he listened to his father on the other end. Carly had seen this look before—it was the same one he had whenever he was trying to hold his temper in check. James might have been an easy-going guy on the surface, but there was an underlying steeliness to him, and when it came to people he cared about, he didn't mess around.

Clarissa, still lounging on Carly's bed, exchanged a look with Tina, Hayley, and Emma, all of whom were now fully invested in the unfolding drama.

"So," Hayley said, flicking her ponytail over her shoulder, "what's the betting odds that James's dad is already tearing through Thames Valley Police's hierarchy to make sure Annabelle gets properly dealt with?"

Emma snorted. "Oh, come on, that's not even a bet worth taking. Of course he is. The guy's a bloody Lord. He probably has the Chief Constable on speed dial."

Tina smirked. "And let's not forget that the Tabor family is involved too. Between Lord Jenkins and Michael Tabor, this might be the fastest-processed harassment case in Thames Valley history."

Carly, leaning against the desk with her arms crossed, shook her head with a small grin. "I swear to God, I wake up every day thinking this radio job is just going to be another dumb promo gig, and then suddenly I'm in the middle of a high-stakes legal battle and a corporate takeover."

"Ah, babe," Clarissa drawled, smirking. "That's what you get for shagging an aristocrat."

James, still on the phone, shot her a pointed look but didn't break his concentration.

Carly rolled her eyes but didn't argue. Clarissa wasn't exactly wrong.

After another minute of listening, James finally spoke again, his voice clipped and business-like. "Yes, father, I understand. Thank you. Keep me updated." He ended the call with a sharp tap, tossing his phone onto the bed before running a hand through his hair.

"Well?" Carly prompted, tilting her head.

James exhaled through his nose, looking half-frustrated, half-determined. "He's already spoken to his barrister. They're drafting the injunction now. As soon as it's processed, Annabelle will be legally banned from coming near you. If she so much as breathes in your direction, she'll be in contempt of court."

Tina let out a low whistle. "Bloody hell, mate. You don't mess about, do you?"

James shook his head, his blue eyes darkening. "I'm done with playing nice. Annabelle tried to force herself on me in Banbury, she's spent the last two months trying to wreck Carly's life, and now Adam Banks is propping her up like she's some kind of victim. I refuse to let her get away with it."

Carly reached out, squeezing James's hand. "You know I love when you go full legal mode," she murmured, "but don't let this eat you up, babe."

James softened slightly, threading his fingers through hers. "I just want it sorted. For you. For us."

Clarissa cleared her throat dramatically. "Alright, lovebirds, as much as I'm enjoying watching this display of emotional depth, we do have another problem to deal with—namely, Adam Banks deciding to pull a full-scale coup against Carly."

Carly groaned, rubbing her temples. "Right. That. Twat."

Emma leaned against the wall, arms crossed. "What's your move?"

Carly exhaled sharply. "I'm not going down without a fight. If Adam thinks he can push me out just to keep his station from getting steamrolled by James's dad, he's got another thing coming."

James smirked. "So, what's the plan? Because if I know you, Hemsworth, you've already got one."

Carly's grin turned wolfish. "Oh, I definitely do."

****

"Ah, Mr Jenkins, Miss Hemsworth, I'm glad you're here," Carly heard Adam say as she and James walked into the Brookes Vibes studios. Carly knew that James was doing a cover shift on the evening show, as one of the hosts was off sick with a cold, also known as a hangover that had been in place since the previous weekend's Christmas party. Carly had tagged along, mostly to see what fresh nonsense Adam Banks was planning to throw her way, and to put her own plan into motion.

Adam leaned back in his chair, arms folded, his usual smirk firmly in place. Annabelle was sat beside him, looking disgustingly pleased with herself, while Lara Knight and Ally Perkins flanked her like a pair of henchmen.

Carly rolled her eyes internally. Christ, was Adam seriously turning this into a mob meeting?

James, standing beside her, didn't sit. He simply crossed his arms and stared Adam down. "You wanted to see us?"

Adam spread his hands in an exaggerated gesture. "Performance reviews, mate! Standard procedure, just making sure everyone's pulling their weight in the team."

Carly let out a dry laugh. "Oh, piss off, Banks. We both know this isn't a performance review—it's a hit job."

Annabelle scoffed. "Oh, Carly, always so dramatic," she purred. "We're just making sure the right people are in place to represent Brookes Vibes properly."

Carly turned her glare on her. "You mean the people who'll do whatever you and Adam say without question?"

Annabelle smirked. "Well, yes. That is kind of the point."

Carly felt James tense beside her, his jaw clenching, but he said nothing—yet. She knew he was waiting, assessing, letting her handle this.

Adam, still lounging in his chair, tapped his fingers against the desk. "Look, Hemsworth, let's be honest here. You've been great for the Babes, really. But things are… changing. After Banbury, after everything, we've got to make sure the team has the right leadership moving forward."

Carly tilted her head, feigning curiosity. "You mean leadership that won't press charges when their members get sexually assaulted?"

Annabelle stiffened slightly, but Adam remained unbothered, simply grinning wider. "Now, now, let's not get nasty about it. This isn't personal, it's business."

Carly's smirk was pure venom. "Oh, Adam, you think it's business. But for me, it's very personal."

Adam's smile faltered slightly, just for a fraction of a second, before he covered it up. "Well, be that as it may, here's how it is. Annabelle is taking over as lead of the Babes. You'll still be part of the team, of course, but in a… let's say, reduced capacity. And if you don't like that, well—there's always the option to step down."

Carly pretended to consider it for a moment, before leaning forward, resting her hands on the desk in front of her. "Here's the thing, Banks. I'm not stepping down. You can shove your fake demotion up your arse. I am the Brookes Babes, and everyone knows it. You might try to shove Annabelle in front of the cameras, but she's got all the charm of a used tampon. You need me. Whether you like it or not."

Annabelle bristled. "Oh, for fuck's sake, Carly—"

Carly held up a finger, silencing her. "Ah, ah, sweetheart. The grown-ups are talking."

Adam laughed, shaking his head. "You've got guts, I'll give you that. But guts don't mean shit if I take away your airtime."

James, who had remained silent up until now, finally spoke. "Except you won't."

Adam looked at him with amusement. "Oh? And why's that, Jenkins? You planning to start doing promos too? Fancy slipping into some booty shorts and handing out flyers with Carly? Oh, yeah, you already do because you need this job... hang on, there again, with Lord Jenkins as your father, I guess you don't really need it, do you?" Adam smirked, leaning back in his chair, his eyes filled with thinly veiled contempt.

James simply smiled. It wasn't the kind of smug grin Adam was used to from him—it was cold. Calculated. "No, Adam, I don't need this job. But you do."

The smirk faltered.

James stepped forward, placing his hands on the desk, mirroring Carly's posture. "You see, you've been trying to play king of the castle, but the problem is—you built your castle on sand. And that sand, mate, is slipping away fast."

Adam scoffed, but Carly could see the way his fingers twitched slightly, his confidence shaken just a fraction. "Oh, for Christ's sake, Jenkins, don't start with your posh boy monologues—"

"No, no, let's talk about this properly," James interrupted smoothly. "You're desperately trying to cling to control of the Brookes Babes, trying to sideline Carly because she's the only one who can stand up to you. You've thrown your lot in with Annabelle because she's an easy puppet. But that was a bad move, Adam. Because what you should have done was cut her loose when Banbury happened."

Annabelle bristled, her eyes narrowing. "Excuse me?"

James didn't even look at her. "You should have realised that associating with Annabelle was a liability, not an asset. And now, because you backed her instead of cutting her off, it's coming back to bite you."

Adam forced a laugh. "Oh yeah? And how exactly is it coming back to bite me, Jenkins? You think I'm scared of you?"

James smiled again, that same unnervingly confident smirk. "You should be."

****

CHAPTER 17 – Breaking Point
Saturday 20th December 2003

It was Saturday, and James was at the Summertown studios of Brookes Vibes, when he saw Carly storm out of Adam's office with the kind of fury that could set the entire building alight. Her fists were clenched at her sides, her face flushed with anger, and her Essex accent was cutting through as she muttered every curse word under the sun.

James barely had time to push his chair back before she spotted him, her sharp gaze locking onto him like a heat-seeking missile.

"Fucking Banks," she spat, tossing her Brookes Babes lanyard onto the floor. "He's finally lost the plot."

James stood, frowning. "What's he done now?"

Carly let out a sharp laugh, throwing her hands up. "He's only gone and put me in a bloody kissing contest, hasn't he? 'Kiss the DJ', he's calling it. Like I'm some desperate fresher looking for a free drink. It's a 'fun little game' for the lads, apparently—see which of the Babes can get the biggest reaction by snogging some tosser off the drive show. Not here, in the studios, but in, and you'll find this hilarious, Pleasuredome. The dodgiest, sweatiest club in the whole of Oxfordshire. I swear to God, James, I'm done. I'm so fucking done."

"Which one? Dave, Chris or Carl?" James asked, hoping it wasn't Dave Adams, a 21 year old who James knew was an absolute creep when it came to the promo girls. He had a reputation for getting far too handsy at station events, and James wouldn't put it past him to take full advantage of Adam's latest stunt.

Carly scoffed, folding her arms. "Fucking Carl," she seethed. "Like I'd want my face anywhere near that slimy prick."

James groaned, running a hand down his face. Carl Nicholson was one of the most unbearable arseholes at Brookes Vibes. He was exactly the kind of DJ who thought he was God's gift to radio, despite getting sacked from 10 different radio stations in his 5 year career in local radio. A washed-up, overgrown fresher who thought being on air made him untouchable.

Looking towards Adam's office, James knew that the promotions manager would either be sitting with another babe, as Annabelle was currently suspended and so had been replaced in the office by Lara Knight, or he'd be on the phone to some poor unsuspecting local business trying to squeeze them for sponsorship money.

Having been in Adam's office too many times, James knew that there were several things that Adam valued on his walls and desk, from the framed photo of GWR head honcho Ralph Bernard shaking hands with a young, smug-looking Adam, to the shrine to Adam's Trent FM days, when he had been the middle man between the Trent Promotions coordinator and the Thunders there, and how he had nailed half of the Thunders during his time at the East Midlands station.

Then, on the desk, was his hallowed Trent FM and Ram FM mugs, as the two stations were sibling stations back in the day before GWR restructured everything. Adam liked to pretend he was some kind of commercial radio genius, but really, he was just another ex-GWR hack who had been shuffled around enough times to convince himself he was important.

Carly wasn't having any of it. She kicked the discarded lanyard across the studio floor with enough force to send it skidding under one of the desks. "I swear to God, James, I've put up with a lot of shit since I joined this station, but this? This is taking the piss. I didn't sign up to be a bloody cabaret act for some greasy local DJ who thinks Lynx Africa is a personality trait."

"You know, on his door, he has a GWR payslip for Core, right?" James said, grinning.

James leaned against the desk, watching as Carly paced back and forth like a caged animal. He could see the rage rolling off her in waves, her hands twitching as if she was barely holding herself back from marching back into Adam's office and launching his precious Trent FM mug straight at his smug face.

"Are you actually quitting, then?" James asked, arms folded.

Carly hesitated for a fraction of a second, but then her expression hardened. "Yeah. I think I am," she said, exhaling. "I can't do this anymore. Every time I think it can't get worse, Banks finds a new way to push it. First, he tried to make Annabelle the Queen Bee. Now, he's treating me like some cheap bit of totty for a promo night. I didn't sign up for this, James. I signed up to have a laugh, maybe get some radio experience, not to be paraded around like a piece of meat."

James ran a hand through his hair. He'd seen Carly angry before, seen her fight back against Annabelle, seen her go toe-to-toe with Adam Banks over stupid promo stunts, but this? This was different. This wasn't just Carly being defiant—this was her reaching her limit.

"You know what this means for me, though, don't you?" James said carefully. "If you leave, Banks is going to make my life hell."

Carly turned to face him fully, her eyes softening just a little. "I know," she admitted. "And I'm sorry, babe. But I can't do this anymore. I won't."

James exhaled, pressing his lips together in thought. He understood, of course he did. Adam Banks was the type to push people until they either broke or snapped back. Carly wasn't the breaking type, but she wasn't going to stick around just to prove a point either.

"You know, there is another way," James said, chuckling. "My father still has that bid in to buy the whole Home Counties Radio Group, and if he and Michael Tabor get their way, Adam Banks is out of a job before the new year. There again, he's like a bloody cockroach, Adam. If there was ever a nuclear fallout in commercial radio, he'd be the last one standing, clinging onto some dodgy local breakfast show in the arse end of nowhere. Anyway, you did promise me that you'd tie me up on the Babes Takeover and torment me live on air. That's the only reason I agreed to this shift, you know."

Carly burst out laughing, despite the fury still simmering beneath the surface. "Oh, babe, trust me, you'd have loved it. You, tied up in that crappy old chair in the studio, me and the girls reading out listener dares, making you squirm while the webcam feed went out live to the student halls. It would've been radio gold."

James smirked, leaning closer. "Yeah? And what exactly would these 'dares' have involved?"

"Oh, you know, just a bit of harmless fun." Carly's voice dripped with fake innocence. "Maybe a few ice cubes down your shirt. Maybe making you read out some very suggestive texts from listeners. Maybe a well-timed can of whipped cream—"

James held up a hand. "Alright, alright, I get the picture. Remind me to never underestimate how devious you lot are."

Carly grinned, but it quickly faded. She let out a long breath, running a hand through her hair. "It doesn't matter now, does it? Annabelle's getting my slot. Adam's already trying to push me out. He's just forcing my hand at this point."

"But Sarah's the manager of Brookes Vibes, not Adam," James said, sighing. "She makes the programming choices, not that tosser."

The sound of Avril Lavigne's Sk8er Boi playing from one of the studio speakers cut through the tension in the room, its pop-punk defiance almost poetic given the situation. Carly let out a short laugh, shaking her head.

"Fitting," she muttered. "Honestly, James, I don't know what I'm supposed to do here. If I stay, I have to put up with Adam's bullshit. If I leave, he wins."

James sighed, running a hand through his already-messy hair. "Not necessarily. If you leave on your terms, not his, you take the power away from him. You make it clear that you're not being forced out—you're choosing to walk away because you won't put up with his crap. And trust me, Carly, that'll sting a lot more for Banks than if he thinks he's got one over on you."

Carly exhaled, crossing her arms. "Yeah, but that doesn't fix the fact that he's screwing me over. He's making me look like some diva who can't handle a bit of promo work."

James watched as Carly paced the corridor, her frustration radiating off her in waves. He knew she was right—Adam Banks was screwing her over, and he was doing it in the most public way possible. He wasn't just trying to push her out; he was trying to humiliate her on the way out the door.

"Alright," James said, leaning against the desk. "So, let's hit back."

Carly arched a brow. "And how exactly do we do that?"

James smirked. "Simple. We don't let Banks control the narrative. You don't just walk away—you own your exit. You go out with a bang so big that when people talk about Brookes Babes, they don't talk about Annabelle or Adam. They talk about you."

Carly's lips curled into a slow, wicked grin. "You mean, make sure that when I leave, everyone remembers it?"

"Exactly." James folded his arms. "And I think I know exactly how."

Carly leaned in, intrigued. "Go on."

 "We hijack Babes Takeover before Annabelle can get her claws into it."

Carly's eyes flickered with interest. "Go on…"

"You do the show," James said. "And you get your faction to make it your show, not Adam's, not Annabelle's. You make sure everyone knows you're still the real leader of the Brookes Babes, whether Banks likes it or not. Anyway, Annabelle is suspended, remember, because of the whole Banbury incident. That means she technically can't lead the Takeover unless Sarah overturns it, and I don't think she's in a hurry to stick her neck out for Banks."

Carly mulled it over, her lips pursed. "So, what you're saying is… we pull a fast one on Adam. We do the Takeover our way, make it so massive that everyone talks about it—and then I walk away, on my terms."

James grinned. "Exactly. Leave him scrambling, make it impossible for Annabelle to fill your shoes, and make sure everyone knows that Brookes Babes is nothing without you."

Carly chuckled, her anger finally morphing into something more dangerous—determination. "James, you devious, beautiful bastard."

James smirked, crossing his arms as he leaned against the desk. "You love it."

Carly exhaled sharply, her hands on her hips as she thought through the plan. "Alright. If we're doing this, we're doing it properly. I want every single Babe on my side when we go live. No weak links, no hesitation. This needs to be the biggest, loudest, most chaotic student radio takeover anyone has ever seen."

James nodded. "Clarissa, Tina, Hayley, Emma—they'll be with you. Sally Clinton's already on your side. Ally and Lara are too far up Annabelle's arse to be swayed, but if we make enough noise, they won't matter."

Carly chewed on her lip, mind racing. "And Annabelle? If she tries to interfere?"

James arched a brow. "She's still suspended. If she so much as sets foot in the studio before it's lifted, she's in breach of station policy, and Sarah will have no choice but to throw her out. If she tries to push it, we get Security involved."

Carly grinned. "Now that would be a sight to see."

James chuckled, but then his face turned serious. "Carly, this isn't just a radio stunt anymore. If we go ahead with this, you're making a statement. You're showing Banks and Annabelle that they can't control you. But you're also drawing a line in the sand. This will be your last stand at Brookes Vibes."

Carly took a deep breath. "Good. I want them to remember me."

James grinned, reaching out to tuck a loose strand of hair behind her ear. "Oh, trust me, babe. They will."

Carly let out a sharp breath, determination hardening in her eyes. "Right then. Time to plan a fucking coup."

"You know, love," James said with a grin, "there's something we can do before that…"

Opening the door to Studio 3, which was empty apart from Mark and Clarissa on the mixing deck, both naked as the day they were born, Carly let out a loud groan. "Oh, for Christ's sake, Mark, Clarissa! Again?"

Mark, completely unfazed, stretched lazily in his chair, the 19 year old electrician and Clarissa, who was on top of him, Carly's friend being ploughed by the 19-year-old electrician, looked over his shoulder with an unapologetic grin. "Oi, don't judge, Hemsworth. We've got to entertain ourselves somehow."

Clarissa smirked, completely unbothered. "If you're going to burst in, Carly, at least knock first. Bloody rude, that."

James, having the decency to at least pretend to be horrified, dragged a hand over his face. "Jesus Christ. Carly and I were going to use this as our shag pad for the next half hour, because Adam, in his infinite wisdom, decided to ruin our Saturday. But clearly, we've walked in on some sort of electrical maintenance."

"What?" Mark said with a grin, still not bothering to shift Clarissa off him. "You think I'm just an electrician? Nah, mate, I'm a problem solver. Clarissa here needed a good... shock to the system, and who am I to deny her that?"

Clarissa giggled, rolling her eyes before giving Carly a pointed look. "You two were going to use this as your shag pad, were you? You hypocrites!"

"Anyway, James is a runner, he has a nook in the server room where he skives," Mark said with a pointed grin. "Why don't you two use that? It's quiet, it's dark, and, best of all, it doesn't currently have me in it."

James groaned, as his 'nook', so to speak, was a secret area in the server room which held some of the Christmas presents he had got for Carly, Clarissa, Mark and the Babes that were on the faction that Carly was leading. The last thing he needed was Carly snooping and finding her Christmas gift early.

Carly, crossing her arms, raised an eyebrow at Clarissa and Mark, who were still very much... occupied. "Honestly, you two have no shame."

Clarissa smirked. "None whatsoever. Now, are you just here to judge, or are you actually going to do something about Banks?"

Carly huffed. "Oh, don't worry, we're sorting it. Just as soon as I bleach my brain from this."

James, still looking thoroughly traumatised, grabbed Carly's hand and tugged her towards the door. "Right, let's go before we get scarred for life."

As they stepped out into the corridor, Carly let out a breath and turned to James. "So, your nook, then?"

James gave her a look. "You just want to snoop, don't you?"

Carly grinned wickedly. "Obviously."

James rolled his eyes but smirked as he led her down the hall to the back of the building, where the dimly lit server room was tucked away behind layers of tangled cables and old station equipment. He pushed the door open, letting Carly slip inside first before following her in and closing it behind them.

The room was quiet, the faint hum of the servers filling the space. Carly took a step forward, scanning the stacks of boxes and wires before turning to James with a teasing grin. "So, where's this secret hiding spot of yours, then?"

James sighed dramatically. "You're relentless, you know that?"

Carly pouted. "You love it."

James muttered something under his breath about bloody Essex girls before moving to the corner where a small gap had been cleared between two server racks. There, tucked behind an old mixing desk, was a shoebox.

Carly, immediately suspicious, snatched it up before James could stop her. "What's this, then?" she said, shaking it slightly.

James groaned. "Carly, put it down."

Carly grinned. "Oh no, Jenkins, this is happening now."

She pried off the lid, her smirk widening as she took in the contents. Inside, there were neatly wrapped gifts, one with her name on it, alongside smaller ones labelled for Clarissa, Mark, and even a few of the Babes.

Her eyes softened slightly as she looked up at James. "You got me a present?"

James rubbed the back of his neck, suddenly looking sheepish. "Well, yeah. It is Christmas next week."

Carly ran a finger over the wrapping paper, her heart giving a small squeeze. For all the chaos surrounding them, James had still taken the time to get her something.

She looked up at him, smiling. "Can I open it now?"

James rolled his eyes, though his lips twitched. "No. You can wait until Christmas, like everyone else."

Carly pouted. "Ugh, fine. But if this is some posh, upper-class nonsense, I swear—"

James smirked, stepping closer. "You'll love it. I promise."

Carly studied him for a moment before setting the box down carefully. "Alright. I trust you."

James arched a brow. "That's a first."

Carly shoved him lightly, making him laugh before she sighed. "Alright, back to business. We're taking over the Takeover."

James nodded. "Yeah. And we need to be smart about it. Banks won't just roll over."

Carly smirked. "Oh, don't worry. I fully intend to make sure he never forgets the day he tried to screw me over."

James grinned. "Now that is the Carly Hemsworth I know and love."

Carly playfully poked his chest. "You'd better, Jenkins. Because I'm about to bring the fucking house down."

James laughed, leaning down to press a quick kiss to her forehead. "Let's do this."

And with that, the battle for Brookes Vibes had officially begun.

****

CHAPTER 18 – The Babes Takeover
Friday 26th December 2003

"You're listening to Brookes Vibes, live on Boxing Day, and I'm Carly Hemsworth, the Queen of the Brookes Babes. This is the Babes Takeover, and yes, I've got the Legal Eagle himself, the Brookes Vibes Hunk, James Jenkins, here, tied up, sitting in the studio chair, looking like a man who's just realised he's made a terrible mistake."

Carly looked at the time—exactly 1pm. This was it. The moment that would define her legacy at Brookes Vibes. She, Tina, Emma, Hayley, and Clarissa were running the show, and in the background, the Brookes side of the Babes, led by their temporary leader, Lara Knight, were lurking like vultures, waiting for their chance to wrestle control of the broadcast.

James, who had been covering the previous hour after Big Bam inevitably called in "sick" (which everyone knew was just a polite way of saying "still hungover from Christmas"), was now securely taped to the studio chair, hands bound to the armrests with thick black gaffer tape, his posh blue shirt slightly crumpled, and his dark hair an absolute mess. The only thing untied was his mouth, much to his misfortune.

James groaned into the mic. "I'm starting to think agreeing to this was an absolutely *horrific* idea."

Carly smirked, nudging his chair with her foot. "Oh, Jenkins, don't be such a baby. You signed up for this. Well, sort of. You got outvoted."

Tina, standing at the sound desk, grinned as she flicked on the studio webcam. "Right, so for everyone listening, if you want to see what's happening, we've got a live stream running on the Brookes Vibes website, and trust me, you want to see this."

Emma leaned into the mic. "I can confirm that James looks both deeply uncomfortable and weirdly attractive in a hostage situation. Make of that what you will. Now, if you want to decide on the torture Carly, Tina, Hayley, Clarissa and I are going to perform on James during the final hour of the show, then just give us a ring, our phone number is 01865 570248, or text us, starting with Y6NW4, on 60777, that's 01865 570248 or text Y6NW4 on 60777."

Carly chuckled, as, apart from her, it was the other Babes' first time on the radio, and each had crib sheets while she and James, while he was tied up, were assisting in directing which faders, which buttons, and which screens to look at. The controlled chaos of live student radio was unfolding beautifully, exactly as Carly had planned.

Carly chuckled, as, apart from her, it was the other Babes' first time on the radio, and each had crib sheets while she and James, while he was tied up, were assisting in directing which faders, which buttons, and which screens to look at. The controlled chaos of live student radio was unfolding beautifully, exactly as Carly had planned.

The fact that Studio 2, where the show was being broadcast, had been upgraded from CD based playout to a new system called Myriad, which allowed for better scheduling and automation, was both a blessing and a curse. A blessing because it meant Carly and her team could queue up jingles, callers, and music with ease. A curse because none of the other Babes had ever used it before, and they were now relying entirely on Carly and a tied-up James Jenkins to guide them.

"Right, first up," Carly continued, "Tina, on your screen, you need to select the 'Voice Mic' fader, make sure it's on, then queue up the next song in Myriad. It's the Michael Andrews and Gary Jules version of Mad World. You got it?"

The fact, Carly knew, that her mic was on air, so her instructions were being broadcast across most of Oxfordshire, from Thame to the outskirts of Banbury, made it all the better. It wasn't just a show; it was a statement—one final, chaotic, beautiful middle finger to Adam Banks before she walked away from Brookes Vibes for good.

Tina squinted at the screen, her tongue sticking out slightly as she navigated Myriad like someone trying to defuse a bomb. "Uh... I think I've got it?" she said hesitantly.

Carly smirked, watching James shift uncomfortably in his chair. "You better, Tina, otherwise Jenkins here is going to be trapped in this studio forever, and I really don't fancy dealing with his father's lawyers. Anyway, to start off this first hour of two of the Babes Takeover, its your Christmas number 1, as announced last Sunday by Foxy himself, Dr Neil Fox, its Mad World by Michael Andrews and Gary Jules!"

As the first notes of the haunting piano cover began to play, Carly looked at the running order of the show, and knew that this was only the beginning, as the tracks scheduled, a mix of Christmas number ones, twos and threes from the past 10 years, as well as several tracks that had been listener requests, made for a show that was about to go down in Brookes Vibes history. This wasn't just a standard student radio special—it was a carefully crafted final stand.

Looking at the list of key points to mention on air, Carly chuckled at the competition they were going to do in the second hour, one where the winner would get a pack of WKD Iron Brew, 12 bottles of the finest fluorescent orange alcohol available to students on a budget. The competition was a simple one—listeners had to call in and guess how many times James groaned in despair over the course of the next hour. Whoever got the closest number won the booze, along with a Brookes Vibes hoodie that had been 'borrowed' from the station's promo stash.

She knew that James was aware of the competition, as, even though the WKD came from one of Adam's left over promo stockpiles, the idea of reducing him to a glorified drinking game was, in his words, "a severe violation of human rights, but admittedly good radio."

"Carly, how do I cue up the next track?" Emma asked, glancing nervously at the playout system as Mad World played softly in the background. She was still getting to grips with Myriad, and Carly knew they had about 30 seconds before they needed to move things along.

Carly leaned over, pressing a couple of buttons. "Right, you see the list of songs? Click the next one, then hit 'Auto' and it'll queue itself up. Don't panic, babes, we've got this."

Emma nodded, her fingers hovering uncertainly over the keyboard before she followed Carly's instructions. A second later, the system flashed green, confirming the next track was ready. She let out a relieved breath. "Okay, we're still on air. No dead air. This is progress."

****

"It's ten to 3, here on Brookes Vibes, and it's the Babes Takeover. We've got the winner of the WKD Iron Brew challenge coming up, but first, let's check in on the star of the show—James Jenkins, the man who's just spent the last two hours tied to a chair while we made his misery into entertainment," Carly announced with a wicked grin, glancing over at James, who was still very much taped to the studio chair, looking half-amused, half-defeated.

The fact that, while taped to the chair, James was currently speaking to the caller who had won the WKD Iron Brew, recording the conversation, getting their details so Hayley and Tina, who were about to leave in the Babemobile for an outside broadcast at the Student Union, could deliver the prize, only added to the absurdity of the moment. James had somehow, despite his predicament, remained semi-professional throughout—well, as professional as a man taped to a chair in a student radio station could be.

"Right," James then said, after taking the details of the winner, grinning as he turned to the microphone which was on air, "I've got Hannah from Thornhill on the line, our lucky winner of the WKD Iron Brew Challenge! Hannah, congratulations—you correctly guessed that I would groan 47 times over the past two hours. Which,

255

frankly, is 47 more times than I ever wanted to, but here we are."

Hannah laughed down the line, her voice crackling slightly through the studio feed. "Honestly, James, mate, I thought you'd crack 50 at least. You lasted longer than I expected."

Carly smirked, tapping her nails against the sound desk. "See, Jenkins? You do have endurance. Who knew?"

James shot her a glare. "Remind me why I'm still friends with you?"

Emma, barely containing her laughter, chimed in. "Stockholm Syndrome, probably."

"So do I actually get my WKD?" Hannah asked eagerly.

Tina, now standing at the back of the studio with Hayley, lifted up the crate of fluorescent orange chaos. "Oh, absolutely. I'll be personally delivering it to you at the SU in about twenty minutes. Keep an eye out for the Babemobile—we'll be the ones pulling up looking far too enthusiastic for people who've been running this station for two hours straight."

"Oh my God, buzzing! Cheers, girls!"

"Not a problem, babe," Carly grinned, before cutting the line and turning back to the studio webcam. "Right, so that's our first official winner. But don't worry, there's still plenty more chaos to come before we wrap this show up. And speaking of chaos—James, its coming up to the final hour of the show, and the listeners have been phoning in and texting us since we started, and the next hour, folks, James will be doing exactly what

"Not a problem, babe," Carly grinned, before cutting the line and turning back to the studio webcam. "Right, so that's our first official winner. But don't worry, there's still plenty more chaos to come before we wrap this show up. And speaking of chaos—James, its coming up to the final hour of the show, and the listeners have been phoning in and texting us since we started, and the next hour, folks, James will be doing exactly what the listeners tell him to do!" Carly finished with a mischievous grin, spinning her chair towards the webcam with the kind of energy that promised absolute mayhem. "We've been taking your texts, your calls, and your slightly concerning suggestions all afternoon, and now it's time for the ultimate revenge on Oxford's poshest student radio lackey."

"What in the hell is going on in here?!" Annabelle, who walked into the studio as if she owned the place, screeched, her eyes wide with a mix of rage and disbelief. "Get that tiara off your head, you Oxford skank. I'm the Queen of the Babes, not you!"

Carly, still spinning slightly in her chair, casually reached up and adjusted the tiara that she had been given back in October in the mud wrestling match that she and Annabelle had fought in—and that Carly had very much won.

The fact that they were on air, meaning the whole of Oxford city centre, as well as most of the county, could hear what was about to unfold only made it all the more delicious.

"Quick, Tina, press 'sound effects', then 'wrestling bell sound'," James said, and Carly threw an angry look at him before turning back to Annabelle. The sound of a wrestling bell rang through the studio speakers, punctuating the moment with perfect comedic timing. The text control screen on the computer was already lighting up with messages from listeners, with people egging them on and taking bets on whether Annabelle would try to physically rip the tiara from Carly's head.

"The following contest is scheduled for one fall," James said with a grin on his face, and Carly internally groaned at how James was now fully committed to turning this into some sort of wrestling event. *The absolute bastard,* she thought, looking at her boyfriend.

Annabelle, still standing in the doorway with all the grace of a furious reality TV contestant, clenched her fists, her manicured nails digging into her palms. "This is MY show! You had your fun, Hemsworth, but it's over. Take the tiara off, end this pathetic little power trip, and GET OUT."

Carly, utterly unbothered, leaned back in her chair, crossing her legs as she smirked at Annabelle. "Oh, babes, I would, except… I'm still on air. And last time I checked, you were still suspended. Anyway, if I remember rightly, there's an order which is also called a restraining order, against you, one that the Courts decided was quite necessary after your little… incident in Banbury," Carly added, her smirk widening as Annabelle's face twisted into something between rage and horror.

James, still very much tied to the chair but now fully leaning into the spectacle, chuckled into the mic. "And just to clarify, that means Annabelle Young is legally required to not be in the same building as Carly Hemsworth, let alone screaming in her face while we're live on air."

Clarissa, who had been watching the scene unfold from the sound desk, leaned into her mic with a delighted grin. "Oh, and we should probably mention that Sarah Linton is listening right now. You know, Sarah? The actual station manager? The one who did not authorise Annabelle's suspension to be lifted?"

Tina, her eyes twinkling with mischief, dramatically pressed a button on the soundboard, triggering a DUN DUN DUUUUN sound effect, which sent the studio into barely contained fits of laughter.

Annabelle let out a furious screech, her hands trembling as she pointed an accusing finger at Carly. "You BITCH! You think this is funny?! You think you can humiliate me like this and get away with it?!"

Carly shrugged, adjusting her tiara. "Oh, babes, I don't think I can. I know I can. And I just did."

James, still very much tied up but clearly enjoying the chaos, grinned. "And let's not forget the best part—this is all being recorded for playback later. So, if anyone missed Annabelle's total on-air meltdown, don't worry! We'll be sure to upload it to the Brookes Vibes website for future generations to enjoy."

The text screen, already on fire with listeners' reactions, was now completely losing it.

Carly knew that both Adam and Sarah were off at home, as both were off for the Christmas period, Sarah being married and having children, and Adam in some dive bar getting drunk no doubt, and that the senior person on site was technically Mark, Clarissa's boyfriend, so there was absolutely no one in a position of authority to stop this from escalating further. And Carly, sensing the absolute goldmine of entertainment this was turning into, had zero intention of letting Annabelle walk out of this with any dignity left intact.

James, his grin widening despite the fact that he was still taped to the chair, looked over at Carly. "So, Hemsworth, what do we do now? Because I think our guest here has just delivered us some of the best unintentional content in Brookes Vibes history."

Carly pretended to think for a moment, tapping her chin dramatically. "Hmm. Well, seeing as Annabelle is both illegally trespassing and violating a court order, we could always... I dunno... call security?" She turned towards the studio webcam with a mock gasp. "Or even Thames Valley Police?"

Annabelle's eyes widened in sheer horror. "You WOULDN'T."

Carly smirked. "Oh, babes, I so would. In fact, I'm pretty sure the Chief Constable already has you on a watchlist." She leaned towards the microphone, addressing the audience. "Listeners, let's take a vote. Should I have our lovely Babes-in-the-field—Tina and Hayley—ring up security and report a rogue banshee loose in the Brookes Vibes building? Text us starting with Y6NW4 on 60777 whether you think Annabelle should be escorted out by actual security professionals or not."

The studio erupted into laughter as the text screen immediately lit up with responses, the Brookes Vibes audience fully invested in what was quickly turning into the greatest student radio showdown of all time.

Tom in Summertown: *CALL SECURITY. DO IT. I WANT THE FULL JERRY SPRINGER EXPERIENCE.*

Holly in Headington: *My flatmates and I are SCREAMING. Throw her out!!*

Jamie in Cowley: *Thames Valley Police better be listening to this live. Give the people what they want, Carly.*

Ben in Jericho: *I will PAY MONEY to see Annabelle escorted out of the building in disgrace.*

James, despite still being taped to the chair, managed to somehow look both delighted and deeply entertained. "Well, Carly, it seems the people have spoken. You know, I could call my father and have his barrister get in touch with the local police force directly. I'm sure they'd be delighted to enforce a legally binding restraining order, live on air."

Annabelle looked as though she was about to explode. "YOU CAN'T BE SERIOUS."

Carly, still utterly unbothered, leaned into the mic. "Oh, babes, I am deadly serious." She turned towards the webcam, flashing a grin at the audience. "Right, listeners, we've taken your feedback into account, and in the spirit of giving you the best radio we possibly can, let's get this mess sorted properly. Here's a bit of Blur, with Parklife, here on Oxford's Brookes Vibes."

As the opening bars of Parklife blasted through the studio speakers, Carly leaned back in her chair, crossing her arms with a smirk as she watched Annabelle go through the five stages of grief in real-time. The studio was a perfect storm of chaos—Tina and Hayley were already on their way to the Student Union for the outside broadcast via Hannah from Thornhill's house, Clarissa was still grinning like the Cheshire Cat from the sound desk, and James, despite being physically unable to move, was clearly revelling in the sheer absurdity of the situation.

Annabelle, however, was still standing there, seething, her nails digging into her palms as she tried to figure out how to salvage what little was left of her reputation.

"You lot are pathetic," she spat, her voice dripping with venom. "This is a joke! Brookes Vibes is my station! My brand! Not yours, you stupid Essex slapper."

Carly's smirk froze for just a fraction of a second before it widened, her eyes darkening with a look that could rival any EastEnders Christmas special showdown. She slowly removed her headphones, placed them carefully on the desk, and leaned forward towards the mic, her voice dropping into a low, dangerously amused tone.

"Oh, Annabelle, babe. You really shouldn't have said that."

James, despite being taped to a chair and usually the voice of reason in any given situation, winced slightly. "Oh, you definitely shouldn't have said that."

Carly got up and grabbed Annabelle's hair, the force of the yank making Annabelle stumble slightly. The studio erupted into gasps, but Carly's grip was firm as she dragged Annabelle closer.

"Say that again, babe," Carly hissed, her voice low, deadly. "Go on. Call me a slapper again. I dare you."

James, despite still being tied to the chair, sighed loudly. "Oh God. This is how it ends, isn't it?"

Clarissa, who had been watching with rapt attention, let out a delighted cackle. "Carly, love, if you're gonna slap her, at least wait till we've got the webcam in full screen."

Annabelle, for the first time, looked genuinely rattled. Her bravado faltered as she tried to yank herself free from Carly's grip, but Carly wasn't budging.

"You know what your problem is, Annabelle?" Carly continued, her voice still dangerously calm. "You think you're untouchable. You think you can walk in here, throw a tantrum, and people will just let you have your way. But guess what? I don't work for Adam Banks anymore. I don't answer to you. And I sure as hell don't take orders from some two-bit, desperate, washed-up promo girl who got kicked out of Banbury for trying to assault my boyfriend."

Annabelle's face contorted with rage. "You're pathetic, Carly. You and your little gang of slags. You think you're so clever, playing radio presenter, but you're nothing. You're just some sad little girl who's going to be forgotten the second you leave this place."

Carly let out a low laugh, finally letting go of Annabelle's hair and stepping back, brushing her hands off as if she'd just touched something filthy. "Oh, babe. You think I'll be forgotten? You really don't get it, do you?"

She turned towards the microphone, her grin widening. "Listeners, let's take another vote. Who do you think should really be leading the Brookes Babes—me, or this pathetic excuse of a human being standing in front of me? Text us now on 60777, starting with Y6NW4. Oh, and Annabelle? You might want to check how many people are watching the webcam feed right now, because I think we've just hit record numbers."

****

CHAPTER 19 – Invasion Of The Other Babes

Saturday 10th January 2004

Brookes Vibes had barely recovered from the carnage of The Babes Takeover when a new problem arrived—an invasion.

The Buzz Beats Babes from Reading's Buzz Beats and the Cambridge Buzz Babes from Cambridge Buzz, both sister stations of Brookes Vibes under the Home Counties Radio Group, had descended upon Oxford for what was being touted as a "joint promotional day". In theory, it was meant to be a networking and collaboration exercise between the three teams. In reality, it was an excuse for the Reading and Cambridge promo girls to storm into Oxford, flex their so-called superiority, and attempt to prove that their teams were better than the Brookes Babes.

The fact that the Brookes Babes were the original blueprint on which the Beats Babes and the Buzz Babes were modelled on meant nothing to them, even though the Oxford ones were 4 months old, the Reading ones a month old and the Cambridge ones only just formed a week earlier, meant that they had no real legacy to stand on. Yet, that didn't stop the Cambridge Buzz Babes from walking in as if they owned the place.

Carly knew exactly what was happening.

It was a plan by the Home Counties Radio Group bosses to try and fight back against the takeover bid by Lord Jenkins and Michael Tabor, the barrister and the businessmen who had their eyes on swallowing up the whole network. The bosses needed to consolidate their promo teams, reinforce their image, and, crucially, weaken Carly's growing power in Brookes Vibes before she became an even bigger problem for them.

Carly wasn't stupid. She saw through the charade immediately.

Waiting at Gloucester Green bus station with Tina, Hayley and Clarissa, Carly knew that the incoming X5 coach from Cambridge would be hosting a posse of a round dozen highly confident, self-proclaimed elite promo girls, all eager to assert dominance over Oxford's radio scene. The Buzz Beats Babes from Reading, on the other hand, were arriving by train, and she knew that Ally, who was now the leader of the Brookes Uni half of the Brookes Babes, had been instructed by Adam Banks to greet them with open arms. Carly, however, had no such plans.

She knew that Adam had been on the interview panel for both the Reading and the Cambridge Buzz Babes, meaning he had personally picked their so-called 'leaders'—and Carly was willing to bet that he had chosen girls who were either desperate to impress or easy to manipulate.

"I can't believe Emma's left the Babes," Tina said with a sigh, folding her arms as she leaned against the metal railing at Gloucester Green. Carly sighed, as Emma was one of their close friends, part of the Oxford Uni faction that Carly led of the Brookes Babes, and her decision to step down after The Babes Takeover had been a tough blow. It wasn't because she didn't support Carly—far from it—but because she wanted to focus on her studies, and the radio station politics had pushed her to breaking point. Carly respected it, even if it stung to lose an ally.

"Yeah," Carly murmured, rolling her shoulders. "I get why, though. This is getting bigger than any of us thought. She didn't sign up for an all-out war."

Clarissa let out a scoff. "Oh, babe, let's be real—she just didn't fancy dealing with Adam Banks' bullshit for another term. And I can't blame her."

Tina pulled her jacket tighter around her as the January wind whipped through Gloucester Green. "You reckon these new Babes are gonna be that bad?"

Carly exhaled sharply, eyes locked on the approaching X5 coach from Cambridge. "They're gonna be worse."

The coach pulled into the station, the large Stagecoach X5 branding flashing as the doors hissed open. A moment later, a group of twelve girls, all immaculately dressed in identical Buzz Babes jackets, stepped off like they were making an entrance at a red-carpet event. At the front of the pack was a tall, blonde girl with piercing blue eyes and the kind of entitled strut that screamed Daddy pays my rent. She was flanked by two brunettes, both equally polished and self-assured.

Following them were 9 more of the Cambridge students, and Carly groaned, as the natural rivalry between Oxford and Cambridge was bad enough as it was—throw in promo team politics, and it was about to get nuclear.

The blonde at the front flicked her hair over her shoulder as she spotted Carly and her group waiting for them. Her eyes raked over them with an expression that could only be described as judgemental.

"You must be Carly Hemsworth," she said, her voice crisp, with the unmistakable tone of someone who had spent a term in student politics and believed herself to be an expert in everything. "I've heard so much about you."

Carly forced a tight smile. "That's funny, I've heard absolutely nothing about you."

The brunette to the blonde's right let out a scoff of laughter, but the blonde didn't falter. Instead, she extended a perfectly manicured hand. "Annika Fairchild. I run the Cambridge Buzz Babes."

Carly noticed that James, who was there purely because Adam wanted a porter for the incoming Babes invasion, was starting to look uncomfortable with Annika's presence. Carly could tell instantly—James Jenkins, the smooth-talking legal mind who could handle Oxford Union debates and student radio wars with ease, had stiffened ever so slightly at the sight of her.

Carly narrowed her eyes. *Oh, great. What's the story here*, she thought, noticing the tension in her boyfriend.

She ignored Annika's outstretched hand. "Well, Annika," she said coolly, "welcome to Oxford. You're about four months late to the party, but we'll try to make you feel at home."

Annika smirked, lowering her hand without missing a beat. "Oh, I don't need to feel at home, darling. I'm here to show you how it's done."

Clarissa muttered a very audible *oh, fuck off* under her breath, and Carly had to fight back a grin. She was already mentally tallying up the ways in which this was going to go horrifically wrong.

Behind Annika, the rest of the Cambridge Buzz Babes were watching like a pack of wolves, all subtly adjusting their jackets and hair as if waiting for their leader to give them orders. They had the air of a team that had been assembled for one reason—to replace, or at the very least, overshadow, the Brookes Babes.

James, standing slightly behind Carly, cleared his throat. "Annika," he said, his tone measured. "Didn't expect to see you here."

Carly shot him a look. *Oh, so he knows her,* she thought, internally groaning.

Annika turned her gaze to James, her smirk sharpening. "Oh, James," she purred, tilting her head slightly. "You should have expected it. I mean, your father did try and betroth us several years ago, and I did say that I intended to go to Cambridge one day."

Carly remembered that another of James's past acquaintances, Arabella Johnstone-Carter, had also been an attempted match by his father prior to joining Oxford—so the fact that yet another one of James's past almost-fiancées had crawled out of the woodwork was almost laughably predictable.

Carly turned to her boyfriend, raising an eyebrow. "James, darling, you really need to warn me when one of your ex-arranged marriages is about to crash-land into my life."

James sighed, running a hand down his face. "She's not an ex—well, not technically—look, it was a thing our parents talked about, it was never serious."

Annika smirked, her blue eyes glinting with amusement. "Oh, but James, I thought we had such a connection." She stepped forward, placing a manicured hand lightly on his arm. "After all, our families thought we were such a perfect match."

Carly, already irritated by this entitled Cambridge princess, stepped between them, physically removing Annika's hand from James's arm. "Alright, Annika, I know the Cambridge elite like to think they own everything, but I'll make one thing very clear—James is mine. You're a few years too late for the Lady of the Manor act, babes."

James muttered something about "not being a bloody possession" under his breath, but wisely stayed quiet as Annika withdrew her hand with a slow smirk.

"Oh, darling," Annika said smoothly, folding her arms. "I'm not here for James. I'm here for Brookes Vibes."

Carly let out a short laugh. "You? Here for my station? Cute."

"Not just me," Annika said, glancing behind her, where the other Cambridge Buzz Babes were standing in a perfectly synchronised formation. "We're here to bring Cambridge class to Oxford's… rough edges."

As Carly led the group through the City Centre from Gloucester Green Bus Station to Market Square, where Adam had arranged for yet another mud wrestling match to take place, Carly was already seething. Of course, Adam Banks had set this up. He was nothing if not predictable. His go-to move was to stir the pot, keep the promo teams fighting amongst themselves, and then sit back and reap the benefits while they tore each other apart. And now, he had his newest protégée, Annika Fairchild, leading the charge.

As they crossed the High Street, Carly turned to James, her voice low. "How serious was this 'arrangement' between your families?"

James groaned. "It wasn't serious at all. Just some posh parents trying to secure a merger through marriage."

Clarissa snorted. "Like a corporate takeover but with wedding vows?"

James nodded. "Exactly. And trust me, Annika was never interested either. She just likes playing games."

Carly's fists clenched. "Well, if she wants to play games, she's come to the right place."

By the time they reached Market Square, the Buzz Beats Babes from Reading were already there, standing around the makeshift wrestling pit that had been hastily erected for the occasion. It was a repeat of the infamous Brookes Babes mud wrestling promo from September, only this time, instead of Annabelle trying to claw her way into power, Carly was facing an invasion from two sides.

Standing near the edge of the pit was a group of girls in black and orange jackets, the colours of Reading's Buzz Beats. The leader of this faction, a curvy, red-haired girl named Bianca Sterling, spotted Carly approaching and smirked.

"Well, well, if it isn't the Queen of Oxford," Bianca drawled. "Still wearing that tiara, Hemsworth?"

Carly shot her a saccharine smile. "Oh, babes, you know I never take it off. It drives people like you mad."

Bianca laughed. "Don't flatter yourself, darling. We're just here to show Oxford how it's done."

Annika stepped forward, the smugness radiating off her like heat. "Indeed. This whole Brookes Babes thing—it was a good first attempt, I suppose. But Reading and Cambridge? We're here to take it to the next level."

Carly folded her arms. "Oh, I see what this is. This isn't about networking. This is about Adam trying to replace me. Again." She looked between Annika and Bianca. "And you two are his latest lapdogs."

Bianca rolled her eyes. "Oh, don't be so dramatic, Carly. We're not here to replace you. We're just… improving things."

Carly smirked. "Babe, I am the improvement."

James sighed behind her. "Here we go."

Carly could see the ever hungover Big Bam, who had a sickness record the length of the M25 and was meant to be the Sunday morning host on Brookes Vibes, was DJing for the assembled crowd, a mix of families and uni students who were already in Oxford for the upcoming terms at both Oxford and Oxford Brookes. There was already some cheering, which was due to Big Bam falling over as the Babes had just arrived.

Carly turned to Clarissa and muttered under her breath, "This is going to be an absolute circus."

Clarissa smirked, arms crossed as she surveyed the scene. "Oh, babe, this isn't a circus—it's a full-blown wrestling pay-per-view."

As they reached the edge of the pit, Adam Banks sauntered over, his ever-present smirk plastered across his face. He was wearing his Trent FM-branded jacket again, as if it was some sort of sacred relic, and the way he was practically buzzing with excitement told Carly everything she needed to know. He'd engineered this entire mess, just like she'd suspected.

"Ladies, ladies, welcome to the Ultimate Babes Battle!" Adam announced grandly, spreading his arms. "We've got three teams, one pit, and one massive prize—bragging rights as the best promo team in the Home Counties Radio Group!"

Carly scoffed. "Oh, piss off, Banks. This isn't a 'friendly' competition. This is you trying to manufacture drama to take the heat off the fact that Brookes Vibes is a mess under your leadership."

Annika smirked. "Oh, Carly, don't be such a sore loser before we've even started."

James, still looking profoundly unimpressed, folded his arms. "So, what exactly is the plan here, Adam? You expecting them to rip each other apart so you can sit back and pretend this is all 'team-building'?"

Adam grinned. "Oh, Jenkins, mate, you know me too well. But let's not be negative! This is about entertainment!" He clapped his hands together. "Right! The rules are simple. Each team picks two representatives. We have three rounds. Mud wrestling, relay race, and… a 'mystery challenge'… and… a special guest referee…"

Carly groaned, as James had been the special guest referee the last time a mud wrestling match had been held, back in September. And if Adam had dragged him into it again, she was going to murder him right here in Market Square.

"Let me guess," Carly said, already exasperated, "James is refereeing again?"

Adam smirked. "Oh, babe, close but no cigar. James was my first choice, obviously. But, after the absolute scenes at the Babes Takeover, I decided we needed someone with a bit more… authority."

Before Carly could question what he meant, a familiar, very unwelcome voice rang out over the sound system.

"Alright, Oxford! Let's get ready to ruuuuumble!"

Carly's stomach dropped.

Annabelle.

The speakers crackled as Annabelle Young's voice boomed across Market Square, and a moment later, she strutted onto the makeshift stage near the wrestling pit, microphone in hand, looking far too pleased with herself.

Carly clenched her fists. "You have got to be kidding me."

Clarissa groaned. "Oh, for fuck's sake, Adam, I thought we got rid of this psycho!"

James, meanwhile, pinched the bridge of his nose. "Why does she always turn up like a horror movie villain? I swear to God, she just respawns every time we think she's gone."

Annabelle, now perched dramatically on the side of the pit, twirled the microphone between her fingers before grinning down at the assembled Babes. She was wearing a fitted stereotypical referee outfit, with a mini-skirt and a black-and-white striped top that looked more like something out of a dodgy fancy dress shop than an official referee uniform. She flicked her blonde hair over her shoulder, flashing a saccharine smile that dripped with condescension.

"Oh, Carly, babe," Annabelle cooed, as the gathered crowd murmured with interest at the tension in the air. "You didn't think you could get rid of me that easily, did you? I'm like a bad penny—I always turn up." She paused for dramatic effect, then smirked. "And this time, I'm in charge."

Carly was about ten seconds away from launching herself at Annabelle and dragging her into the mud pit herself. She turned sharply to Adam, who was grinning like a

Cheshire cat, clearly enjoying the absolute chaos he had manufactured.

"You gave her the referee spot?" Carly hissed, barely containing her rage. "After she got suspended? After the restraining order? Are you actually trying to get us sued?"

Adam held up his hands in mock innocence. "Oh, come on, Hemsworth, let's not be petty. Annabelle's had her little slap on the wrist, and she's here in an official capacity." He gestured at Annabelle's outfit. "Look, she even has a whistle."

Annabelle blew the whistle dramatically, winking at the audience. "That's right! And if anyone disobeys my orders, there'll be consequences."

Carly's fists clenched. "The only consequence is going to be me throwing you headfirst into that mud pit."

Annika, still watching with the kind of smug detachment only Cambridge students could pull off, sighed dramatically. "Ugh, this is already so unprofessional. I thought we were here to showcase excellence."

"Shut up, Annika," Carly and Clarissa said in unison.

Bianca, the leader of the Reading Babes, folded her arms, amused by the entire situation. "Oh, I don't know, Carly. Maybe Annabelle being here isn't such a bad thing. I mean, we were all thinking it—it's about time someone put you in your place."

Carly shot Bianca a death glare. "You want a mud wrestling match, babe? Because I will ruin that overpriced salon hair of yours in five seconds flat."

Annabelle clapped her hands, grinning. "Oh, I love this energy! And lucky for you, Carly, you'll get plenty of chances to prove yourself, because you, my dear, are competing."

Carly narrowed her eyes. "Who the hell said I was competing?"

Adam leaned in, still grinning. "Oh, babe, you are. You see, you're the face of the Brookes Babes. Your lovely little faction thinks you're untouchable. And what better way to prove it than by going head-to-head with the best of Cambridge and Reading?"

Carly groaned, as she suddenly heard Annika muttering how Carly was an 'Oxford skank who looks like she's about to go on the game, not act as a respectable promotions team leader'. That was it.

Carly turned, locked eyes with Annika, and in one fluid motion, snatched the referee whistle off Annabelle's lanyard and chucked it straight into the mud pit.

"You posh little snake," Carly spat, stepping right up into Annika's personal space. "If you've got something to say, say it to my face, instead of muttering like a Tory in a sex scandal."

Annika smirked, unfazed, adjusting the sleeve of her pristine Buzz Babes jacket. "I just think it's hilarious," she said smoothly, her voice dripping with superiority. "You've got this whole queen bee act going on, but at the end of the day, you're just another insecure little Essex girl, clinging to relevance."

Clarissa let out an audible, "Oh, you've fucked up now, babes," as James instinctively moved to place a hand on Carly's arm, likely to stop her from full-on launching herself at Annika.

Annabelle, now standing smugly beside Adam Banks, laughed. "Oh, this is too good," she said, folding her arms. "I was worried this would be boring, but Carly, babe, you never disappoint."

Carly's blood was boiling, but she knew better than to let them get the reaction they wanted. Instead, she plastered on the most saccharine, condescending smile she could muster and took a step back, smoothing down her Brookes Vibes jacket as if Annika's words hadn't even touched her.

"You know what, Annika?" she said, voice eerily calm. "I am clinging to relevance. Because I built this. I took this promo team from some sad little stunt Adam cooked up for his own ego and turned it into the brand that Home Counties Radio can't ignore. And you? You're standing here, wearing my hand-me-downs, thinking you're special because Banks let you have a go."

"At least my brother didn't get himself blown up by an IED, unlike Stanhope's," Annabelle then say, smirking cruelly as the words left her mouth.

The world seemed to go silent for a second.

Carly knew that a week earlier, in Iraq, Clarissa's elder brother, Carl Stanhope, a junior officer in the 20th Armoured Infantry Brigade, had been killed by an improvised explosive device near Basra. It had been a devastating blow to Clarissa's family, and while she had kept up appearances, Carly knew her best friend was barely holding it together.

Clarissa's expression darkened immediately, her normally sharp tongue momentarily stunned into silence. For a split second, there was nothing but pure, seething rage in her eyes.

And then, before anyone could react, Clarissa moved.

The sound of her fist connecting with Annabelle's face cracked through Market Square like a gunshot.

Annabelle staggered back, eyes wide in shock as she clutched her now-bloodied nose. Gasps erupted from the crowd, followed by a few scattered cheers from those who knew exactly how far Annabelle had just crossed the line.

"Clarissa!" James grabbed her arm, trying to pull her back, but she shook him off, breathing heavily.

"You absolute piece of shit," Clarissa spat, her voice shaking with barely controlled fury. "You think you're funny, Annabelle? You think bringing up my dead brother is some clever little power move? You're disgusting."

Annabelle, still cradling her nose, managed to smirk despite the blood now dripping onto her pristine referee shirt. "Oh, boo hoo," she sneered, her voice nasally from the hit. "It's not my fault your brother was stupid enough to get himself killed in some pointless war."

Clarissa lunged.

Carly barely managed to get between them in time, grabbing her best friend around the waist before she could throw herself at Annabelle again. "Clarissa, no," Carly hissed, tightening her grip. "She's not worth it."

But Clarissa was shaking with rage, her entire body tensed like a spring about to snap. "Let go of me, Carly," she snarled. "Let me fucking end her."

James stepped in beside Carly, eyes hard as he looked at Annabelle. "You need to leave," he said, voice dangerously low. "Now."

Annabelle wiped at the blood on her face with the back of her hand, glaring at James. "Oh, what, now you're her knight in shining armour?" she scoffed. "Please. You're just as bad as the rest of them."

James clenched his jaw, but before he could respond, Adam Banks finally decided to intervene—though, predictably, not in a way that was actually helpful.

"Bloody hell," Adam muttered, rubbing a hand over his face like this was all just an inconvenience rather than an actual incident. "Alright, alright, everyone calm down. Christ, this was supposed to be a promo event, not an episode of EastEnders."

Carly turned on him, eyes blazing. "Are you serious?" she snapped. "She just mocked a dead soldier—Clarissa's brother—and you're acting like this is just some petty argument?"

Adam groaned. "Look, I don't give a shit about whatever personal beef you lot have going on—"

"Personal beef?" Clarissa let out a sharp, bitter laugh. "My brother is dead, Banks."

Adam hesitated, clearly realising he'd walked straight into a minefield. "Yeah, uh, look, I didn't mean it like—"

"No, you never mean anything, do you?" Carly cut in furiously. "You just sit back and stir the pot, letting the girls fight it out so you can keep your shitty little power trip going."

Annika, who had been watching all of this unfold with an unreadable expression, finally spoke up. "Look, I don't condone what Annabelle just said," she said, voice clipped. "But this whole thing is descending into chaos. We came here to showcase our skills, not get involved in whatever this is."

Carly scoffed, stepping away from Clarissa now that she was at least somewhat composed. "Oh, spare me the 'we're so professional' speech, Annika. You've been stirring the pot since you got off the coach."

Annika raised an eyebrow. "Well, if you can't handle a little healthy competition, Carly—"

Carly had had enough.

"Oh, babes, this isn't competition," she said sweetly, stepping forward until she was toe-to-toe with the Cambridge girl. "Because you're not even on my level."

****

CHAPTER 20 – The Years End
Saturday 3rd July 2004

It had been over six months since the Reading and Cambridge Babes had invaded Oxford, and things at the Brookes Babes had changed, albeit only slightly.

Sarah Linton, the station manager at Brookes Vibes, had resigned, her tolerance of Adam Banks had finally run out after nearly a year and a few months of working with the promotions manager at the Summertown station, and had gotten a job at BBC Midlands, as a Deputy Head of Region for the public service broadcaster.

Annabelle had gone on maternity leave a few weeks ago, as Adam and the former GWR executives on the board of the Home Counties Radio Group had rehired her after Sarah had sacked her following the fiasco involving the Babes Takeover and the invasion of the Reading and Cambridge promo teams. Of course, Adam had spun it as a "second chance" for Annabelle, but everyone at Brookes Vibes knew the real reason—she, like Carly, was one of Adam's old guard, one of the few people still willing to stroke his ego, and he needed all the allies he could get.

A new station manager, Clive Atkinson, a former Granada executive who had made the move from television to radio, was now in charge of Brookes Vibes, and had curbed some of Adam's more excessive antics, but had largely left the promotional teams to their own devices. The one move that Carly had to admit that she liked was that she had been specifically handpicked by Atkinson to be the head of the street team, not Ally or Lara, the two who were on Annabelle's side. That, at least, had been a victory.

It was the summer holidays, the end of the second year at Oxford, and the time had finally come for Carly and James to pack up their student flat and head home. Except, this year, "home" was a more complicated issue.

Carly zipped up the last of her suitcases, glancing over at James, who was sat on the bed, scrolling through his phone with an expression of mild disbelief.

"What's up?" she asked, lifting a brow. "You look like someone's just told you there's no ice in your G&T."

James sighed, tossing his phone onto the duvet. "My father lost the bid."

Carly blinked. "What? The takeover for Home Counties Radio?"

James nodded. "Yeah. Lord Jenkins and Michael Tabor have officially failed in their attempt to buy out the Home Counties Radio Group. Apparently, Ralph Bernard has decided to block his shares being sold. Anyway, I'm not heading back to Henley this summer… Father is going to New York for the summer to appraise some horses and buy yet another property to add to his personal portfolio. Mother, on the other hand, wants to plan our wedding, even though we agreed that, while I popped the question to you last week, we agreed that we wouldn't actually wed until both of us pass our degrees and get settled in our careers. She's already booked a meeting with a wedding planner at Claridge's and tried to put down a deposit on a stately home in Surrey. I had to remind her that I want to wait until at least 2007, if not slightly longer."

Carly chuckled, as two weeks earlier, James had took her to a restaurant called Le Manoir aux Quat'Saisons in the village of Great Milton, a small village just outside Oxford. Le Manoir, a 15th century manor, had two Michelin stars and was one of the most exclusive restaurants in the country. James had booked a private dining room, the kind of thing Carly would have laughed off as "ridiculously posh" had it been anyone else, but when it came to James, she had to admit—he knew how to do things properly.

Saturday 18th June 2004

The sound of soft classical music played in the background, the gentle clinking of cutlery and hushed murmurs of well-dressed diners filling the elegant dining room of Le Manoir aux Quat'Saisons. The candlelight flickered against the dark wooden beams of the 15th-century manor, casting warm glows across the crisp white tablecloths.

Carly felt completely out of place. Not in a bad way—just in the this is far too posh for an Essex girl who grew up eating chips in the back of a Ford Fiesta kind of way. She was dressed in a sleek black dress, one of the few 'proper' dresses she owned that wasn't bought specifically for a club night, and she'd even worn heels, despite her intense dislike of them. James, of course, looked effortlessly at home in a tailored navy suit, his hair styled just so, his usual smirk softened into something more nervous than usual.

"You alright there, posh boy?" Carly teased, taking a sip of her wine. "You look like you're about to tell me you've run up a massive gambling debt and we need to flee to Spain."

James let out a short laugh, shaking his head. "No debts, I promise. Just—" he hesitated, shifting in his seat before clearing his throat. "—Just something I need to say."

Carly arched a brow. "Oh no. If you're breaking up with me, at least let me finish my dessert first."

James rolled his eyes, but there was something undeniably nervous about the way he reached into the inside pocket of his jacket. Carly's stomach flipped as he pulled out a small velvet box and placed it on the table between them.

Her breath hitched.

No.

No way.

Not here. Not in the middle of a ridiculously posh restaurant where the cheapest thing on the menu cost more than her monthly phone bill.

James exhaled, meeting her gaze. "I know we said we'd wait," he said quietly. "That we wouldn't rush into anything until after we graduated, but—" He paused, his fingers brushing the box. "—Carly, I want you to know I mean it. That this isn't just some uni relationship that'll fizzle out once we get into the real world."

Carly swallowed. "James…"

"I love you," he said simply. "And I want to spend the rest of my life with you. So, no, I'm not asking you to marry me tomorrow. Or even next year. But I am asking if you'll marry me someday."

Slowly, carefully, he pushed the box towards her.

Carly stared at it, her pulse roaring in her ears.

She wasn't the romantic type. She didn't daydream about weddings or dresses or any of that nonsense. But looking at James—at her James, the boy who had been by her side through all the madness of the past two years—she knew there wasn't a single part of her that wanted to say no.

She reached out, fingers trembling slightly as she flipped the box open.

Inside was a ring. Not a massive, flashy diamond like she'd expect from a posh boy like James Jenkins, but a delicate, vintage-style ring with a deep blue sapphire in the centre, surrounded by tiny diamonds. It was her. Somehow, James had found a ring that felt right.

Carly exhaled, laughing softly. "You really want to marry an Essex girl, do you?"

James grinned. "Absolutely."

She bit her lip, looking down at the ring, then back up at him.

"Alright then, posh boy," she said, her voice soft. "Let's do it."

As James slipped the ring on her finger, Carly sighed, as she knew that James would be her one and only.

Saturday 3rd July 2004

Carly smiled as she glanced at the ring on her finger, its sapphire catching the light from the afternoon sun that streamed through the window of their student flat. It had been two weeks since that night at Le Manoir, two weeks since she had officially agreed to marry James—eventually. And now, they were here, packing up their Oxford lives, ready for the summer.

James, however, was still looking at his phone, his brows furrowed.

"My father's going to be livid," he muttered. "He really thought he had Home Counties Radio wrapped up. He already had people lined up for executive positions—he was going to ship them in from the US, Europe and Australia, people who were experts in commercial radio takeovers. But Ralph Bernard pulled the rug out from under him at the last minute. Apparently, he decided Home Counties Radio needed to remain 'independent'—which, translated from radio exec speak, means 'not in the hands of a Jenkins-Tabor empire'."

Carly smirked as she folded the last of her jumpers into a suitcase. "Poor Lord Jenkins. Must be a hard life, having a media monopoly snatched from his grasp."

James huffed, running a hand through his already-messy hair. "You joke, but this is the first time in years he's actually lost something he wanted. He's been banging on about this takeover since Christmas. I wouldn't be surprised if he disappears to New York just to sulk about it."

"That, or buy another racehorse out of spite." Carly zipped up her bag and glanced around the room. "So, we're all set, then? Last-minute check for anything you might have hidden in some posh-boy nook of the flat?"

James, who did have a habit of stashing things in the oddest places, glanced towards his old desk. "Maybe. Give me a second."

As he rifled through a few stray papers and notes from his second-year law course, Carly leaned against the window frame, watching the street below. The past year had been chaos, but she wouldn't change a second of it.

The Brookes Babes, the radio wars, the fights with Annabelle, the ridiculous student politics—it had all shaped their lives more than they ever could have imagined. And now, they were leaving it behind for a summer in Essex.

Carly suddenly heard her own mobile ring, and, looking at the screen, saw that it was her best friend and partner-in-crime, Clarissa, who, when the duo had spoken the previous night, was stopping in Oxford, but not for Brookes Vibes.

Instead, it was because she and Mark Harrison were dating, and had been since October, meaning that the pair would have had been navigating the world of long-distance relationships, had Clarissa gone to her home in Kent and not stayed in Oxford. It was ironic, really, that the Canterbury girl had fallen for someone who had not even got any A Levels, but had become an electrician at the age of 16, training on the job for 3 years before he left school, his father being a plumber and his uncle an electrician, meaning that he had grown up in the trades. Carly still found it hilarious how Mark—who had once spent most of his time winding up the Brookes Babes by walking around the studio half-naked—had somehow ended up in a proper relationship with Clarissa, the most sarcastic and sharp-tongued person she knew.

Answering the call, Carly put the phone to her ear.

"Alright, Clar?" she said, propping herself against the windowsill.

"Alright, babe. You packed yet?" Clarissa's voice was as dry as ever, but there was a slight edge of amusement beneath it.

"Just about," Carly said, glancing at James, who was now staring at a pile of legal notes with a confused expression, as if trying to remember why he'd ever bothered keeping them. "James is currently having a crisis over whether to take his second-year notes with him or leave them for the next unfortunate law student to deal with."

"I say burn 'em," Clarissa said. "Symbolic and all that. Anyway, just thought I'd let you know that I'm still in Oxford for a bit. Mark's got some extra shifts, and I figured I might as well stick around." Carly grinned. "So, what you're really saying is, you'd rather spend your summer shagging an electrician than go home to Kent?"

Clarissa snorted. "Listen, love, you and James are practically married, so don't start judging me for actually having a boyfriend for once. Anyway, I was thinking—before you head back to Essex, why don't we have one last night out? Proper send-off. Get the old gang together, one more round of drinks at The Bridge before we all disappear for the summer?"

Carly hesitated for only a second before nodding. "Yeah, alright. I'll see if James is up for it. He'll probably say yes, just so he can watch you and Mark argue over the best way to wire a plug."

"Oi, we've only had *one* row about that," Clarissa shot back. "Anyway, bring posh boy and meet us there at eight. First round's on me."

Carly smirked. "You just want an excuse to drink shots, don't you?"

"You *know* I do," Clarissa said. "See you later, babe."

Hanging up, Carly turned to James, who had finally decided to stuff all his notes into a box labelled *'Unlikely to ever need again'*.

"Clar wants us to go out tonight," she said. "Last Oxford night out before we head back to Essex." James raised an eyebrow. "Let me guess—she's buying the first round so we all get too drunk to say no to the second?"

"Obviously," Carly said. "So, you in?" James considered this for a moment, then sighed dramatically. "Well, seeing as my father's latest business empire has crumbled and I no longer have to pretend to be interested in media monopolies, I suppose I can allow myself one evening of debauchery."

"And you're sure about Essex?" James asked, glancing over at her as he tucked his folders into a box. "You do realise that my father is going to absolutely loathe the idea of me spending a summer in a semi-detached house in Romford instead of the family estate in Henley, right?"

Carly grinned. "Oh, I know. That's half the appeal."

James gave her a look, but he was smiling too. "My mother will call you, you know. Try to persuade you that I need to be somewhere with a butler and at least four sitting rooms at all times."

Carly snorted. "Well, she can try. But my mum's already planning to have us redecorating the kitchen, and I've promised my little sister that we'll take her to Clacton for a proper British summer holiday. So, unless Lady Alexandra Jenkins wants to swap her afternoon teas at Claridge's for fish and chips on the Essex coast, she'll have to get over it."

James chuckled, standing up and stretching. "You really do enjoy winding her up, don't you?"

"Oh, absolutely," Carly said, beaming. "Besides, I like the idea of us doing something normal for once. No student politics, no radio drama, no posh boys in cravats telling me how 'unique' my accent is. Just you, me, and a summer of bad telly, cheap pints, and my mum telling us to move all the furniture every two weeks."

James shook his head fondly. "Romantic."

"You love it."

"I really do," James admitted, stepping closer and wrapping an arm around her waist. "Even if my father is going to have an actual coronary when he realises I'll be living in Essex for the summer."

Carly smirked. "Well, if it makes you feel any better, I won't make you eat jellied eels."

"That does make me feel significantly better," James said, pressing a kiss to her forehead. "Alright then, Essex girl. Let's go."

As they wheeled their suitcases out of the flat and down the stairs, Carly couldn't help but feel a strange mix of nostalgia and excitement. Oxford had been the centre of their world for two years—but now, a new chapter was waiting for them.

And something told her that, with James Jenkins by her side, life was only going to get even more interesting.

****

Books by Thomas Brant

Broadcasting Boundaries Series
BROADCASTING BOUNDARIES
BROADCASTING CHAOS
BROADCASTING DISRUPTION

The Wirral Gal Series
THE WIRRAL GAL... IN SPEKE
THE WIRRAL GAL... NOW A MAM

Standalone Stories in the Manic Radio Universe
THE BROOKES BABES

www.ingramcontent.com/pod-product-compliance
Lightning Source LLC
Chambersburg PA
CBHW031252120726
47906CB00003B/708